WASTED

HENRY GRAY
HG
PUBLISHING

Granada Hills, CA
"Select books for selective readers"

Cover illustration by Benton Jew.

For information, contact: henrygraypub2022@gmail.com

Publisher's Cataloging-in-Publication Data:

Names: Park, Sam F., 1956—.
Title: Wasted/ Sam F. Park.
Description: Granada Hills, CA : Henry Gray Publishing, 2025 |
Identifiers: LCCN 2025921621 | ISBN: 9781960415561 (hbk.) |
    ISBN: 9781960415578 (pbk.) | ISBN: 9781960415585 (ebook)
Subjects: LCSH: Western stories. | Alcoholics – Fiction. |
    Ranchers – Fiction. | Outlaws – Fiction. | Identity (Psychology) –
    Fiction. | Redemption – Fiction. | Wyoming – History – 19th
    century – Fiction. | BISAC: FICTION / Westerns. | FICTION /
    Action & Adventure. | FICTION / Historical / 19th Century /
    General.
Classification: LCC PS3616.A75 W37 2025 | DDC 813 P—dc23
LC record available at https://lccn.loc.gov/2025921621

Made in the United States of America.

Published by Henry Gray Publishing, 17020 Chatsworth Blvd. #1125,
    Granada Hills, California, 91344.

All names, characters, places, events, locales, and incidents in this work are fictitious creations from the author's imagination or used in a fictitious manner.

For more information or to join our mailing list, visit HenryGrayPublishing.com

WASTED

Sam F. Park

Thanks

There are so many friends that have helped me over the years. Here are a few: Kerry Gammill, Clay and Madeleine McBride, Willie and Beth Mays, Brian Faerber, Katherine Tomlinson, Peter Lenkov, Bill Todman, Jr., Tom Cohen, Kenneth Hall, Sharyn Essman, and her editorial skills.

And especially writer, director, and raconteur Courtney Joyner, without whom we wouldn't have this book.

Dedication

To Mom and Pop

To Frieda, an Arkansas farm girl turned English teacher and
later a state educational department administrator; for her en-
couragement to my making art and becoming an artist.
This support of my writing and art during lean times
means more the older I become.

Belief in the impossible to forge a reality is a rare gift.

To Tom, Jr., an Arkansas farm boy turned WWII vet,
German P.O.W., history teacher, principal, and superintendent
of schools; for his love of *Gunsmoke* and watching it religiously in
our house for its entire run—and the repeats.
And for him telling this story from some Western he watched
once: A rough cowboy walks into a saloon and yells, "When
I drink, everybody drinks!" The crowd leaps up and claps the
cowboy on the back and drinks up. The cowboy finishes his drink
and pulls his gun and shouts, "And when I pay, everybody pays!"

Yep, Pop. We all pay in the end.

Prologue:

No Sleep For The Wicked

Mountainous black clouds had rolled out of the prairie night in Wyoming and engulfed the moon and stars so suddenly and completely it seemed almost biblical. Except it was just Wyoming. The sky was buried and below came a flood of its shadow that swallowed all the light from the 1880s frontier town of Spirits Bend. The world had become a black void to the eye but not to the ear and nose. A warm breeze had risen, carrying the prairie tang of wet dirt and hay from the fields. Nearby a husky whisper told of long blades of grass bending and caressing under the gentle wind. Off behind a hill a lonely calf bleated for the lost moon and stars.

A stronger gust pulled on a backyard fence, stretching the rusty nails to creak in protest at its planks while a loose pane of glass rattled in the house's front window. Dirt and grit sailed along to scrape against the town's wood and brick making tiny scratching sounds like restless ghosts roaming through the unseen streets.

This puff of wind settled down as a train whistle floated softly in from the outer hills on the thick moist air and then slowly faded off, dreamy and lost. The quiet was soothing and languid. A male cricket chirped and waited, unsure exactly what for.

A loud cough broke the quiet night like a hard knock on a door past midnight. Startled awake in the dark a man cried out.

"Ruby!" his voice carried so far it made a slight echo against the hills. Rising up fast in a panic, he kicked the gravel loose beneath him with a slight rattle. The man stared out at the impenetrable black night. An old fear gripped him as he strained to hear a sound, any-

thing, to signal he was alive and not in damnation. Coughing again, he tasted the cheap phlegmy liquor on his tongue and was relieved. He knew this hell. The drunk let go his breath, sucking gulps of air before settling into a slurred wheezing. He wearily hummed an old tune but his waking senses could not quite grab hold of the words.

Beyond him a speck of white ignited like a coal spark on a black curtain. It moved. Slowly. From the right to the left and then it settled into itself.

The drunk's humming became mumbled words in a broken chant from a soaked memory. *"Take...my hand...dar-lin. Take...my hand... my hand..."*

The distant white spot burned a little brighter.

"Take my hand...my darlin'
In...savage land
Hold me in...the garden
My soul...God's true plan..."

The old hymn called him and he sang louder and clearer to hold off the dark.

"Take my hand...my darlin'
In this savage land
Hold me in its garden
My soul to God's true plan..."

The glittering spark blazed as a rhythmic chuffing roiled the air behind it. The drunk sang louder to its light.

"Along the way...you left me
I didn't see you...go
Left alone...to wonder why
Dear God, I'll never know..."

A deep grumbling rippled the air. A hysteria gripped the drunk's voice. He sang faster as the light grew closer.

"Along the way you left me
I didn't see you go
Left alone to wonder why
Dear God, I'll never know..."

The drunk's voice shouted the hymn, rushing and fumbling the lyrics over his lips.

"May His peace fill your soul
Let your happiness grow and grow——"

Within the light a rushing train headlamp emerged. Frozen in its glare between two steel rails, the dark shape of the drunken man sat waiting for a salutation from God. The huge engine roared down upon him.

The drunk howled into its blazing circle of light. *"We all come to Jesus in the end!"*

He screamed from the bottom of his lungs. An erupting halo whited out the man's pitch-black silhouette as the world disintegrated in the din's explosion.

The train screeched by, the large cars clickety-clacking over the rails in a deafening swell of thundering fury. A blur of windows trailed overlapping rectangles of bright yellow. Abruptly the train's caboose ripped past, disappearing down the tracks with smoke, red cinders and leaves flying whipsaw in its wake.

～

A quiet bleakness filled the hole left by the train. The clattering noise receded into the dark and faded with the wind. For several moments nothing moved or made a sound.

Out of the night an animal shrieked. Its terrified bleating desperate and trapped until it was choked into loud sobbing. Slowly the wailing slipped into soft defeated whimpering. Lying to the side of the tracks the sad broken man began mumbling again.

"We...We all...come to...to Jesus...in the...end..."

He fumbled through the lyrics of the old hymn, the words shrinking softly to ebb away. The man drifted into sleep on the sharp gravel and damp earth.

From the tall grass nearby that defiant cricket furiously rubbed its wings again, producing another loud churr. The insect stopped and waited for its answer. An answer to its purpose.

A weedy sound hissed from the man's nose like a broken whistle.

If a cricket could be mocked the mating urge surged through its entire insect body. The cricket's wings trilled loud and called out for—

Silence.

It sliced the bug's song like with a hatchet. Out of the dark sightless void a black widow sank its fangs into the cricket's head, ripping it from the thorax. Powerful forelegs seized the insect in a flurry, tearing its wings and legs apart. Broken and twitching the cricket had assumed a new purpose beyond creating life to one serving death. A slaughter for the ravenous spider who feasted. Eating the cricket the black venomous creature with the blood red hourglass turned its victim to a new task as she spun a bundle of webs. Inside the predator's swollen abdomen a legion squirmed for the nourishment to set them free, and she obliged.

In that moment the night that ate the stars pulled its shroud tighter around Spirits Bend. Inside this black sleep a venom of nightmares was growing its way through a shattered man who cried for death and it answered with life. A novel cause called to him just like the spiderling eggs released from their venomous mother into a dark cocoon of possibilities.

Chapter One:

Spirits Bend

———

Thin morning light cut gunmetal shadows of storefronts along Spirits Bend's wide main street. The night's darkness had withdrawn into the town's corners and under its boards but remained close as always. Out of this waking gray the outlines of hoof tracks, dropped clods of dried manure and wagon ruts appeared in the sand and clay soil and slowly filled in the view. The March weeds and tufts of grass along the edges reemerged green against the brown of the dirt street and under the rising sun.

Burton Ardway, the owner of the newly constructed Ardway Hotel, stepped out from inside the building and onto its boardwalk. He gazed along the street in the gathering light.

Ardway was dressed stylishly in a whiskey-colored, wool frock coat with leather lapels and matching waistcoat. The new boots practically sparkled, polished to a bull shine that cavalry grunts would envy. Embroidery of expensive gold and green thread lined a brown Western bow tie that accented Ardway's green eyes. A large Stetson "Boss of the Plains" hat with a slender leather band shaded his tanned, lined face. Too symmetrical or perhaps too delicate for his likes, Ardway had caved in the big hat's left side with his fist to rough it up.

Dressing like a well-to-do rancher could not hide Ardway's thirty-plus years working long hours moving cattle and horses. His strong build was honed like a keen blade against the territory's fierceness.

Ardway had taken this all on and still had his scalp, despite several close shaves. His gaze was open but sharp as cold steel in its appraisal. He wasted no time in sizing things or people up nor chewing and spitting them out if needed.

To the locals it was quite out of the ordinary when Ardway was dressed to beat the drum and especially when he was pleased to show it off. He stepped down into the street and walked along its center, taking in the town with pride because his fortune had a large hand in building it. Down the strip an older man rode his horse toward him with an easy lope. They tipped their hat brims slightly to each other, smiling warmly as neighbors do when passing. Ardway inhaled a deep breath, relishing the morning's cool clean air. He marched on with his mission but with a lighthearted swing to his gait.

Along the street a few storekeepers hustled around in white cotton or leather aprons, brooming their front walks, swatting at rats scurrying back to their nests. An old black dog with a missing ear and a stringy-haired calico cat worked viciously as a team. The dog had just managed to clamp its jaws on an escaping rat's tail, stopping it in its muddy tracks. The cat jumped, sinking its fangs into the rat's neck. Together they pulled and ripped the rodent to pieces, wolfing down torn chunks of red meat. No one watched. This was just another morning in Spirits Bend. Work needed doing just like animals got to eat and rats got to be killed. As the two former enemies shared their meal: brawny young shop boys stepped out of the establishments in rolled-up sleeves and sweated to carry heavy wooden boxes piled up with goods. They set them down for show on the planked sidewalk and trudged back for more.

Wives and daughters, dressed in dark grey and blue to better hide their sweat stains, bustled about efficiently behind the store windows arranging items for display. Two stores had the latest "Gay Paree" attire from St. Louis and rolls of cloth and lace, sold by the foot or cheaper by the yard. Three shops sold handguns, double-barrel shotguns and rifles along with farm and hand tools. There were also cocaine and morphine remedies for stomach sickness and headaches alongside rawhide bags, belts and hats. Men were supposed to have little sense for arranging these store items for show. But that was a lie, just like it was a lie that women could not run a ranch or farm. Wyoming understood that well enough to give women the right to vote in 1869 long before any state or territory in America. It was common knowledge throughout the territories and down to Texas that Wyoming women did not take offense lightly and their tongue-lashings, gunplay expertise or horsewhipping exhibitions were to be highly avoided. The use of honesty with a little honey was the best approach to business, courting and engaging with the territory's women.

Ardway passed full-tilt down the street, eyes ahead and not wishing to partake of conversation with the store-keeps working at their plank storefronts covered in their brighter colors of green, yellow and white paint. He knew many of the recent store owners but not personally and it always felt uncomfortable trying to make conversation with them. They were prone to talk around an issue instead of getting to the point.

Ardway slowed his pace a little when he got to the older log-stacked buildings while staring at their familiar knots and holes and the patched roofs that sagged in the middle. Ardway knew their owners well and shared their histories without varnish. He passed a worn storefront that was shedding red and brown flakes from the gray wood underneath. It made him think of the old times of adding rusty nails to milk to make paint. The color wasn't consistent but Ardway thought that was its charm.

This brought Ardway back to memories of coming to Spirits Bend, a frontier town proud of its bloody days of killing the Lakota, Sioux and Cheyenne for their lands. And how it revered those that were killed in turn by these original people. Ardway thought of the many white men who spilled blood and brains with each other for the right to hold land which he was guilty for now. No wooden buildings were erected in those times. It was a village of tents and huts. A few old-timers, the ones that wore wide brim or old beaver hats with tattered linings, continued to run their freight wagons and pelt businesses from great patched tents to the east in the "old" part of town. They still slept outside in the back behind their tents and shacks.

Every last one complained how soft and mollycoddled the townspeople were who lived in wood homes and boarding houses. Especially the brutishly large muleskinners who fought poor damn strangers who rode into town on weekends. They baited the unknowing outsiders into ruckuses over their remarks praising the railroad. The Bighorn Wyoming Railroad had recently added a stop to the town and made a deep cut into the skinners' business. Those big ass muleskinners knocked their way through their worst problems with their fists and their backs but the railroads couldn't be manhandled. Ardway's money was on the scrawny ones that could sweet-talk a mule to go twenty miles more without resorting to a whip or axe handle. They were the ones that could figure out how to survive the town's changes that were coming with progress. Best stay away from those big lunkheaded ones until they died out or were run off. Unless you happened to enjoy having a big sore knot on your noggin. Unfortunately he had learned that lesson the hard way when he first came to Spirits Bend.

Ardway walked on and pondered over the future that people like those humongous skinners hated. A few disjointed blocks from the dusty tents was the writing on the wall—the Ardway Hotel—that he had just come from with its forty rooms. Rooms where the thinkers met and hustlers made plans to build businesses and bring money to themselves and to Spirits Bend. The building was three stories high and covered in red brick, imported from the Hydraulic Press Brick Company, again, from St. Louis — that city of the river boats and railroad. Ardway glanced back over his shoulder at his hotel. The Ardway Hotel dominated the town with its unheard-of height, width and the way the orange brick absorbed the light. It glowed at sunset like a hot coal. He was proud of that building and what it represented and loved to watch its orange flare on the horizon in the evening. Nothing like it for hundreds of miles. Also located on the facilities was a Chinese laundry with sewing, a barber shop and a dining establishment unpretentiously called Sticks (as in "sticks to your innards"), run by the locally famous trail cook and former girls school teacher, Mrs. Pettigrew. Truth be told she practically ran the whole hotel and made him a lot of money doing it. Ardway just signed the checks and nodded when she had an issue.

Pettigrew had worked for Ardway a few years before on the trail rides. His men loved the tough old lady like a favorite aunt and not just for her cooking. She was high morals but with a bit of the gutter to her. She had been married once but would not talk about it. Ardway set her up teaching school but she quit after the first year. Pettigrew told him she could not hack dealing with young children anymore having rode with burly men. It was her idea to build a brick hotel, which seemed crazy at the time but now he realized that Mrs. Pettigrew was smarter than he and his men ever were. She ran the dining room and served meals in strict accordance with proper table etiquette according to her rules. Meaning that you washed up and dressed clean and respectable and you damn well acted accordingly. The renown of Pettigrew's meals and proper table manners did more for bringing civilization to Spirits Bend than any preacher or lawman. Even the town's preacher-sheriff would swear to that on the Bible.

Ardway paused a moment to stare at a worn old shop that had been turned into a church and officiated by his oldest friend, Sheriff John Gammill. A makeshift sign with a wooden cross made from two carved tree limbs hung above the door. Painted in uneven block letters it stated:

ALL ARE WELCOME

A sly smirk crossed his face. His old friend, a former slave, was no angel when they arrived in Spirits Bend and neither was he. Your hide meant more than your soul in those days. Shaking off the memories Ardway's long legs strode in and out of the lengthening sunlight and shrinking shadows cast by the stores, bright then gray then bright again on the shiny boots. He moved a little faster, excited to see his destination.

Up ahead was the new railroad station. The tracks ran through the town but the building was still under construction. Ardway saw the wood frames nailed up for storage rooms along with the framed arch entrance. The pine wood studs and beams glared white in the morning light. Ardway stepped up on a new stone and mortar ramp with a few damp spots that lingered. He walked up to stand on the station platform that was piled up high with several stacks of lumber. No one saw as his head raised back, eyes to the sky, arms flung out wide, giddy like a child on a hill. The tall cowboy turned around basking in the smell of the sawed wood and feeling the sun on his face. Ardway had not felt so young and happy in years. He lived a lifetime in that instant, savoring his past and future.

Slapping his arms to his sides in mirth he almost skipped along the tall rows of raw yellow and red timber cut in long planks. Ardway headed for the only section of the station that was complete and with a roof, the ticket office and loading area. He passed a freshly painted green sign with white letters, expertly crafted with a knowing hand that read:

SPIRITS BEND

WYOMING TERRITORY

Ardway stopped and looked back at it. Grinning with satisfaction he walked on.

Inside the ticket office Ardway appeared at the counter, looking around, clearly pleased by the smell of the freshly-painted decor and knowing that his town had finally achieved this successful point in time. His sharp eyes searched around for the station manager. Seeing no one he turned and noticed a large, oval-framed mirror leaning against a wall.

He stepped toward it and cocked his head left and right, studying his appearance. Ardway hefted his pants up by the leather belt and pulled his vest and coat down, then stroked his finger along his top lip to smooth out his trimmed chestnut-colored mustache. He leaned closer to squint at its few gray hairs. Satisfied he smiled back at his reflection. At fifty-six years old Ardway could be handsome in the right mood, even with the inch-long pink scar splitting his right eyebrow.

～

Ardway walked out of the station's office and blinked in the bright sunshine. He stared down the tracks that led into the Wyoming hills. Glancing around and finding he was alone, Ardway reached into his jacket's inner pocket and withdrew spectacles along with a folded paper. He placed the glasses with their small and rounded lens over his nose to find the right distance to focus them. Finding the proper length he held the paper out and read its note. A polished gold pocket watch glinted in the sun as Ardway pulled it forth from his vest to check the time. Ardway peered with a cheery anticipation down the tracks as if all the world was riding on it to Spirits Bend.

From behind a corner two horses slowly pulled a weathered Shuttler farm wagon, its wooden sides worn and gray from many trips. The driver guided the creaky-sounding wagon up beside the station platform. He strained at the reins and sighed a deep breath as the animals stopped. The man's drained face was beaded with sweat which he wiped at with his damp shirt sleeve before lifting a canteen to his mouth and taking considerable gulps at the water. It was clear that during the last night a great deal of whiskey and beer passed over those lips. In the back of the wagon two hungover men with their faces hidden under their hats were stretched out next to each other in a deep sleep, quiet and unmoving like corpses.

Hearing the wagon pull up Ardway turned to see. His sunny smile dropped, turning his mouth down at the edges into a tight slit.

A man rose slowly from the floor under the wagon's cracked leather seat. Shirtless, his tanned skin showed its miles with three hardened bullet scars. A knife wound had healed raggedly down one side. Some animal with long teeth had chewed at his right shoulder. Lean corded muscles shifted across his chest and arms. Two long flaxen and gray-colored Indian braids framed the sharp cheekbones while the rest of his long hair had fallen loosely about his face and shoulders.

Ash Fendris gazed up. His pale blue eyes squinted with an irritable glare in the morning sunlight. At sixty years his face was lined but lean like a younger man's, its features that of a Swede mixed with one of the native peoples. His eyes adjusted and focused on Ardway. A crooked smile formed under his shaggy mustache and goatee.

"Ardway! You're a sight..." Fendris comically imitated Ardway's glasses with his fingers and thumbs in circles held to his face, "...for sore eyes."

He pulled a deep breath as he climbed tiredly up and sat upon the seat, then exhaled with a, "Woof!...Ain't seen you since..." he looked to the tracks to think. "Hmm, the first train came through, 'bout...five months ago."

Ardway self-consciously folded his glasses and slid them back into his coat before speaking. "Fendris..." nodding to him, "looks like the last train ran over you."

Fendris's bloodshot eyes looked down over his bare chest and dusty pants. His face broke wide in a burst of laughter, then contracted with a pained reaction for the effort. Recovering through it, he enjoyed Ardway's fun at his expense.

"Damned if I do, Burton! I sure do!" he shouted.

The two men in the back of the wagon woke up and roused themselves in miserable regret. Bleary eyes shifted from their boss over to Ardway. A prostitute in her hard thirties tumbled out from under the seat and squinted out at them with a vexed expression, obviously not a morning person. Rouge and mascara ran red and black in smeared lines down her cheeks. For a moment Fendris and his men were confused, unsure where, or how, they had picked her up.

Unnoticed over by the tracks the drunken man who had tried to commit suicide the night before, sat up. He blinked up in pain at the sunlight. Stiff from having slept on the damp gravel and grass, he struggled with his limbs to rise and stand.

"Blazes, what are you doing here, Burton, and all dressed—" Fendris's eyes expanded wide. "Junior! Home from schooling back East." He whistled. "That's it! Only thing'd drag you into town from your...'Ardway and Son' ranch."

Ardway made no answer, turned his eyes back to the tracks.

Fendris made a slight knowing smile, sensing an old wound. "You sure he's coming, Burton? S'been a few years..."

He snickered to his men. "He might just want to stay in ol' Philadelphia," and chuckled loudly to goad Ardway. "Same as Burt's wife."

Ardway rotated slowly, revealing a face more stone than human.

Fendris drew back at Ardway's glare, delighted. He reached over and hugged the dim whore to him. He kissed her roughly but his eyes remained locked on Ardway. He finished and turned to his men. "I sure miss Patricia. Burt's wife was the finest and prettiest lady ever lit the streets of Spirits Bend." He shook his head at Ardway. "It's a damn sin, Burt. The way you run her off."

Ardway's eyes squeezed tight, exposing pinpoints of fierce light. His voice spoke low and with disgust, "Flappin' your gums...and with mud, Ash? Was never your way."

He pulled both flaps of his coat back, revealing twin holstered Colt .45 pistols. "Or mine."

Fendris's eyes dropped their humor. He rose and was followed, reluctantly, by his jittery men. The men's hands trembled. Sweat leaked down their faces, gray and drained of blood.

The prostitute blinked in irritation at the men a few seconds as her mind fought to clear the night's residue. A candle sparked on concerning the situation as her runny raccoon eyes expanded in shock. She bolted off the wagon, falling flat in the dirt and stumbling up fast to disappear down an alley.

Ardway stood resolute and ready. He had not killed in five years. That was the day that his wife had left him.

Fendris's face glowed with the old wildness. His men saw its awful expression and knew there was no backing down.

Ardway stared his hard eyes into the sweating faces of the driver and two hungover men. They squirmed in their damp sticky shirts, nervously licking at their dried lips. He smiled with a devil's knowing grin. The men grimly realized what Ardway saw. The bloodshot eyes and shaking limbs showed to all the world what easy pickins they were and there was not a goddamn thing they could do about it. Fendris saw this fear in his men and his manic excitement cooled down a few notches. And there was something else digging at them. Ardway was not in his usual riding clothes but dressed up slicker than an undertaker. At a funeral. Their funeral? His eyes blazed a calm light and the hands were steady. Each man felt a dread that froze their heart. Like the feeling a person gets when falling off a running horse over rocks.

Ardway raised his arms slightly up with fingers curved out, feeling unhurried, but ready. He felt their fear. It made him even more serene. He was the one in control here.

Defiantly Fendris stared into Ardway's cold eyes with an iron determination despite wildly overplaying this move.

A clamor of laughter froze the moment.

Everyone looked suspiciously to it. Out of nowhere the drunk stumbled up between Ardway and Fendris and right at the moment before pulling triggers. He continued to laugh while announcing, "Gentlemen! Gen-tle-men." The men's eyes flicked shocked glances at each other. Who was this queer fish?

The drunk twirled around with his arms out, laughing to each man in the circle. "Laughter, gentlemen! Laughter with friends! Good times! And..." A silly thought had crossed his face, then blurted out in song, "And we all come to Jesus...in the end!"

The drunk laughed uproariously at his private joke while Ardway, Fendris and his men blinked on in astonishment. For in this morning light the drunk's appearance was a walking horror. His stringy, matted, dark hair had not been washed, combed or cut in over three years. The long filthy beard was a tangled mass of knots crowded with bits of dried food and dead insects. Apparently he was in his late twenties but it was a hard row that got him there. His coat and clothes were threadbare with ripped holes and atop his head there was a crumpled hat that would have insulted a scarecrow. Grime and dried mud were caked over his oily skin and garments. But worse, much worse than his appearance, he was completely oblivious to the sure death coiling about him; a crippled rat fallen into a nest of snakes.

"So, in that good Christian spirit, could you gents see into your friendly hearts...and spare some coin for a man recently fallen down on his luck?" The grinning wreck held out his dirty hand with its grit-encrusted fingers. Each man glanced around to the other, unsure how to react. The drunk dimly sensed something was off. His mood turned timid and desperate. "I'm sorry, Sirs. It's just...I need a little something. You know. My nerves. I..." He trailed off at their looks of shock and revulsion, seen so many times before. His voice raised higher, turning into part squeal and part whine, "Please-eee-eee..."

Fendris was gobsmacked for once. He glanced over at his men's edgy, desperate faces. His eyes darted to Ardway's startled expression. And in that moment he found his way out of this black hole he had dug.

Fendris began to chuckle, then his guffaws led to a great roaring howl. The men heard, saw and were relieved. So much so they started sniggering and chortling along. The drunk looked stupidly at them and joined in. Which sent them all into deeper convulsions of laughter.

A visibly irritated Ardway took a deep breath, his arms lowered and he waited for the men to quieten down.

Still chuckling, Fendris fished a silver dollar out of his pocket. "Here's a dollar, boy. Damned if you didn't earned it!" He flipped the coin in the air over to the drunk. The drunk reached for it, fumbled the coin, but with a quick surprising move, snatched the silver dollar before it dropped on the ground.

Fendris gave his men a look and nodded sternly over to the drunk. They quickly pulled their change out and pitched it. The coins rained about the excited drunk. He dropped to his knees, clawing the loot out of the damp mud.

Fendris signaled with a glance to his driver who eagerly grabbed the reins without sitting and slapped at each of the horses. The wagon took off with a jolt. Fendris fell down into the seat and snatched up a half-full whisky bottle rolling on the floor. He raised it to Ardway. "Here's to your Junior, Burt. And all that goes with him." He took a long draw on the bottle as the wagon rolled down the road.

Ardway watched the wagon go, unsure what had happened. Then he turned his attention to the drunk, digging coins from the mud. The drunk looked up at Ardway cheerfully and held out his grubby hand.

Peering at the drunk with vicious contempt Ardway reached inside his pocket to withdraw a silver dollar. It caught the light with a flash. The drunk eagerly leaned forward toward the money. Ardway pulled back and lobbed the shiny coin high and down the street. The drunk bolted, shambling after it. With his eyes locked on the money, he shouted over his shoulder to Ardway. "Thank you, Sir! Thank you kindly!"

Mystified and annoyed Ardway watched the hunched, broken man stagger and weave down the dirt street. A train whistle blasted its approach. Ardway snapped around. Gray smoke rolled above the incoming train in the blue morning sky like a snake twisting through clear water. Forgetting the drunk and Fendris, Ardway hurried to meet it.

Chapter Two:

Shot in the Neck Drunk. Again.

The train rumbled slowly into the station, brakes hissing and screeching to bring its stop. Ardway appeared, feeling the throb of the powerful engine as a pressure valve released a great cloud of steam about the platform. He waded through it, too excited to wait while searching each of the cab windows.

At the first car's exit opening a man was looking down, his face hidden by a gray hat. Ardway's eyes sparkled with anticipation.

Jurant finished tying the thin straps holding his black leather gun holsters to his legs. He rose to his six feet, two inches height, dressed in a trim wool suit and a burgundy-colored vest. Jurant was surprised to catch Ardway, an obvious man of means, staring so intently up at him. He returned Ardway's gaze with coal-black eyes while his fingers cautiously stroked his holsters in readiness. The men gauged each other for a quick second. Ardway's face dropped in disappointment and he walked briskly away. The rangy Cajun pulled off his hat and ran his fingers through his dark wavy hair with puzzlement and relief. Jurant gazed after Ardway who was eagerly eyeing each cab window down the platform. Satisfied that he wasn't being watched Benton Jurant turned and grabbed his worn leather military valise and the Spencer repeating rifle. He stepped down to stroll easily off the platform and wandered into town.

Ardway stood at the end of the train and stared around in confusion. No passengers had gotten off except that tall stranger. A despondent looking woman clung to her two tired children in the last car. She stared through the window down at the expensively-dressed cattleman who seemed lost and worried in the moment. A smile parted her grim features and she laughed out loud. The alarmed children looked to each other in confusion. They had been watching their mother slip away from them and everything from the moment that she stepped on the train. Now she was laughing, something she hadn't done since Pa left.

Ardway walked slowly back along the train while glancing up in the windows. His eyes stared close at every face but their hopeful energy ebbed away with each step.

Outside the ticket office a young black porter rolled a large gray travel trunk down a ramp from the train's storage coach. He wheeled it expertly up to a section outlined in white paint marked "Luggage Section" and settled it against the office wall and set the dolly next to it. He turned and walked back, lifted the heavy ramp up, shoving it back into its slot under the coach. He held out his arm and signaled by pumping a fist at the conductor at the rear, who signaled with a blue flag to the front. The cars clanged as the engine pulled at their slack. Without looking back the young black man took three easy leaps to jump up into the coach. Leaning out he waved ahead to the engineer.

The train's whistle shrieked as the engine's large wheels rolled faster and pulled it out of the station.

Ardway stepped back from the moving train, unsure what to do. His mind replayed the time for arrival as he gazed at the cars rolling past him. *Eight in the morning* said the telegram. The caboose finally clanked by and shrank down the tracks leaving only the train's drifting smoke and steam. Ardway stared at their gray trail until it disappeared into the blue.

The station manager appeared, startling Ardway back into the moment. The cheerful manager handed Ardway a light brown envelope addressed to him. Ardway gawked at the envelope and back at the manager before taking it.

"Your trunk is right this way, Mr. Ardway." He turned to extend his hand toward the trunk and they walked to it. "Do you have transportation?"

Ardway was still processing what was going on. He absently nodded, no.

"I'll see to that." The manager smiled broadly, "A trunk from Philadelphia! I'm sure you can't wait to see what is inside."

The manager hurried away as Ardway was left alone to stare at the trunk. He remembered the envelope in his hand and swiftly tore it open and withdrew a handwritten letter. Ardway pulled his glasses out, held them to his eyes and read the neat cursive script. After a few lines he whipped his glasses away, too overcome to finish the rest.

He placed his hand on the trunk, holding on to keep from falling. Tears stung his eyes and for a moment the world swirled around Ardway as the blood rushed from his head. He wiped at the tears with his hand and saw that he was crying. Gruffly he coughed and abruptly stood straight, glancing about to see if anyone noticed him in his calamity of weakness.

He rubbed at his face with the sleeve of his coat when a man with a dolly came up and thumbed to a wagon. Ardway turned away, waving the man to load the trunk. He waited to the side as the trunk was placed in the wagon. Ardway paid the man and stepped up into the wagon to sit. For a long moment he just stared off while holding the reins. Finally he glanced back at the trunk in a sadness that held his eyes a long moment. Then with a sneer, Ardway willed his misery into contempt.

Ardway slapped the leather strips with an angry yell. The horses jumped, bouncing the wagon as it raced down the street.

Behind a window in a market the tall proprietor looked up from patiently arguing with a man over the price of a can of beans. He stared at the dust flying behind Ardway's speeding wagon, wondering to himself who got shot. The dingy pug of a customer noticed and turned to see. They both leaned over to follow with their eyes on the wagon tearing down the street.

Ardway jerked the reins back, pulling horses and wagon to a sliding stop next to Molly's Saloon. He jumped off the wagon and nearly knocked down two men who grabbed hold to him for support. The angry rancher jerked loose without a word, stared ahead with one thought and marched into the saloon. The baffled men shrugged and went on their way.

The shopkeep leaned back from the window and peered down at his customer. "This ain't good."

"Hell no, it ain't! Last time Ardway went into Molly's that dandered up he came out drunker'n he was shot in the neck." He gazed off, remembering. "Those bushwhackers...thought he'd be an easy roll outside of town. Blew two of 'em's brains out and he was half-blind at the time."

The grocer shivered, "Jerked the knife out of own body and stabbed the one what stabbed him. Slit his throat..." He closed his eyes trying to hide that image, "Looked like a kilt hog with his head a-hangin' by a cord of skin."

The man put a nickel and a penny on the counter and took a second can of beans. "Somebody better go get Sheriff Gammill."

"Sheriff's at a revival over at Pottsmouth." The leggy man knotted his face in thought. "Rolfe, the banker. He might be who could slow him down."

The customer scooped up his cans, hurried to the door and turned, "You tell him. Ardway's too rich and too damn tough to mess with in this town. I'm not setting a foot out of my shack until Ardway's back out to his ranch." He scampered off.

Over at Molly's the people nosed up over each other while they peered in the windows. The trunk sat in the bright sunlight while the day heated up. It was still there hours later when the sun had moved and its shadow began to edge across the wagon's floor. People had stopped looking in the window. They crossed the street now to avoid the saloon.

～

Inside it was quiet. A few men drank about the room but the conversation was low. Like in the woods, trying not to let a bear or wolf's ears on to your whereabouts.

Ardway squinted at his poker cards. There was a full bottle of whiskey on the table. It waited behind another half-empty bottle. There was a broken bottle on the floor that had not been swept up.

Glasses of beer lined round the table along with used shot glasses. The wood top had sticky puddles from spilled whiskey. Three other men in suits sat stiffly while waiting on Ardway's call, their cards laid face down on the table before them. Alice, a saloon lady with a pitcher served water for them with a sharp eye on Ardway. They drank the water, leaving the beer on the table. Glen Jeffords, the city clerk, wiped the sweat off his long neck as another man stared up at the ceiling. The fat one with a red mustache closest to Ardway pulled his watch out to look at it. He began to rise.

"Sit down, Fred."

Frederick Rolfe tried to be nonchalant. "Well, Burton. The bank is—"

"My bank's president is on a holiday. It'll get by. 'Sides I need players with bucks and bits to make the cards interesting." Ardway spoke without his eyes leaving his cards. Rolfe slowly sat back down and picked up his cards with a nervous cough. Ardway looked over to him with an exaggerated conspiratorial grin. "That's good, Fred. You know who butters your biscuit."

The other men glanced away. Ardway saw their discomfort and laughed. He snatched up the full bottle and filled their shot glasses, whiskey spilling sloppily over the table. Spirits Bend's leading businessmen glanced nervously around to each other then reluctantly raised their glasses to Ardway.

"Drink up, damn you dudes! We're celebrating! More whiskey!" he proclaimed. "Alice!" He swatted at Alice's backside and she went for another bottle. For a second Ardway's excitement trailed off as something took hold deep inside. He grew quiet. The word came out small, with pain. "Celebrating..."

Then he looked up with that wild energy, "My son!" He threw his head back and knocked back the whiskey to stare at Rolfe. The banker sighed and lifted his shot glass to pour its whiskey over his lips, sputtering and coughing it down. Resigned, the others tipped their shots up and drank. Ardway watched them finish. Alice came over with a new bottle. He laughed wickedly, then louder. But it was hollow and a little too hard...and a little too long.

～

Outside, the trunk's shadow stretched longer too and grew darker before Ardway staggered out of the saloon. Dusk was just beginning to gather its purple in the sky. He stared up and down the barren street. Ardway cackled to himself, realizing why the streets were empty. His eyes locked on the top of a building outside of town. Something primal shifted inside him. He pulled himself clumsily into the wagon and flung the reins, yelling, "Shake your tails, you bastards!" The horses leapt to charge down the street. On the outskirts of town the people stopped and stared after Ardway's wagon and its dust. They shook their heads nervously to each other and hurried away.

Half an hour later at the north end of town the wagon with its trunk stood parked as a pale yellow, half-crescent moon rose above the darkening horizon. The horses drank water at a trough next to a small corral holding a few other horses with a locked shed for feed. A thick grove of wild Gambel oak and aspen snugly wrapped about the grounds including a two-story building with its ramshackle additions tacked on here and there, added as business grew over the years. The trees and brush served to cloak the wild yelling and laughter coming out of the odd-looking whorehouse known as Fancy Nancy's Palace.

The twilight's blue tint shone through an open window on the second story. Rising up through the floor the muffled sounds of a piano played at some frisky music. In the shadows of a small room the staccato huffing and grunting of two battling lovers bounced off the walls. A squat round candle burned languidly on a nightstand, its yellow flame swaying to each shift of air as bodies clashed on and around a brass bed.

Ardway stood on the floor while grinding himself into a woman with her back on the mattress and her legs extended up in his arms. His shirt was half off his torso with his pants hanging around his legs, piled atop his boots. Ardway grabbed her thick long thighs, pulling her higher to him. The woman was no wilting flower. She arched her back, sturdily raising herself to Ardway. Suddenly she flipped over and reached back with one arm, guiding him into her new position. Ardway was growling and slamming his body into hers. He raised his hand and slapped her round white hips violently again and again. She moaned and shifted to his rhythm, smashing her hips against his groin, playing rough to his tumble. Faster. Harder. Ardway was riding her like a wild horse, angry with her stamina matched to his, her denial of his sexual superiority. His focus swelled inside himself against the liquor and pain like a hot beam of light driving his anger. Ardway's head snapped up, veins strained across his neck, his sweat-drenched face gripped within the throes of his frenzy for the jolting climax. Ardway grunted to the ceiling three times but found no joy in his body's release. He gasped with a deep inhaled breath. His body sagged, his inflamed memories not forgotten nor forgiven. He exhaled heavily and hoarsely, blowing out the candle's flame. Finished, he pulled up his pants and grabbed money out of a pocket. Ardway carelessly pitched it to fall haphazardly over the prostitute's body. She grabbed and tossed it up in the air, giggling to herself as Ardway shambled to the door. As he opened it, the hallway's white glare cut a slender shaft across the floor to the naked buxom woman covered in coin and bills.

"Burt..." she said. He stopped with his back to her. "...try not to kill anyone." Ardway walked out and closed the door, leaving her laughing in the dark.

Rouget's Mill was a few doors down from a muleskinner's place on a street more weeds than road. No light came from the closed shacks next to the saloon. It had been a tiny leathersmith shop ten years ago, now turned into a bar by throwing up some rough planks over barrels and salvaging chairs out of the trash with sawdust thrown over a dirt floor. Liquor bottles lined a warped wooden shelf behind the counter. At three in the morning the yellow flutter of candlelight left only faint outlines of figures and objects in its shadows. Wearing an old yellowed apron, owner Rouget was resting his considerable gut on a small barrel under the counter. He held his tired head in his hands propped up by his elbows on the sagging board. Three men sat around a barrel in a dark corner, too stoned to talk or move. Like pale specters etched on the gloom they occasionally reached out to the whiskey bottle they shared and sipped it for a little warmth while it sucked the same out of them.

Rouget normally would have closed up hours ago but Ardway stumbled in and ordered a bottle, throwing his money blindly over the bar. Ardway had steadied himself, holding to the counter with no hat or coat, his shirt open and hanging over his pants muddy from a few tumbles on the way over. The barkeep had gasped at his condition but recovered at the sight of the silver coins. He quickly walked Ardway to a chair and shared some drinks with him for extra profit. But Ardway only wanted company long enough to make it proper before he slid back to drinking alone. Some of his friends came in to check on him and tried to get him to go back to the hotel but he pulled his Colts and that ended that. He had come to the worst shit-hole bar in town for one reason—to drink and not to be riled.

Ardway was slumped in a chair with his legs up on a barrel, too drunk to move. His earlier pattern was that he snored, woke himself up, yelled for a bottle and would fall back to sleep. Rouget was obliged to get him a new bottle at every holler and was keeping a tab. Ardway even bought the old sots in the corner a bottle—or at least it sort of sounded like he did to Rouget. Nights like this maybe happened once in a lifetime and the old fat bartender was going to ride it for all it was worth.

Ardway had started to snore again, low and guttural. After about a minute something moved at the next table. Fingers slowly extended out of the shadows to lightly place themselves on the whiskey bottle held to Ardway's chest. Gently and carefully the bottle was pulled from Ardway's grip. It slid from his fingers, the glass neck almost drawn away when Ardway woke with a start. He caught hold of the bottle's neck like it was falling. His eyes blinked open and saw a man stealing his whiskey. Ardway jerked his gun out and shot. The bottle exploded, throwing liquor and glass about the table and floor.

The man screamed like boiling water was dumped on his lap. The three men in the back turned their ghostly faces to the noise with no heed.

Ardway jumped up from his chair, holding his cocked pistol on the quaking man. He looked down, saw the neck of the severed bottle in his hand and pitched it away. Ardway bent down, squinted at the man groveling at his feet. His face drew back with recognition, "You!"

The ragged drunk from the railyard stared up with eyes bulging as he pissed himself. "Lord, please! D-d-don't kill me!"

Ardway seized the wailing drunk and jerked him to his feet. Ardway slapped him across the face with the gun barrel and the drunk began to make with loud moaning sounds. Frustrated Ardway grabbed the man's long beard and slung the screaming boozer about the room, crashing into walls and over barrels and chairs. Rouget and the other drunks jumped up and tried to stay out of the way. Ardway worked a path over to the front and tossed the bearded man out the open door into the deserted street.

"Help! Murder!" screamed the terrified drunk, crawling on his belly through the mud of the street.

Ardway could barely walk but lurched into the Mill's doorframe. He stepped out and over to the drunk where he furiously jerked him up by his ragged coat to his knees. Ardway jammed his Colt's long barrel against the man's nose and cocked its hammer.

Rouget appeared at Ardway's side, his hand gripped his shoulder. "God's mercy, Mr. Ardway! He can't help it. He's just a...poor drunk."

The drunk squealed, "Oh God, yes! Please! Mercy!"

Ardway's finger twitched about the gun's trigger. A thought crossed his clouded mind and then to his wild face. He smirked dementedly at Rouget then leaned in to study the quaking man, slobbering and crying in the street. Ardway's disgust soured, curling his lip as he un-cocked the Colt's hammer.

Without warning Ardway brutally smashed the barrel over the drunk's skull. The man's whimpering cut off with a groan as he collapsed unconscious into the mud. Ardway reached down and seized the lapel of his coat and the back of his pants. He dragged the limp body over to the wagon and slung the drunk up onto its floorboard to sit. For a moment the drunk's face shone in the moonlight, white and dripping in blood. Ardway got the man's hat off the ground and roughly pulled it over his bleeding head and let go. The ragged man slumped back in a rumpled pile next to the trunk. The rancher pushed the drunk's legs inside, slammed the tailgate shut and locked its deadbolts.

Ardway staggered to the front of the wagon. With an effort he pulled himself up onto the seat. Drawing a deep breath he seized the reins. Rouget stepped forward before the horses to make sure Ardway would see him.

"Wait. What are you doing with this man?"

In the shadows of the street Ardway's face was hidden as by a black mask but his eyes shone with light like torches flickering in the distance.

"Man?" He nodded back at the drunk. "This worthless tub of guts ain't a man!" Ardway hoarsely spat, "But I'll make him one, dammit, I will! Unless God calls him first."

Ardway slapped hard at the reins. The horses charged forward, knocking Rouget to the ground. The wagon wheels blurred by inches from his face.

Rouget steadied his hand to a roof post, rose and watched Ardway and the wagon disappear. He stared uneasily at his saloon and then to the black road leading to Ardway's ranch. Rouget's hand quickly traced the sign of the cross over his chest as he lowered his eyes. The fat bartender hugged against the post, sighed loudly, and pushed away. Rouget walked past his three ghost drinkers. They watched as Rouget walked quickly inside his dark saloon and slammed the door shut. The lock clicked loudly like a signal and the ghost drinkers heard and faded away into the shadows.

Chapter Three:

Purgatory's Road

T he horses charged along the rough trail, tossing the wagon up and down under the moonlight. Ardway knew the uneven road, traveled a thousand times and more during his trips during night or day. He cracked the leather straps attached to the horses' bits, pushing the team on and faster. In the back the large trunk and the man bounced against each other again and again. Each slid violently around the floorboard like worthless stone and dirt sloshed in gold pans mined in the nearby stream over forty years ago.

The drunk was pinballing between his body's suffering and death. Reality and nightmares collided through a mirror, smashing it with glass flying everywhere in a thousand reflections. Pain battered his head from the wallop of the gun barrel and something else. His guts and brain were shaken and bounced about like a rat in that black dog's jaws. This and the fear that he was speeding to some greater and unknown horror. He was tossed from the floor to flying in space and slammed back over and over. His thoughts and energy splintered unhinged, slipping from his shuddering heart and soul while rushing out into the black universe through his limbs and fingers. He was coming apart at the seams of his existence when an island touched him in the storm. His arms found it first, then his legs and feet. He wrapped to it like a leech on a wound. The damn trunk. In and out the drunk fell through his visions and this torture but as long as he held to the trunk he knew something existed beyond the madness.

The drunk had tried to look and see where he was, open his eyes, but the tossing and inertia were too much. Images splashed and swirled. His fears and reality flew around like broken glass shaken in a box.

The drunk caught glimpses of hills and valleys, shrub and trees, all blurred past in obscure chiaroscuro images under the moonlight. Creatures trotted in and out of the black void. A coyote ran beside him, snapping and howling. It faded into the distance. A fox laughed and jumped over the wagon to float up to the crescent moon. A huge bear peered out of dark woods, eyes glowing and teeth white, growling as it disappeared within the swaying tree branches. Ravens glided overhead on extended wings to stare down on him holding to the trunk. They merged into one giant bird and blotted out his vision, cawing for him to sleep or die. But the pain, the ache, it would not let him sleep or rest. A hard rain blew in, cold and wet as he clung to the trunk for warmth. It offered none but it did shield him a slight cover from the wind and some of the rain. That meant that the trunk must be real. It did not pop in and out with the visions but remained and that was everything to his sanity in those moments.

The drunk saw Ardway look back over his shoulder to stare at him. Ardway's face was manic and feral. The wind and rain whipped his hair about his head like a raptor's wings. The features contorted under the silver and shadows of the moonlight and became a devil grinning at him and laughing with the thunder. The face became blotted with swirling shadows and then a new face emerged. A woman of mixed blood stared at him, beautiful with long black Native American hair that spread into the night like spider webs. The French eyes were green, smiling seductively and teasing a secret. For the first time the drunk felt a dread so real his lips pulled back over his yellow teeth and a ragged scream escaped. The pain from his head wound throbbed but something different had been added. Something from deep inside. Familiar but so far away. An old sorrow filled him then. And with it the blackness flowed in from the edges and the drunk let go and passed out into a grateful oblivion.

Chapter Four:

Hell Has a Gate

In the pale gray light of morning the fog parted as the wagon crested a hill. In the distance a handsome two-story house of log and stone moved closer and into view. As they neared the house a great rustic barn and a long stable appeared. This was followed by a low-slung bunk house with its kitchen/dining structure along with various sheds. Cattle and horses sought to bathe in the rising sun and its warm shafts of light while grazing lazily behind a long row of fence rails. A few cowboys rode on horses up trails leading into the surrounding hills.

The drunk woke up sensing the change in temperature and peeked out from under his hat. He blinked in the dawn's light, unsure, sick and afraid. Was this real? The wagon's trailing dust plume ignited in orange flames in the ruddy light. High overhead they passed under a large hanging sign slung from two large columns made of mortar and brown rock. The drunk believed a gateway had opened and swallowed him whole. A sign, "ARDWAY AND SON RANCH," had been crudely hewed by axes in its weathered wood as if left by ancient people. The great horned skulls of two steers blazed with the sun's fire and leered down over him. The drunk pulled his hat back tightly over his eyes.

At reaching the house Ardway pulled back on the reins, drawing the horses to an exhausted stop at a trough where they inhaled the water. Two men walked up fast to meet him. His head foreman Jed Wilson and the large junior foreman Seth Kroeber were smiling until Ardway jumped off looking like he'd dragged in under the wagon. Sweat poured down Ardway's unshaven face in grimy streaks. His dirty clothes were ruined. His hair hung down over his eyes in a tangled mess. Their mouths formed "O"s in shock at seeing Ardway. He hoarsely barked, "Wilson, close your trap and get this trunk up to Junior's room."

Wilson stared a moment before asking, "Where is—"

"Dammit, he ain't here! Can't you see? Quit asking fool questions!"

The foreman looked around, motioned to the trunk and two men standing nearby. They jumped to and quickly leaped into the wagon. Both were caught off guard by the slovenly pile of rags only to realize a man was inside. His eyes trembled like a kicked dog from under all the hair and the squashed hat. They roughly stepped over him and slid the trunk to the back. They jumped down, jerked the trunk off and carried it, following Wilson to the house. Ardway shouted to his second foreman, "Kroeber!" He pointed at the drunk. "Put this sorry addle-pot to work. South Range."

The drunk raised himself up. He weakly stared over the wagon's sideboards. "Water..." he rasped. Ardway quickly stepped over to the trough and pulled a bucket out of it. He tossed the water full into the drunk's shocked face. The drunk sputtered and gasped for breath.

Ardway stared at him. "What do we call you?"

The drunk coughed, "I...I don't know..."

"Your name, you corned sot!"

"I...ain't got one. Something happened. My...my mind is...broke."

Ardway shook his head at Kroeber. "Sort this out. Take care of these horses first." Kroeber hesitated, repelled at the disgusting sight of this filthy man. Ardway didn't hesitate. "Kroeber!"

Kroeber jumped into the wagon, slapped leather and the wagon rolled away. The drunk bounced about, grabbing the sideboard to steady himself. He leaned over and called to Ardway. "Mister! Your whiskey. I'm sorry. I just...just needed a drink!" He nervously stared around at the ranch, fear in his eyes, worried of what was going to happen. He looked back to Ardway. "What are you doing? I don't know...What's going on?"

Ardway ignored him and walked toward the house. He went inside and slammed the door shut.

The frightened drunk looked around the yard. Everyone went about their work giving him no heed. Panicked, he glanced about and yelled, "For God's sake, help me somebody!" A few men looked up but no one showed any care or concern. He sank down on the floorboard and whimpered to himself, "Help...me..."

Chapter Five:

The South Range and a New Name

The long green grass barely moved in the gathering heat of the morning sun when Kroeber drove the wagon with the fresh horses through and while passing three men digging mounds of dirt from post holes with clam shell diggers. It was brutal hard work on their arms and shoulders and each was covered in sweat. The humidity was climbing at nine o'clock and wouldn't slow until around four. It was going to be a long warm day. Kroeber drew back on the reins, stopping the wagon. He wiped the sweat off his brow with his large muscled forearm. He stepped over the seat and stood next to the sleeping drunk. Smiling to himself the hulking Kroeber raised his big boot all the way back for momentum, and brutally kicked the pointed toe directly into the man's tail bone. The drunk screamed himself awake, flopped about the wagon and fell out the end in a squirming heap on the ground.

The men nearby turned to see, startled at the man's bawling. They saw the strange bearded man on the ground with Kroeber looming over him on the wagon. It wasn't their business but everyone hated that big rattler Kroeber. Just once they would like to see him getting his tail bone kicked like that.

Kroeber jumped off the wagon to tower over the cringing drunk who held his hand out in a feeble defense. "Please! I'm sick. I can't—"

Kroeber's ham hock-sized fist smashed down into the man's face. The drunk fell like a rock dropped to the ground. He lay there unconscious as his blood gushed from his nose into the dirt.

The men stared away uneasy.

Kroeber bent over the body to admire his cruelty. He glanced over at the men.

"When he wakes up, make him fetch water for you. If he can hold a bucket. What a soft horse. Be sappy for weeks, maybe months."

The men looked bewildered at the drunk. None dared asked any questions. A thin young man with a wispy blond mustache, Bailey, approached and bent down over the unconscious man. He peered closely at the bearded filthy mess. "He...he looks like something a coyote shat." Suddenly Bailey squinched his nose up, coughed violently and quickly backed away. "Uh! Smells like it, too! I swear, I never seen anything so...wasted. What's his name?"

Kroeber's face lit up with a thought, his lips spread wide and laughed. "That's it, Bailey!" Bailey wasn't following, his brows turned up in confusion. "We'll call him, 'Wasted'."

Everyone leaned in to gawk at Wasted's senseless face pressed in the dirt with the blood, and his pupils rolling around.

Wasted. The drunkard. The amnesiac. The demolished man. Whoever he was that name followed him down as he bobbed in and out of consciousness. Wasted. A name for ridicule or...what? He fell further down into a deeper...

Black.

A flash of expensive white lace swept before his eyes turning...

Black.

Two gunshots boomed explosively in a dark room, echoing into silence.

A beautiful raven-haired woman stepped out of the shadows, part Native American, part French, in an expensive white lace dress...and turned with a grace and assurance beyond her years. Her stunning green eyes stared directly over her shoulder at...

Wasted's eyes. Younger. Desolated. Lost.

The thunder of three quick gunshots wiped the image away into...

Black. Silence.

Light exploded the moment open. Somewhere on the South Range Wasted was bent weakly over a dropped bucket of water on the ground. The water covered his tattered shoes as it drained into the ground. Wasted looked about, unsure and confused. Men were repairing a rail fence to a small corral. The red-faced Kroeber stormed over to him. Wasted's arms and legs trembled like things apart as the alcohol withdrawal gnawed at his insides. He stammered gibberish at the huge man, unable to focus his words, like a baby. Kroeber reared his huge fist back, punching Wasted in the face...

Black.

Wasted made slow stunted steps into the bunkhouse that night, his body twisted like a crippled old man's. He was late and missed the cook's supper of rabbit stew and rolls. A few lanterns along the walls cast a golden sheen with heavy black shadows about the room. Men played cards at a table. Others sat on their bunks talking or reading. Some washed their clothes around a tub of water. One sewed a ripped pair of pants. As Wasted hobbled by they looked up. The chatter immediately died in their mouths as each dropped open.

For most of the crew this was their first eyeballing at the living mess of hair, dried blood, sun-burned skin and dirt called Wasted. He stared at the floor, having to concentrate with a focus just above unconsciousness. Each unsteady step was a triumph over agony. His eyes hurt, mere slits to permit just enough information inside his mind to move. He had been told his bunk was at the very back. He moved toward it with an all-consuming desire to lie down and die. Any excitement at getting closer was dragged out of him by the pain coming from every spot in his body. The men moved out of his way, not that he noticed them. The back of the room was all that mattered. For a moment he had to stop and gather his thoughts. Where was he? He was walking. Where? His body swayed. Bailey stood up from his bunk and walked over to stand close.

Oh, Wasted remembered. The bunk. He moved on with short halting steps, dragging his feet. When he saw the empty bunk he almost cried tears. But tears were a bet he couldn't meet. His body didn't work right and he did not care. Nothing mattered but the bunk, where he could let go and let nature do with him as it willed. Life or death. He did not care. Suddenly a man stepped toward him. Wasted realized that it was the big man. For the first time on this long journey to his bunk he felt something besides pain. Kroeber was there making sounds. His lips moved but Wasted did not hear anything.

He was fighting to stop a wave of nausea clawing up through his intestines like rats on fire. It was too much. Wasted felt the vomit coming up, his mouth opened and...he puked all over Kroeber.

The men of the bunk house froze in place, eyes ready to pop out and bounce on the floor over to Wasted. The only sound was Kroeber gasping in shock. The only movement was him stepping back a foot too late, Kroeber's arms up and waving uselessly as pale liver-yellowed vomit dripped down his shirt and pants to cover over his boots.

Wasted looked up at Kroeber's incredulous expression. The smell of the vomit hit the junior foreman's nostrils and he gagged, helpless to his own violated senses. In that moment Wasted knew what was coming but was too sick and worn out to care.

"Kill me, or...," he spoke as he walked away. Wasted collapsed into his bunk as the edges of the room's whiskey-colored light crumbled around him into...

Black.

The days went in and out like this as Wasted bounced between his body and mind rejecting reality and the alcoholic forced to deal with it. Ardway had come down hard on the men. No "firewater" for Wasted. Indians used to pay him to buy them whiskey for the price of a bottle. The irony galled him now. The men drank on weekends and all that Wasted could do was watch and hate them all for it. He tried begging but that just got him a hard kick in the pants. Wasted took it because he had no damn choice. He learned that lying around got more of a beating by Kroeber than being out on the range trying to work, even if he was slow as an old grandpa about it. His insides hurt like someone was in there kicking and punching to get out. And maybe there was, the person he used to be before he became this pathetic mess. God, he wanted a drink every second he was awake. He wanted to kill Kroeber for a shot of whiskey—or sometimes just for a spit of water. The blackouts were a blessing. Sleep was hell for the dreams. What the devil did it mean? No memories of his past except a woman and guns. Hell, how did he ever end up here in the Wyoming Territories? These thoughts went round and round and ached his body as much as his mind. He was sick with the not-drinking and sick inside dealing with the mystery of himself. Nothing mattered but being lost in the black. The black was a void untouched with a sweet solitude and peace from himself.

And then came a time when he was in the void that he remembered voices and sounds...

Black.

Kroeber yelled, "Get out of the way, you sot!" The sound of a fist crunched loudly against Wasted's face.

Black.

Jordie, another ranch hand, gently spoke, "Wasted, come on. Get up."

Black.

"Wasted! Stop your puking or by God, I'll kill you!" bellowed Kroeber.

Black.

Wilson said, "Good job on splitting those logs, Wasted. You're finally getting some muscle."

Black.

Tom was angry, "Slow down on those beans, Wasted. Your bunk is next to mine, damn your asshole."

Black.

"Finished? You?" Kroeber couldn't hide the surprise in his voice. "Well...start on that hay over there. And Wasted. Don't let me catch you loafing."

Black.

Bailey was shocked, "You're still awake past dinner? Boy, Wasted! That's a new one."

Black.

"Thanks, Wasted. 'Preciate the help." Tom's tone was genuine.

Black.

The next day, or month, or maybe it was a year later the blistering sun was close overhead, yellow and hot. Wasted was having a rough time sorting his jumbled memories with the pain and sickness as much as the days and moments. Four men worked hunched over a wagon nearby with a missing wheel. Wasted hauled a bucket of water toward them, hanging from his drooped arms barely an inch above the ground. His shoulders and back ached. His muscles felt stripped raw. A knowing horror crept over him as he watched his hands start to shake. The bucket dropped to the ground, its water spilling. His head jerked up, darted nervously about looking for Kroeber. He was nowhere to be seen. Wasted's body sagged in relief. He wearily picked up the bucket and trotted back to the stream.

After refilling the bucket he staggered over and placed it on the ground by the men. The one named Jordie, a wide barrel of a man, looked up and wiped the sweat from his eyes. He took a few steps over to the bucket. He cupped his big wide hands in the water and lifted some up and drank. Wasted was leaning against the wagon, ready to pass out. Jordie was partially disgusted with Wasted but hot himself and saw that the dragged-out looking man was doing the best he could. He gave Wasted a nod to lie down under the wagon. "I'll keep an eye out for Kroeber."

Wasted dropped to the grass, shooting Jordie a pitiful glance of thanks before shutting his eyes. Immediately he was snoring.

Black.

It was a chilly Wyoming spring night meaning it was as cold as a Kansas winter. Wasted, the low man on the totem pole, staggered back from the woodpile with an armload of chopped lumber. He tottered along over the bumpy ground in the dark to the bunkhouse. He followed the faint streaks of light streaming out of the cracks surrounding the back door. His body had recently lost some of its pain that had been torturing him since he got there. He was moving like a man of sixty years now instead of eighty. Abruptly his foot slipped down in a hole and he took a tumble with the cordwood falling to the ground. Wasted landed on his knees, then to his hands, gasping hard for breath. He waited and prayed that this abrupt shock to his back and arms would pass. The fall brought all the old pain back. That familiar feeling twisted up through him. He was still on the hook of alcohol. Wasted convulsed uncontrollably with the dry heaves for ten minutes before his body relented and allowed him to breathe. Wasted felt about the grass finding the wood and picked it up. He rose shakily as Bailey stepped out the door to look around for him. Wasted walked inside looking like nothing had happened and past Bailey saying, "Thanks." After he had piled the wood by the stove he climbed into his bunk and pulled the blanket over his head and welcomed the near instantaneous...

Black.

Chapter Six:

Bocephus

Coming back from having spent the day in the heat shoveling and hauling manure by wheelbarrow, Wasted walked along the stable shed dead to the world. "Walked" was the wrong word; he shuffled his feet forward while dragging the dust. Slowly by rote he placed one foot in front of the other toward the bunkhouse. The smell of shit and piss had inured his nostrils and senses to the world outside of his work and now to this task. His mind would kick loose his next goal once he got to the bunkhouse, which was to scrub water over his face and hands and get his sense of smell back. Then he had planned to grab a biscuit and a slice of beef, eat it at his bunk and pass blessedly out. It was a good plan. Only he hadn't counted on Bocephus.

Bocephus had the reputation of being the meanest and strongest damn mule on the property and perhaps in the entire territory. Earlier that day Bocephus had been indignantly rousted from his favorite shady spot under a barn eave by Wasted who was given the job by Kroeber to shovel the mule's shit and cart it away, for which you would think Bocephus would be grateful. He wasn't. Bocephus chewed on grass along the fence all day in the hot sun while eying Wasted wiping at his sweat as he shoveled among the flies and the stench. Wasted didn't move or act like the other cowboys, he was slow and weak, and that vexed Bocephus. Never had a slower cowboy been on this ranch. That odd behavior along with the length of Wasted's long black beard and hair spooked Bocephus like a snake or coyote would. And Bocephus stomped snakes and coyotes that came too near the stables to death, which is why Ardway and the rest tolerated him. He would have stomped the dogs, too, but they learned fast enough after some kicks and bites to give him his berth. So as Wasted shuffled in that strange slow way along the barn Bocephus galloped through it and nosed open the latch on the far door. He trotted out and carefully nudged up to the corner and hid out of sight. Wasted was so bushed he had to stop trudging along and rest on the worn path by the barn. It was just after he had crossed the end corner. He leaned over and placed his hands on his knees to gather his breath.

Off about thirty yards away Tom looked up from shoving food scraps into a hog trough and saw Bocephus angling to turn around backwards. Then he saw the mule carefully move with his tail end out behind Wasted. Tom's eyes sprung wide as he realized what was happening. He started running toward Wasted and shouted. Wasted looked up, confused about the commotion when—

Black.

It took a month for Wasted to recover from Bocephus's how-do-you-do. He had the most gruesome bruises blotted along his back and torso, with a jaundiced color running through and crowding around the black, blue and purple. The boys would gaze at it in wonder with a mix of respect and horror. They all had a war story about Bocephus becoming familiar but this ugly medal was his worst ever bestowed. Tom swore that Wasted was in flight for at least a minute and had ascended straight up twenty feet and sailed over fifteen yards. But as bad as it hurt Wasted something awful he was grateful for one thing. Miss Claudine, Ardway's cook and superintending housekeeper, had checked him over and pronounced that he had to stay in his bunk and not move. Just sleep. Which was all he could do anyway. No one gave any lip to Miss Claudine or they answered to Ardway. Not that she needed his help. Miss Claudine could skin bark off a tree just by raising her eyebrow. She also insisted Wasted be given a pot to keep by his bed instead of trying to get up to use the latrine.

Kroeber hated this "easy" treatment for the "worthless bar rag" and told anyone that would listen that Wasted was stretching a blanket to get out of work. He ordered Wasted out of bed to work after three days but when Miss Claudine heard, she practically ran down to the bunkhouse with her horns on.

"Mr. Kroeber." She paused and gave him a look that made the others back up a step. "If you do not let this young man heal properly, I shall have the men put you in a harness. Then I will hitch you to the backside of Bocephus, where he can kick God's mercy into your thick skull until you find the grace to repent."

Needless to say Kroeber knew that Miss Claudine wasn't barking at a knot and he stomped away to go shout at some other unlucky cowboys.

Wasted was alone and sleeping in the afternoon. The weather had become warmer and the bunkhouse had heated up more than usual. This made Wasted toss and turn and did him no favors with that big bruise over the side of his body. He woke up with a loud yelp at turning his body too much. Lying there waiting for the pain to ease he realized he needed to pee. Cursing, he worked to get his body turned right to drag the pot out from under his bed. He lined it up just right on the floor so he could swing up and get his legs on either side of it, then he could lower himself down to the pot. Or so he thought. After much howling and cursing of Bocephus while trying to get up, he finally made it. But Wasted was exhausted from the effort. He sat there while wiping at the sweat on his face when he saw the young woman with black curly hair standing inside the open back door. She stared at Wasted with a mixture of concern and amusement. Shocked, Wasted quickly reached for a sheet to cover himself with and yelled out in anguish at the resulting pain. The woman lost her smile and rushed over to Wasted. It was then she saw the horrible mark on Wasted's side and back.

"Oh my Lord and stars!" She leaned over and reached out to help.

Wasted jerked the sheet to cover himself, making him cry out again. He stared into her eyes with pain and embarrassment. The woman realized how much her presence contributed to the moment. "I'm sorry, I heard you crying outside. I thought something had happened and I..."

Wasted saw that she was only trying to help. "Well, you caught me trying to...use the pot. Not the kind of thing you want a stranger to walk in and see. Especially a woman."

The woman smiled again. Despite the embarrassing moment Wasted liked her smile. She had a few freckles under her eyes hinting at growing up with lots of sunshine. She wore loose denim pants and a print work shirt and stood before him in old boots with a wide brim hat hanging off her neck on a leather stampede string. Her body was lean and wiry like a girl that had grown up on a farm jumping fences and swinging from trees. It was her open gaze that put him at ease. It was warm, not calculating and mean, such as the kind he got tossed from hard women over the last few years.

"My name is...ah, Alice. I work at Molly's. Mr. Ardway said I could come out and see myself around his ranch. I grew up on a farm so...I used to see you around in town. You ah, look a lot better. 'Cepting for that awful looking bruise'n."

"Alice. If you're walking around this property alone, just be on the lookout for the meanest mule in Wyoming."

"I'll remember that. Ah, I had five brothers. I can see you might need, ah, some help..."

Wasted quickly spoke up, "No! I mean. Thank you, ma'am, but I can manage. If you could give me a little privacy?"

Alice gave a little jump. "Oh! Yes. I'll go back outside. But let me know when you're done. I'll come back to say goodbye."

Wasted nodded. Alice went out the door and waited. Wasted got up yelling like the devil and sat on the pot.

Teasing Alice called from outside, "Sure you don't need some help?"

"I'm good!" shouted Wasted. Then in a low voice to himself, "You damn woman." Alice called, "What did you say?"

"I said, how did you know Mr. Ardway?"

"I met him that night he tied one on for the books at Molly's. I got whiskey and beer for his table. He was torturing the richest men in town, making them play cards and drink. Afterwards he tipped me twenty dollars! He told me he had a ranch. Well, hell, we all knew that. When I said I grew up on a farm he said come out and see his place. So here I am. I see he's still drinking. Fell asleep on me visiting in the parlor. Miss Claudine told me to go look around the property for an hour and come back and Mr. Ardway would never know. It's nice out here but way bigger than the farm I grew up on."

Wasted finished peeing and yelled and cussed some more while he crawled back into bed and covered up. Gathering his breath, he called to the door, "Finished."

Alice came back in and up to his bunk. There on the floor was the pot filled with urine that he had forgot to shove under the bed. Wasted saw and almost killed himself trying to get up. Alice laughed and reached down and picked up the pot. Wasted watched in panic, "No, I can get..."

Before he could move, Alice turned with the pot, walked and carried it out the back door. She took it and threw the smelly contents in the grass twenty yards away close to the latrine. She noticed a water pump out in front of the bunkhouse and went and rinsed out the pot with a few pumps of water. Alice came back in the house from the front door and walked back to Wasted's bunk. She bent down and shoved the pot back under it. Wasted leaned back on his bed in resignation but with a grateful shine to his eyes. He could not remember a woman ever being so generous to him.

"I appreciate your kindness. I'm just so...whupped up. I hope I can repay you—"

"Oh, posh. It wasn't nothing. Glad to help. Anybody would have done the same for a person who got kicked by a mule...Hey, what's your name?"

Wasted's eyes glanced about, embarrassed again. "Well. They call me Wasted. 'Cause of I can't remember my name. Or anything else either."

Alice thought about it a second and then smiled with her farm girl warmth, "Wasted. That's a new one. If you come into town, stop by and see me at Molly's. But cut some of that beard and hair off and surprise me, huh? That's probably what scared that ol' mule. Sounds like he ain't as stupid as you think." She turned and walked down through the bunkhouse, turning at the front door. "See you around, Wasted!" And like that, Alice was out the door and gone.

Wasted closed his eyes and lay back on his pillow wondering if she had been a dream. He smiled. Suddenly a voice yelled, "Wooee!" and he looked up at an excited Bailey staring over him, "Wasted!

How the holy blazes you got a woman coming out the front door? You ol' bunkhouse Belvidere!"

When Wasted went back to work after two weeks Wilson made sure he was given easier jobs until he could walk like a regular human being again. He drove a wagon mostly, delivering supplies all over the ranch. Wasted was glad to become familiar with the property without having to work it for a change. After another week of this Kroeber finally got to have his way. It was decided Wasted needed to ride a horse and do some range work. Wasted couldn't recall ever riding a horse before. Kroeber chortled over the chance to get him up on a bronc. Bailey was assigned the task of getting Wasted "saddle ready" along with the help of the rawboned black, Nat Ware.

Wasted was quickly taught all the dos and don'ts of keeping a horse healthy, fed and clean then putting its saddle on and off. He found he liked that, especially brushing the horses down and talking to them. Wasted would sneak a carrot or one of the apples off his plate to his favorites. So after a bit of training, up he went into the saddle. The horse took off with Wasted fighting to stay upright while bouncing around like a fishing cork on a line in a rocky stream. That horse grew tired of Wasted's nonsense and bucked him flying into the air, hanging for a second like caught on that fish hook, then plowed into the dirt as a squished heap of hair. Wasted pulled himself up slow and awkward, stretched his limbs, checked if he was broken, but found nothing too painful. Note, this was in accordance to the Bocephus pain level indicator which left a man grateful that anything less than an attack by that damn mule was a blessing. So Wasted was determined to go again. Sometimes he managed to beat the horse's buck and jump off but hell, that was a tumbler too. Wasted didn't get better as much as he got pissed off at the horses. And also with that big lump of lip Kroeber laughing his ass silly at him over each toss. He worked harder and listened to every word and watched Bailey and Nat intensely, both of whom made riding a horse look as natural as a frog swimming in a pond. Wasted strained harder to pull the reins and use his legs. It took strength he didn't have but it was coming. And that's the thing that made the difference with the horses. They were used to rough men putting them through their paces and Wasted had to learn how to be rough. It began to come to him. His whupped body was filled with a new kind of pain at the end of the day but Wasted had decided it was a good pain. So much so that he was barely able to finish eating his supper at the end of the day, wanting only to make it back to his bunk to curl up into the...

Black.

All the hard work paid off and Wasted was trusted now to go on tasks about the property on a horse without a nursemaid. After two weeks of this Kroeber announced on Monday after breakfast, "The bar rag has finally got some spit to him. I'm sending Wasted out to the north border. Got some broken fences at the lodge up there he can work at while chasing new calves and cattle to fill it. Make a cowboy out of him."

Bailey spoke up, "Kroeber, he's still too green for that. There's wolves and Indians up there and he don't carry a gun." Others nodded with this.

Kroeber laughed, "You old ladies! Junior needs to walk to school without you holding his hand. Wasted! Get five days' worth of grub, saddle up and hit the trail, pronto!"

An hour later Wasted had packed his gear and saddle bag on a quarter horse named Jackrabbit when Bailey walked up. He checked over everything and gave a tug to some straps. Wasted waited. He knew Bailey had something to say. Bailey pulled out a double-long razor with a handle, filed off to a wicked point at the end. "Here. Take this."

Wasted looked it over and whistled. "Hell. You could shave five men with this and then stick a hog to death." His eyes turned to Bailey. "Thanks. I'll take good care of it."

"You better. I don't want to have to come get it if you don't come back. I hate that lodge."

Wasted smiled. "I'm looking forward to it. Five days without Kroeber barking down my neck."

Bailey's face clouded up a little thinking about it. "You'll be alone. Except for the critters and...just be sure nothing else is barking down your neck."

WASTED

Wasted nodded. He raised his boot to the stirrup and hoisted himself up. With a wave he nudged Jackrabbit with his heels and they bounded off up the trail. Bailey watched until each disappeared over the ridge. He turned away and heaved a sigh, ticked off with that prick Kroeber and feeling worried for Wasted.

Chapter Seven:

The North Lodge and Its Devil

Massive white clouds butted against the mountains with misty gray tendrils floating down the eroded cuts between ridges above the North Lodge. It reminded Wasted of a giant beard and that God must of been staring right down at him while he rode up into the camp. Everywhere the tall grass glowed emerald green with a wet luster that gave the hills an ethereal grandeur that only a heaven could have mustered. It had a feeling of timelessness which made you feel that you could live forever.

The ramshackle old lodge was dug into the steep hill with a thatched roof that extended over two rooms, a two-stall stable and an open work shed. Next to it was a corral about thirty yards across. Wasted got off Jackrabbit to let him loose in the enclosure. The horse was happy to be on flat ground. He munched at the tall reedy grass growing in and around the pen's rails.

Wasted busied himself cleaning the lodge and chasing out large woolly rats and a very angry raccoon that rose up on its hind legs looking ready to wrestle him for the right of ownership. Wasted started a fire and opened the doors to air the rooms out. The corral fence had a few rails that were rotten and repaired quickly with wood from the shed. The grass thatched roof could do with some minor repair but nothing that couldn't be put off until later. There was no sign of leaking inside.

Walking around the front he looked over the stone and mortar foundation that housed the well. He removed the heavy rocks on the hinged wooden cover and drew up a bucket of cold spring water that tasted sweet and coppery. Wasted sat on the edge of the well and ate some beef jerky and rested a bit. The view over the valley was breathtaking, showing the world so big and Wasted so small. He felt humble but alive and grateful for seeing it. A hint of blue smoke trailed over the treetops at the ridge and marked where the ranch house was much farther beyond. Looking out through the haze at the trees and grassland in their patches of green and brown far away made it abstract and unreal at this height. He felt a deep satisfaction about making the trip and the progress that he had already completed. It was about four in the afternoon and even with the clouds there was light. The nearby moo of a calf turned his head to that direction. Wasted yelled out, "I hear you, dogie." It echoed a bit. For the first time he realized how alone he would be out here; a speck in a world that would never miss his coming or going.

Wasted had started over to Jackrabbit when he noticed the calf he had called to earlier had wandered up the hill to investigate. He grabbed his coiled rope off the horse and walked over the forty yards where he faced the idle calf. The animal watched him with a great show of curiosity, having never seen a human before. Wasted thought to himself what an easy start this was. He carefully whirled his lasso, throwing its loop into the air. It landed around the neck of the docile calf and Wasted pulled it tight. The calf cried out and abruptly bolted. Wasted was jerked off his feet and dragged along over the wet sand and clay. Wasted managed to curl himself around and leapt up to his feet to dig in his heels, scooting to a stop. Calling out to the struggling calf, "Whoa, you damned hellcat!" he pulled and tugged until it reluctantly followed his lead back to the corral. By that time it had calmed down and trotted in easy as a kitten as Wasted closed the gate. Jackrabbit gave a disgusted wave of his head at Wasted, seeing a cowboy covered up in mud like that over a little cow. Wasted swore later the horse neighed in such a way as to say, "You're so stupid you can't tell skunks from house cats!"

That evening after a hot meal of dumplings and jerky Wasted unrolled his bedroll under the shed so he could stare up at the bright glittering stars so close here at the lodge. But his full day of riding and work took a hold of him as Wasted's head touched the blanket. Last thing he remembered was he had floated up in the sky and was swimming among the stars.

The next day a heavy squall had blown in as Wasted rode out to search for more calves and scattered cattle. He had found and roped seven calves for the corral while the rain increased. It was lunchtime but he wasn't hungry. He trembled violently and it wasn't because of the cold and rain. He felt sick as a dog and thought of going back to the lodge. But Kroeber would love that. Wasted didn't have a slicker, just his old ragged clothes that were soaked to the bone even with a wool blanket wrapped around him. Without warning an awful pain stabbed deep in his guts, sending him bent over the saddle. He retched a few stomach-clinched moments, puking up that morning's cornpone biscuits. As he weakly wiped the bile from his lips with his coat sleeve he felt a wave of depression like nothing before. His body still craved alcohol, even after being without it for five months. Was it ever going to stop? Wasted grunted at the pain, hung weakly to the saddle and stared at the ground. Behind him about twenty cattle had drifted up this way to be near the calves and were grazing on the hill under the cold gray sky. Wasted was figuring what would be easier, pulling himself back up in the saddle or falling off...when he saw the white bones sticking up through the tall grass.

Wasted slid down from Jackrabbit to check out the calf's remains. It was ripped clean except for some chewed gristle and membrane. The calf had bled out there and left a mottled, reddish-black pool. Probably not more than a week ago. Coyotes? There was a huge paw print in the dried blood. Six inches wide, seven inches long. A goddamn Goliath of a wolf! Even without a memory Wasted knew this was not normal. Wasted wasn't feeling depressed now. A cold dread squeezed his belly, his head jerked up. He glanced about the hill with a cold sweat mixing with the rain running down his face.

Wasted rode back to the Lodge and rounded up the cattle into the small corral with the calves for a snug fit. The afternoon's light was going. He tried starting a fire in front of the gate but the wind and rain put it out in minutes. So he sat down in the work shed under its roof and weighed his options out. Killer wolves. Cattle in corral. Cattle must be protected. No fire to scare wolves away. No gun.

And he felt like shit. He got up and went into the lodge but left the door open. Wasted went to the fireplace and started a large blazing fire. He took off his wet clothes and hung them and the wool blanket over some lines to dry. He grabbed a cot and dragged it over by the open door. A half full bottle of rye rolled out from underneath and spun around on the dirt floor. It stopped with its cork offered up.

Wasted was so shocked that reality fled from him. There was just the bottle staring back at him. Without opening it the old familiar smell wafted up through his nostrils. He could feel a hot sting to his lips. The smoky taste of whiskey flowed over his tongue and the roof of his mouth. Sounds and images faded away as the old sensation of being drunk overwhelmed him. He was swept away from himself and all responsibilities and feeling any pain. Wasted dreamed himself floating on his back in the middle of a gleaming lake made of rye and which filled the inside of that bottle. A cow bellowed from far away and afraid. Somewhere Jackrabbit gave a nervous squeal.

Everything snapped back instantly as Wasted felt the cold. The sun was gone. He could hear the jumbled drumming of the rain outside the lodge. A presence wild and terrible was out there, pacing around the corral and watching. The cattle and Jackrabbit sensed it. Wasted stared out the open door. But his eyes flicked back and forth to the bottle. He went to his clothes. Dry. How long had he been frozen in that spot gazing at that bottle of rye? It beckoned at him from out of the corner of his eye.

He walked to the bottle by the fire and stood over it. The bottle gleamed in the firelight, fused with a golden glow. The rye inside was like dark amber, the flames reflected across its flat surface like a river on fire. His tongue licked his lips. He reached down and grabbed up the bottle.

The call from outside began as a low harsh rumbling. It changed pitch and rose to become a deep-throated howl. Wasted looked out the door into the pitch black of the night. He pulled the wool blanket about his shoulders and ran outside.

Wasted reached the corral as a bolt of lightning froze the scene in silver, a blurred image of animals with wide eyes glowing with fear as etched on one of those glass daguerreotypes. The rain had stopped but the wind was whipping the long grass and black tree limbs about in a frenzy. Wasted clenched the old blanket tighter about his neck while it thrashed about him in the air. The cattle pushed and backed restlessly against each other inside the wooden pen and bellowed for the chaos to end. Some fence rails split loose and flew high away in the darkness. Wasted could see the fire that brightly lined the doorframe of the lodge in a yellow light. His body caught its shine and was gold against the night.

Wasted peered into the darkness waiting for the wolf. He suddenly remembered the bottle. To his body and mind's shock he realized his fingers held its neck tight in his hand. An absurd thought seized at Wasted. What if the bottle had followed him outside, afraid that he would not return? Wasted raised the bottle up before his face. The fire from inside the lodge sparkled upon its glass. He turned the bottle at an angle, looking at the golden liquid inside. Wasted snatched the cork with his teeth and spat it out. Despite the winds rushing around him he believed he could smell the liquor. Wasted's mouth and tongue suddenly felt so dry and parched. He wanted a drink like never before during those awful times. The rye's intoxicating aroma met his nose, burned at his nostrils and flooded his senses in that old intimate way while it was actually the bottle that inhaled at him. Wasted lifted the lip of the bottle up to his mouth. Inside the whiskey's pool reflected the shimmering flames of the lodge fireplace.

Abruptly the winds died down. An eerie quiet fell over the grounds. Wasted didn't care about any of that now. He raised the bottle to drink when he noticed two pinpoints of light dancing in the rye's blaze. Each moved closer, warping from vague soft dots into sharp-edged pools of crimson. In the lodge's glow the outline of an enormous black shadow formed around those orbs.

Wasted lowered the bottle. A massive wolf glared hungrily into his eyes. The creature was over six feet long to the end of its tail, the shoulder height was at least forty inches and it must have weighed two hundred pounds. The animal's expression was ruthless, showing no hint of fear. Every single hair on its body bristled on end like a mat of combed steel fibers, stretched over muscle and sinew hardened and challenged every day of its life by fighting and killing to survive.

WASTED

Wasted was astonished to feel something move deep inside him, an emotion or...an instinct, lurking in a shuttered room that spoke to and understood the supreme confidence behind those hard determined eyes. He knew what this great wolf was thinking: the throat of this weak creature would be ripped open and its blood consumed in the next few seconds. This pathetic man thing, the cattle and the horse would be torn into pieces of fresh dead meat. The wolf and his pack would feed once again and well, thriving on their mountain as soft men come but never stay. Wasted knew this terrible wolf like its blood pumped in his own heart. Like a black widow protected its eggs while a cricket chirped away its life under a moonless night. He knew it like a homeless old dog and stringy cat worked a kill together to feast upon a rat. Somewhere far and yet close Wasted remembered a submerged but familiar urge as he watched the wolf become a blur.

And in that sure moment of the kill...as the savage predator streaked toward Wasted...it sensed something unthinkable...the prey had changed...its smell of fear...was gone...and it welcomed death.

Wasted lowered the bottle of rye as the wolf changed, its body seized by a manic energy and consumed with one pure thought. Kill. In meeting this clarity in the briefest of moments Wasted was transformed. A forgotten instinct was ignited. A lever that controlled the civilized part of him was blown to Hades by some inner lightning. Wasted's body accelerated its movement, his sense of time slowed to a dream state.

As the huge wolf charged, Wasted observed in time's fractions a shocked puzzlement appear in the beast's eyes. The bottle in his grip smashed against the gate, shattering its glass. His closed fist came up with the bottle's jagged long edges glittering in the firelight. The wolf sailed through the air, its trajectory and arcing movements appeared like a snail-paced, distorted hallucination to Wasted. The jaws slowly opened, black lips pulled with inchmeal action over large sharp teeth with foamy droplets of saliva spreading gradually in space from around the pink gums. Then reality snapped back to its relentless speed and death hurtled forward to rip out Wasted's throat.

Wasted jammed the deadly glass spikes beneath the underside of the wolf's jaw, slicing through the the coarse fur and tough sinew of its throat and forcing them up, driving deep into its brain. The long fangs and teeth of the huge creature returned the ferocious gesture and closed about Wasted's neck. The momentum was tremendous, slamming both into the gate, shattering its wooden lock to splinters. Their bodies bounced off the fence rails onto the mud and grass with claws thrashing and fists punching. Consciousness ebbed and swirled about Wasted, his world turning round in collapsing circles of...

Red.

The sun rose the next morning painting the world in hellish scarlet hues. Wasted's eyes twitched open and saw the crimson landscape. He thought of red steer skulls and entering Hell at Ardway's ranch gate. Wasted's head ached. He tried to lift himself but couldn't. His eyes burned as he blinked to keep them open. Everything appeared fuzzy and flushed in a cherry wine color. He squinted his eyelids to focus at the light. Something black suddenly appeared into view. Inside its silhouette the wolf's large eyes gleamed red at him in an odd upturned angle. Wasted realized the wolf's heavy body was spread across him. Wasted also became aware that his neck ached. Something was clamped to it. Wasted managed to get his arms unpinned and his hands up to his neck. Carefully he gripped the wolf's jaws to remove them from about his throat. There was sticky dried blood all over his beard. His blood? It was streaked about the teeth of the dead wolf. He lifted its massive head high, revealing the jagged bottle stuck under the wolf's head. There was more thick clotted blood. The wolf's blood. But Wasted didn't understand this at that moment. He reacted in panic, shoving and kicking at the wolf carcass to push it quickly off him. The effort drained him and he fell back weakly against the corral gate, drinking in fast deep breaths. At last Wasted felt better and rose to sit up. He stared at the dead wolf and the blood over his body and remembered killing it. Wasted raised his hand under his beard to his throat and gingerly felt the teeth marks and his own blood.

Wasted slowly got to his feet. It hurt to move. It hurt to breathe. He walked over to the well and worked the pulley handle to draw up a bucket full of water. Wasted drank long from it, then dumped the rest over his head and down his naked body. The cold well water made him shiver and shake but he was still alive. Alive felt good. He tossed the bucket back down the well. As he waited for the loud plop of it hitting the water he glanced over to the lodge. A white-haired, ancient Native American looked back, dressed in faded leather as worn and wrinkled as his brown face and hands. He was standing before the open door, holding a Winchester rifle in his folded arms.

They both stared at each other for half a minute without any movement or show of emotion. Wasted finally raised his arm to wave his open hand in a show of friendship. The Native American did not react. Wasted was too tired and thirsty to care. He turned back to the well and worked the handle to draw up another bucket of water. The Indian walked over and took over working the well handle. Wasted watched as the bucket of water rose to the top. He grabbed it to set on the flat rock surface. Wasted gestured for the old man to drink first. The Indian set his rifle down and motioned his hand at Wasted's neck. Wasted painfully raised his head. The Indian carefully gathered the long unruly beard and lifted it up, studying closely at the wolf's teethmarks. He then pointed at the thick full beard, indicating with his fingers "biting" at the thick hair and that it saved Wasted's life from the wolf's teeth. It was true. Wasted's uncut beard, at least three years' worth, was too much for even a wolf's fangs to pierce.

Satisfied they had understood each other, the Indian stared into Wasted's eyes and spoke what sounded like a name. The old man placed his hand on Wasted's shoulder and repeated the words. Then he drew a large sharp knife. Wasted's eyes widened for the first time in surprise. The Indian also smiled for the first time. He sliced a minor surface nick in his own neck. Blood drained out. Dabbing his finger in his own blood he held it up to Wasted's throat and gestured. Wasted nodded, not exactly sure what the old man was doing. The Indian lifted the beard, wiped his bloody finger in two quick swipes across the teeth marks on his throat. Then he wiped some of Wasted's blood over his own neck, mixing it with his blood. He pointed to Wasted and then himself. And then repeated the words again.

The old man turned and walked over to the wolf's dead body. He bent down and began cutting at its neck with his long knife.

Wasted went back to washing the blood off his naked torso, making sure he did not wash it off his neck in front of the old man. The Indian finished with his knife and raised the great head of the savage wolf up, its dark blood dripping to pool in the dirt. He showed it to Wasted who politely nodded back because he was feeling weak from hunger and last night's struggles and could do nothing else. Then the Native American pointed to the wood sign above the corral that was crudely burned with the lettering that spelled:

ARDWAY AND SON LODGE

It was faded but legible if you knew what you were seeing. Wasted was shocked as the man said clearly, "Ardway and son lodge." The Indian waited for Wasted who slowly got the message and nodded back. Then the old man did another unexpected thing. With shockingly spry energy he climbed the gate and wrapped leather thongs about the sign to secure the wolf head to the top of it.

After making sure it was strapped down tight, he jumped down. They both stood and admired how damn scary that wolf's head was glaring out from the top of the corral gate. Wasted thought about it and concluded it would frighten the hell out of man or beast that wasn't supposed to be around the vicinity of the Ardway and Son lodge. Maybe this ol' Indian knew a sly trick or two.

The old man bent over and started to drag the wolf's body toward his horse. Though still feeling weak as a sick pup Wasted jumped to and pitched in to help. They both dragged it to the horse and then lifted the body of the wolf up to lay across its back while the old man tied it down. He then turned and looked into Wasted's tired face. His eyes inspected Wasted's wild hair and beard. The Indigenous person reached up to pull the hair hiding Wasted's brow to study a three inch bullet-creased scar. He repeated the words spoken earlier from that of his nation, the Sioux, calling Wasted "Šung'manitu Tanka." That must have meant something about a big wolf but Wasted would likely never know.

The old man smiled again but this time he shook his head. It was unfathomable to him that this strange wasi'chu had killed the legendary giant wolf that had terrorized his people in the hills for many years. He slung himself up on his horse and without a look back he rode down through the trees and disappeared.

A few days later Bailey, Jordie and Tom rode up to help herd the cattle and calves back down to the lower range. Wasted was glad to see them and wanted to hear the latest news of what was happening around the ranch. They laughed and Jordie said that Wasted was the only talk down there. Truth be told they were relieved to find Wasted alive, what with no gun and all. Kroeber, that low-down snake, was taking bets back at the ranch on whether Wasted would came back, and if so would he have all his limbs. The men were surprised at how well the lodge looked from the work Wasted put into it. Usually the men who came up just did the required cattle work and drank themselves silly out of boredom, paying no attention to fixing up the lodge. As they moved the cattle out of the corral and started riding their horses down the hill, Bailey glanced back and saw the large wolf head up on the corral sign. He glanced over at Wasted and drawled, "Huh. Don't remember that big ugly wolf's head before. Looks kinda...recent." He nodded over his shoulder at it to Wasted. "You have a speck of trouble up here?"

Wasted reached back into his bedroll. "Nope. Hey, here's your razor. Didn't have any use for it."

Bailey took it, then reached over and made a playful tug at Wasted's long beard. He gave a light kick to his horse, taking off at a trot. He laughed back over his shoulder and yelled, "Too bad!"

Wasted stroked his long thick beard and then reached under to lightly touch the teeth marks on his throat from the wolf. He looked back at its head. The wolf stared back as pissed as the dickens. Wasted surprised himself by blurting out, "Šung'manitu Tanka," and speaking it correctly with no trouble. With an easy kick to Jackrabbit, Wasted galloped off to catch up with his friends.

A few days later in the evening Wilson and Ardway sat in the courtyard, sipping coffee. Wilson had finished reporting to Ardway about the week's work at the ranch.

Wilson chuckled, "Damn, we sure as rain thought your drunk would have run off by now. Guess he had some sand hidden inside that beard after all. Everybody likes him 'cept Kroeber. And in spite of Kroeber's bullshit he's proven quite tough and smart. He tries hard to help everyone but..."

Ardway nodded to himself, pleased to hear Wasted was working out yet knew there was always something to it. He cocked his eyebrow and made a crooked grin. "But what?"

Wilson shrugged, "Well...There is one big complaint."

Ardway was incredulous when he heard what Wilson related. "What? Five damn blasted months? Take him out and get it done with before he kills someone!"

Chapter Eight:

The Rustlers and the Rifle

Wasted's eyes darted desperately left to right as he backed up. His back rubbed against a wagon. He was cornered. "No!" he yelled at his attackers. He reached into the wagon to find a weapon, His hand came up with Bailey's long razor blade with its sharp filed point. He jabbed it at the air to ward the men off. "I mean it! Stay back!"

Jordie and Bailey stepped closer to Wasted. Jordie spoke calmly, "Now Wasted. Don't make this any worse than it has to be."

"Wasted, you wouldn't stick me with my own razor would you?" Bailey edged a little closer.

Crack! The knot end of a bullwhip wrapped around Wasted's wrist and jerked. The razor was flung from his fingers into the air to fall to the ground. Abruptly a small mob of screaming men charged around Wasted. He punched one as the others took hold of him about his body and limbs. They lifted him into the air as he struggled to break loose. The men carried him a few yards and raised him high above their heads. They hurled Wasted high into the air.

Splash! Wasted was swallowed into rolling, churning water. He surfaced, gasping for air and floundering in the cold mountain stream. His wet long dark hair and beard clung to his body. The men howled in triumph, all dressed in their sweat-stained long underwear. Bailey yelled, "Three years of not bathing. You're lucky we don't shoot you, Wasted. Now. Tear his stinking clothes off!" He held up a horse brush with a handle and large square white bar. "I got the lye soap."

The men jerked Wasted's threadbare clothing off, ripping it to pieces. He tried to rise but they held him firm. Bailey worked the brush along with the soap to lather suds over Wasted's head and naked body as the crew wrestled him to stay in place. Wasted gasped as he bobbed in the water. "Blast it! I...I'll get you...Bailey!"

Bailey smiled. "Dunk him again, boys. Gonna take the whole bar to get this stinkin' pig clean." Wasted's head was pushed under the water as the men laughed and cheered.

Higher up on a hill above this cowboy baptism, Kroeber watched the men. Satisfied, he waved a red handkerchief to someone on the other side of the valley. A red cloth fluttered back in a return signal.

Later that afternoon a warm easy breeze had flowed in out of the south and with it a red-tailed hawk that floated high above in the cloudless blue sky. The raptor appeared frozen in place, framed against the pale white circle of an early moon. It patiently searched for a meal but nothing moved on the green landscape below. It was a quiet and peaceful June day in Wyoming with just enough heat to make the world lazy and satisfied. The men were stretched out along the stream's bank, lulled by the soothing burble of the gently rolling waters. White helixes of fractured sunbeams sparked across the stream and whited the men in flickering spots of light as they dozed while drying in the sun.

Wasted walked up looking over the "new duds" he was wearing. He bent low, knees out, stood up and stretched out his arms wide with a pleased expression at their fit. His crew friends had donated their old castoffs: patched-up jeans, a brown shirt with crinkled-up leather stitched at the elbows, old creased-lined boots but with no holes, a faded black vest and a gray hat with two holes. The clothes weren't the only thing new to Wasted. He stood tall and straight and not like before when he hunched over like a beat dog. There was muscle where fat used to be. His long black hair and beard was cleaned and straightened. It had taken an hour for Wasted to brush out the tangles and knots with a curry and a dandy brush but the effort was quite shocking compared to how he looked before. His "wild man" animal look was gone, now more like a Mennonite off a farm. Wasted stood just off from his sunning friends and continued to fidget and stretch at his clothes with exaggerated grunts for some attention.

Bailey heard and glanced up from where he lay on the bank. He sat up in surprise, a smile stretched big across his face. "Well, praise be! I could mistake you for a genuine human being, Wasted." The others turned heads to look, their faces brightening with the same pleased shock.

Wasted caught his reflection in the water. It shimmered a moment then became still. His face was clean with no grime or sores and the eyes shone bright. Gone was the yellow and red coloring, the bloated skin of a man killing himself slowly on the bug juice. Wasted still could not place that face looking back at him. Would he ever? Shaking it off Wasted looked around at the men who were smiling and delighted. "Thank you for the clothes, boys. I'm mighty grateful. I...I feel like a new man."

Broke-nosed Tom reached up and lifted his wide brimmed hat back from covering his long face and bald head. His thick lids peeled back halfway over his eyes and glanced sleepily at Wasted. Tom's long sideburn whiskers fluttered in the light wind as he spoke up, "Wasted, we're just happy that you smell like one."

The men guffawed and shook their heads in agreement. Wasted tried not to join in and acted like he was insulted. He tried so hard he frowned. This made the others laugh louder and harder, seeing Wasted try to resist and act like he was mad. Wasted fought it a bit longer and then burst out laughing. His friends pointed at him and howled along.

A clatter of hoofbeats rose behind them. The men looked to it while still chortling. Suddenly over the hill forty steers thundered into view. Ten riders, their faces hidden under bandanas, drove the cattle straight at the men. Jordie's meaty face lost its mirth to cry out, "Hell! Them's rustlers!"

The cattle charged through the men, scattering them about. Some crawled under the supply wagon, others jumped in the stream and hid behind its rock ledges. On the other side of the creek in another smaller wagon their guns were laid out next to their clothes.

Wasted turned and ran through the stream, splashing and struggling to get to the wagon on the other side among the rushing cattle. He made the wagon and grabbed a Winchester rifle. Wasted flung himself behind a tree stump and curled up to it. Glancing around at the chaos his eyes turned to the rifle in his hands. Staring at the gun Wasted froze, panicked not by the rustlers but at a dreadful feeling welling up inside. A feeling that the wolf ignited that night at the lodge. Why did his mind fight to hide it? For a moment he sank into the darkness as the woman in white appeared. Her beautiful face flashed and was immediately gone accompanied by those gun shots echoing behind her as they always did. More shots were heard, this time blasting closer. Bullets smashed into the tree stump splintering wood shards over his head and shoulders.

The darkness faded as the paralysis slipped away, jarred by the force of the bullets pounding the stump along with the thundering gun blasts. He rolled around the stump, coming up with the rifle to his shoulder and his eye searching for a target. A masked rustler pointed a rifle at him. Wasted balked a short moment focusing the rustler in the rifle's sight. Not so the rustler who loosed two shots, hitting the stump. Whump! Whump! Wasted sucked in a deep breath, aimed and fired.

The rustler fell back in the saddle from the force of the bullet, grabbing his shoulder in pain. Hurt and shocked, he managed to shove his rifle into its saddle sleeve. Hunched over his horse's neck he gave a kick to its hind legs, sending them both racing away and lagging after his escaping crew and the cattle. They all disappeared in the plumes of their dust.

Three more shots blasted out, two bullets rammed into the stump and one raked the ground by Wasted. He rolled back behind the wood barrier, clutching the rifle tight to his chest, eyes squeezed shut. Death came close that time. His breath came in short gasps. The edges of his mind closed in bringing the darkness, the black void. Wasted's heart was beating furiously. The woman in the white lace dress appeared again, smiling mysteriously at him. Her exquisite green eyes and lips taunted him. The gunshots echoed as before only there were more along with the beating of his heart. No, that was wrong. It was hoofbeats. They pounded closer and louder. The dark moment faded. Wasted opened his eyes to see Kroeber riding toward him. He stood up as Kroeber drew up beside him.

"They drove your horses off. Round them up and get back to the ranch." Kroeber gave his horse a boot and raced off after the rustlers. Wasted stared after Kroeber a moment, then turned and ran to join his friends.

~

Night descended high over the red and yellow streaks of the sun disappearing behind the hills. It was a few minutes after dinner in the courtyard behind the Ardway house. His estranged wife Patricia had designed it with a pleasing simplicity. It was walled with a sandstone that changed colors from pink to brown and orange with the passing of the day's light. A flower garden of purple and red native plants surrounded its center that kept a hand pump next to a well. Kerosene lamps provided yellow light from rusty iron hooks embedded in the walls about the area. Night had begun to cool the air but it was pleasant and no jacket felt needed.

Ardway paced by the dining area's French doors, carrying a tall glass of whiskey. His hair hung loose and was longer than that day in town. So was his mustache. A grey beard stubble of three days growth made him look older. He held the glass out in exasperation, "These damned rustlers don't make sense!"

Wilson and Kroeber sat smoking cigars and watched Ardway walk aimlessly in circles before them, putting together the day's events in his mind. Kroeber spoke up, "Probably just drifters looking for quick money."

Wilson added, "Maybe they thought there would be more cattle."

"Maybe. But my gut says..." He burped painfully, placing his hand over his stomach. "Hmm. This doesn't feel right. Like Claudine's stew tonight." He thought better about having said that out loud. "Don't tell her I said that."

Kroeber shifted uncomfortably in his chair, "What's bothering you with these rustlers?"

"Bothering me? Rustlers steal at night. All they can. And unseen, so they don't get hung. It's a dumb move. All they did was wake snakes under my bed." Ardway burped intensely and loud. "Dammit! I've et that stew for near twenty years and she goes and changes it!"

The men suddenly grew quiet, realizing they were not alone. The thin and stately African American/Cheyenne, Miss Claudine, stood in the doorway holding a tray with an elegant china coffee pot and cups. Claudine's otherworldly ethos was on full display, her noble and highly intelligent manner seemed beyond its time and place. With her chin out she spoke to Ardway, "Burton, I did no such thing." Her spine straightened as her shoulders pulled back, "Too much whiskey is your problem. Hide it from the others but you cannot hide from your constitution."

Ardway's face snapped back tight with surprise and anger. At seeing this Miss Claudine continued, "You are too old for this childish nonsense. Months ago you got stinking drunk over Junior and—"

Wilson jumped up, crossed over to Claudine. "Thank you, Miss Claudine. I'll take this tray so you can finish up, ah, whatever you're in the process of doing." Wilson grabbed the tray and nodded his appreciation to Claudine. "Always a pleasure to sup your good cookin', Ma'am."

Claudine and Ardway glared at each other for a strained moment. Claudine made the tactful effort to turn and smile at Wilson. "Thank you, Jedidiah. It's so nice to have a man with understanding and manners on the property." She put an extra emphasis on "manners." Claudine gave a courtly nod to the men and walked back to the kitchen.

Wilson set the tray down on a small serving table and poured the coffee. He handed cups on saucers to each man. He and Kroeber sat down in their chairs as before.

"As I was saying..." Abruptly Ardway stopped. He turned and shouted to the kitchen, "And I ain't that old!"

The two men looked away until Ardway turned back to them. He let out a frustrated sigh. "Let's see. Oh, yes. Snakes. Trouble. Which always smells like Fendris." He nodded to himself. "He's got a nose in this. Ash wants to rile me. Like that day at the train station."

"Fendris?" said Kroeber. "Why'd he want to dig spurs in you? I don't think—"

Ardway cut him off, "Let's leave it at you don't think. Go back to the bunk house, Kroeber."

The big man looked from Wilson to Ardway. Annoyed, Kroeber shook his head and stood up. He walked over and exited out the courtyard door. Wilson began to stand up. Ardway smiled out of the corner of his mouth, "Not you. You. Can think."

Outside of the courtyard Kroeber kicked at the dirt in his anger. And almost collided with Wasted who stood in the shadows of a pine tree. Kroeber barked, "Watch it, you dumb bar rag!" He started away then stopped and turned to Wasted, "What the hell are you doing here?"

Wasted glanced over at the courtyard wall. "Wilson told me to show up after dinner."

The big man considered this. "You got lucky with that shot, ya sot! When I seen you lying behind that stump, you were white as a sheet." Kroeber leaned in to crowd Wasted. "You're a piece of shit drunk that'll never amount to nothing. Stick your nose up Wilson and Ardway's asses all you wish but they won't trust a drunk any longer than they can throw you." Wasted flinched at that last part, causing Kroeber to smile. He turned and stalked off back to the bunkhouse. Wasted shifted his eyes uneasily to the ground.

~

Inside the courtyard Ardway poured more whiskey for himself. Wilson silently watched, not too pleased but he kept his trap shut. "You say our drunk was the only one to get off a shot? Him? He could barely walk when he got here."

"He's come a long way since you last saw him. I've got him outside."

Ardway shrugged. "He ever remember his name?"

"No. They call him Wasted."

Ardway made a slight frown. "Wasted...Well, let's see him."

Wilson stepped out. He returned with Wasted who pulled his hat off to fidget with it, moving it hand to hand as he stared nervously at the floor. Ardway walked around him, staring with wide shocked eyes. "I'll be...dammed! You look a mite better than before when I first saw you. I wouldn't recognize you 'cept for that Biblical beard and hair."

Wasted raised his eyes. "You...look a mite like I used to, Mister Ardway."

Wilson stared up at the ceiling as Ardway gruffly drew himself up and scowled. "Tell me straight. You got a problem? With me?"

Wasted straightened up, thought about it for a few seconds. "Nope, Mister Ardway. But...you do have a problem. Those rustlers."

Wilson turned to him, "Wasted, you said you were fired on by one. Winged him back. In the shoulder."

Ardway perked up. "You sure?"

"Yes, sir. There was blood left where he took it."

"Good job! That's what I want to hear! Hmm. Wilson says you turned out to have some Buckaroo in you. Doing fine now. A good cowhand." He paused and looked closer into Wasted's eyes. "Ah. You sticking around?"

Wasted stared straight back at him and nodded. "I'm...working on some things. This has been a good place for that. I got some friends here. I'm sticking."

Ardway smiled broadly. "Good. 'Cause I have no problem with you...Mister Wasted." He took a long drink.

Wasted weighed speaking up, then said, "Everybody has problems. Some...they don't even know about. Trust me on that. Well, good night." Wasted turned to go.

Ardway stared after him, wondering how to take what he said. Wasted stopped and turned back. "You had too many men for that rustling. The extra...was riding for protection."

Wasted took a deep breath before giving an anxious look to Wilson and Ardway. "Kroeber. ...Something don't smell right. Watch him."

Wasted walked out through the courtyard door.

Ardway and Wilson stared after him. They looked back to each other. Wasted had said aloud what both were thinking. "Jed, do what he says. Keep an eye on our junior foremen. I'll go into town later this month when things have cooled off about our cattle stealing. Sniff around. See about who got himself shot."

"And what about Wasted?"

"Let's wait and see about whatever it is he wants to figure out." Ardway shook his head. "It's been a doozy so far." Ardway burped painfully but managed to smile about it. "My gut has spoken."

Chapter Nine:

Haben, the Preacher and a Prayer

As promised a few weeks later Ardway was in town. He smiled warmly to the world as he stepped out of the door of the Haben Veterinarian Office, the name painted primly on a large pane glass window next to the door. Ardway's longer hair, mustache and fuller beard showed the passage of time while his exaggerated smile more than hinted that whiskey was affecting his constitution as Miss Claudine had stated. And if you needed more proof he walked along proudly to the Ardway Hotel carrying an empty fifth bottle.

Ardway was almost to the hotel when he discovered that he still held the emptied whiskey bottle. Shocked, he gave a quick look to either side and tossed the bottle under the planks of the boardwalk. Ardway stepped up to the entrance like nothing had happened. Pleased with his resourcefulness he was about to enter the hotel when he noticed a tall man leaning in the open door frame, watching him. The man stepped out and tipped his hat. Benton Jurant smiled, "Mister Ardway," and not waiting for an answer, walked on.

Ardway drew back, perplexed and a mite ruffled. Who was this stranger and what gave him the right to act familiar? Something tugged at the back of his mind when a strong slap on his shoulder made him turn. "Converter" John Gammill smiled warmly. This was Ardway's oldest friend, a big-shouldered African American preacher who made people's full growth look stunted. But to most of Spirit Bend's citizens he was Sheriff Gammill, who slapped down the law on bad eggs who went over the limit. "Heard you was at Vet Haben's office, Burt. He should of gave your face a shear. Looking shaggy 'round your edges, you ol' goat!"

Ardway returned the back slap and with his own wide grin. "Converter John! Yep, had to see Haben about some constipated horses."

"Only hoss full of shit runs your ranch."

Ardway neighed like a horse, making his friend laugh. "John, you must be starving giving out jokes like that when passing the plate at your church."

"My jokes in church are more upright for preachin'. But the inmates in my jail sure laugh hard and plenty at them around feeding time."

Ardway rolled his eyes, "In jail it don't pay to sneer at the sheriff's jokes. Well, I'm buying the grub today so I expect you to laugh at all my funnies, you old jackass."

Gammill threw up two large fingers up behind both of his ears, "Heehaw, heehaw! I'm Burton the burro!"

Ardway gave Gammill a soft kick in the pants as they entered the hotel.

Two hours later in a small private room the men had pushed their plates back and were quietly drinking coffee and enjoying cigars by a window. The bright sunshine through the linen curtains caught the pale blue smoke as it curled from the cigars and their lips. Gammill was staring intensely at his friend, "I don't like it, Burt. You and Ash get to raising hell, innocent folks are bound to be in for some hurt. Then I gotta step in. And you don't want that."

"Tell that to Ash. I'm not stealing his cattle." Ardway leaned forward. "I waited three weeks after that rustler got shot afore I come in to town to the doctor. He hadn't fixed any bullet wounds on folks in months." Ardway drew on his cigar. "So I got our vet Haben all liquored." He blew the smoke out at the window. "Spilled his guts about fixing Dooley Green's shoulder, secret-like, that day after my cattle was stolen."

Gammill's brow knitted in disappointment. "Green's been with Fendris ten years. And he comes to church regular. Sad to hear he crossed the line." He thought back, remembering. "Still, there was that six months we spent on the big pasture in Yuma—"

"Ha! We was full of whiskey and black power back then." Suddenly Ardway lowered his voice, eyes to the door. "'Sides, we swore we'd never speak on that no more."

Gammill leaned back in his chair and puffed at his stogie while recalling those times. "Wouldn't help my preachin'."

Ardway's lips blew a line of smoke, smiling. "Or sheriffin'."

Gammill nodded, "Everybody's got something to hide. I wouldn't trust a man that didn't." Perplexed, he shook his head. "This Fendris trouble is big nuts, hard to crack."

Ardway pulled a flask from his coat, poured whiskey in his coffee. Gammill watched, sipped at his coffee, and nodded no to Ardway when he offered the flask to him.

"Listen good to me—don't fall for Fendris's tricks. He's betting on your damn pride, sure as I'm sitting here."

Ardway nodded like a kid that had heard it before. "Look. You live in town. I hear Ash stays mostly up in the top of his feed store now, instead of out to his ranch. What's going on with that?"

"Nothing. He drinks and howls at the moon from time to time but he's been pretty tame since his boy, Clay, got killed a few years back. That's when he moved into town."

Gammill took a drag on his cigar, slowly letting the smoke out. It rose slowly up to the ceiling. "I thought sure that ended it with both y'all getting old."

Ardway's eyes shot back with a stern look under pinched brows. "I'm not that old! But Fendris is! Maybe he's gone senile and thinks he's been wronged by me." A memory crossed his face. "Like ol' Cliff and Red Bear with that silver spoon and the naked woman on the handle."

Gammill shook his head, remembering. "Shot up half the town over that spoon and all they got was one crippled and the other lost an eye." He cleared his throat and took on his devout preacher appearance. "'You shall not covet your neighbor's house.' Exodus 20, verse 17."

Ardway's face twisted with exasperation at the Bible statement, knowing this wasn't going to end up good for him. "Well, don't waste your Bible sayings on Ash. I'm his deuce." His eyes became hard slits with no light. "He's bucking for a killin'."

Gammill threw the hard stare back at Ardway and added a little of his own granite to it. Both locked eyes for a long moment. "You can be right...and still be a pig-headed jackass about it. I'm asking you to hold up a pinch. Let me try to figure a Christian way out of this."

Ardway wasn't letting up. He sarcastically intoned, "Oh. Amen."

Gammill let that stew a moment. "I'm not done. Miss Claudine told me you shanghaied a poor drunk and near worked him to death."

This hit Ardway between the eyes. He looked away with embarrassment. Ardway glanced back anxiously. "Well, the full story is the man was a drunken sot. I caught him stealing. A whiskey bottle. Working for me...spared the law. And he's much better now. Sober."

The preacher continued his iron-eyed stare, wasn't buying the excuse.

Ardway countered with, "Hell, he's the one that shot Green. When everyone else was runnin' around with their heads in their asses."

Gammill sighed, "Burton. Claudine said Junior's not coming back. You got his letter and his trunk. You got angry. You roostered yourself up. And you forced this sorry man to be a slave out at your place, all because of your pride and pain."

With his back up, Ardway tossed it back at Gammill. "That sorry man's name is 'Wasted.' 'Cause he's got no recollection who he is. No family. No nothing." With that spoken he let out a sigh. "Yes. I was red-eyed loco. At first. But I never badgered him out at the ranch. Wasted worked under my foremen. He's better now. Says he is. And he wants to stay on. Work out his troubles. He can leave any time he likes."

Gammill's hard expression softened. "Luke, Chapter 15, verses 11 through 32. Read it on your own time." He held out his large palms. "Now. Pray with me, Burt." He motioned for Ardway to join hands.

Ardway gazed at those large hands that could crush most men but were offered in prayer. He shrugged and put his hands out to grip the hands of his friend. Both men bowed their heads and silently prayed.

Below the window on the ground floor a potent blend of strong-smelling tobacco smoke wafted up into the air. It was a mix of New Orleans Perique with a Virginia-grown, produced by the shop of Pierre Chenet. Jurant leaned against the brick building and finished smoking his pipe. He had heard enough and took a brown stained rag from his pocket to thumb out the pipe's fire and save the Perique. He wrapped the pipe in the rag and put it in his jacket pocket. Jurant smiled up to the window through which Gammill and Ardway's smoke drifted out when they had discussed Fendris while thinking they were alone. He walked away and down an alley to disappear around its corner. A fragrance of the Perique with its sweet earthy aroma lingered long after Jurant had gone.

∿

A few hours later the painted letters of Haben's establishment appeared like ghostly images in the dying light, merging with the darkness in the office. Inside black and gray shadows crisscrossed the room becoming darker by the moment. No lantern was lit. Haben lay across his desk, still sleeping off the whiskey he had enjoyed with Ardway earlier. A person would have missed him there in the gloom, except for his loud snoring.

The door opened slightly and a small bell rang above its top corner. A hand reached up and stuffed a rag inside the bell, stopping the clapper. A man entered, quietly shutting the door behind him. He waited for his eyes to adjust to the dark while pulling a Colt SSA "Peacemaker," holding it up high and ready. He focused in on Haben's snoring and walked lightly over to the desk.

Jurant stood over the sleeping man. He roughly shook Haben by the shoulder. Haben woke up confused and squinted around at the dark. Jurant spoke, "Haben." The Vet's eyes sprung wide at seeing the gun barrel pointed in his face. "Fendris says you got a wobblin' jaw. Needs fixin'."

Haben gasped. A small bag of feed was thrown over his face, cutting off his yell. Jurant jammed his gun into the bag. A muffled shot made a "whump!" sound. Haben's body sagged over the desk, his head covered by the sack. Grain poured out of a charred hole in the sack along with a rising wisp of gun smoke.

The sounds of Jurant's footsteps went quickly out the door. The rag fell from the bell, allowing one tiny, lonely chime for poor Haben on his way to the hereafter.

Chapter Ten:

Kroeber

In a field next to some woods Kroeber almost expelled a lung delivering his latest harangue while walking around the twenty half-naked cowhands. Some big men worked at heaving sledgehammers and axes for splitting logs to make fence rails. The smaller men tapped iron and wooden wedges with the hatchets' hammer ends to set in the log for making halves or fourths. This was placed to split along the grain where the big men swung the sledgehammers. The new rails were lifted by a group of men that carried them high in the air over to a wagon and filled it up to its sides. None of this was a Sunday cakewalk as the men sweated rivers with their shirts off in the hot morning heat and it was getting hotter by the minute. Kroeber shouted, "Jordie, you fat bastard! I know'd old whores with slits bigger than you're making. Get to choppin' that wood!"

Jordie had finished splitting a large log and was gathering his strength to go at it again with one of its two long halves. He gave Kroeber a dirty look and cursed under his breath. Jordie hefted the heavy sledge hammer to his shoulder and rested a second. He gauged the wood grain to line up right for the sharp wedge that Nat had placed. Splitting rails was as much mind and aim as strength and Jordie wasn't looking to lose a foot, his or anyone else's. Kroeber wasn't having that and quickly marched over to Jordie, "Well? Strike that wood and hurry up, you fiddleheaded lunk!"

Jordie lifted up the hammer and swung it. The aim was off and the hammer bounced off the wedge to fly at Kroeber. He jumped and it missed his shin by a hair. Jordie looked on in pinched horror. Kroeber gasped and sucked wind as his rage purpled his face. He paced back and forth two times and halted. His big fist smashed into Jordie's chin, knocking the stout man off his feet. Jordie lay there semi-conscious, bleeding out of his lip as all the men stopped and gawked. Kroeber seethed in fury, his large chest heaving and blowing heated breaths. His hard eyes dared the men's shocked faces to speak up.

Bailey spat a loogie, riled up and hot. Bailey started for Kroeber when Wasted stepped in his way. Bailey flashed him an irate glance, Wasted shook his head slow and deliberate, signaling with his open hand to wait. Bailey shrugged and made a pissed-off grunt.

Kroeber glared at the men as he raised his immense fists. "You gutless soft horses! Anyone else here want their plow cleaned?" No one moved. "Ha! That's my brave bull nurses. Now get back to work! I'll check when you get in and you better have these wagons full of rails or I'll give you all some of Jordie's medicine."

The junior foreman walked through the men to his horse. Their mouths were closed but their eyes screamed murder. Kroeber didn't care. Big and powerful men had that luxury. He didn't have to take shit, he gave it. Kroeber reached his horse and mounted. No need to look back at their faces, so dull they couldn't cut paper. The only face that mattered was his. He grinned to himself. Kroeber was busting to tell his secret. He planned to be rich and soon! Then he would use his size, strength and good looks to have fine women and never work outside again.

Wasted and the men watched Kroeber ride away to the ranch house. Wasted turned and walked to Jordie, bent low to survey his damage. Bailey brought some water and Wasted dipped a cup and held Jordie's head up, pressing the cup to his lips, tipping it so Jordie felt the water on his tongue. Jordie stirred and drank. His drifting eyes focused and saw Wasted. He took a big gulp of water and spat out some blood. "Hell. I was dreamin' of something with big tits and soft eyes."

Wasted smiled, "You been around these cows too long. You good to stand?"

Jordie answered by getting to his knees, taking a breath then rising to his feet. The gathered men smiled, clapping him lightly on the back. Jordie growled, "I feel like a new man after that little nap." His friends laughed, feeling relief for their tough pardner.

Bailey frowned and squawked, "We need to fix Kroeber's wagon! I'm up to my ears with his beatin's. I say we oughta gang up on him next time in town when he's drunk and beat him 'til he don't know his ass from a hole in the ground."

The men nodded to each other, their anger blazing, fueled in part by the heat and humidity. Some shouted Kroeber's name tagged with obscenities. Wasted raised his hands up and waved for calm. "Fellas, you have every right to beat the living piss water out of Kroeber. And I sure know he's not worth a penny's worth of dog meat. But...why not beat the son of a bitch at his own game?"

Bailey squinted at Wasted, popped one eye wide at him, "What cards you got up your sleeve, Wasted?"

Wasted grinned. Ever since he returned from the lodge there was something different to his manner. He didn't skulk around like a kicked dog anymore. Men noticed how he really listened to what was said. He didn't talk a lot but gave answers that made a person sit up and think. And when he smiled it was like you were in on a secret with him. Something good was up.

"Well, before we all hang for hanging Kroeber let's get this rails business finished. I been studying it a bit."

Bailey grinned, "Oh, here we go."

"Boys, we can either do this the Kroeber way and be all knotted up and mean and angry, or we can work like people playing poker. Like, as we play the hand given to us we work to the cards' strengths and throw away those that don't pay."

The men looked to each other, unsure.

Bailey had on his sidekick face. "Wasted, I'm a little slow. Spell it out for me, okay?"

"Alright. So ol' Kroeber gets us up in the morning and throws everyone on the jobs with no thought of what's what. All so he can yell and cuff us about 'cause it's expected. I say, let's work smarter than that pile of cow patties." Wasted glanced around with a sly hint of the conspiratorial. "Put the big bruisers on the heavy work. Have the little guys on the fast work. We'll take turns and trade off. And take some short breaks regular, so a man ain't worn out early. Work steady and hard but most of all, work together...to beat the dealer."

The men still showed a bit of puzzlement but with a willingness to try. Bailey was convinced and stepped forward, "Where you want me, Wasted?"

Wasted went to work. First he divided the men up by size into three groups. Next he put the biggest men, "the grizzlies," to work on hefting hammer and axes and the "quick foxes" on the wedge work. The third group were the tall and slender, "the Bocephuses," better for picking up and carrying the rails to the wagons. This proved a source of joking all day about who was the biggest ass. Wasted made sure the men could trade off jobs but with the regular breaks everyone stayed fresh and up for more. No one fussed or complained. Wasted did work at every job. And he discussed it, or cussed it, with the men. By the end of the day no one felt cross. Tired, yes, but in that satisfied way. They felt included in the planning, understood their roles and with set goals. Like a team. They filled up the wagons in record time. They could have stopped but Wasted pointed out if they left a pile, hidden in the trees, they could use it the next day and finish the work with more breaks and in less time. Tom drawled, "Damn, Wasted. After we kill Kroeber we'll put you in for his job!"

They piled in the wagons and gustily sang a song on the way back to the bunkhouse, "By Golly, Miss Molly Needs A Man!" Up on the hill and unseen, Wilson got up and stretched from sitting on a log while watching the men work. He had ridden out when he saw Kroeber cross over to check the men working the other side of the range. He climbed up on his horse and trailed the wagons at a distance just out of sight on their way in. Back at the ranch a pleased Kroeber gazed over the wagons full of rails, assuming the good work was due to his natural and tough bossing.

A few days later Wilson sent Wasted out on Jackrabbit to the lower end of the property to chase any rogue cattle in that part of the scrubland. They had a small shack and corral there to keep the strays rounded up. While exploring around the property's border in the late morning Wasted picked up on a calf's tracks and was having a little trouble following her through the brush. It was easy for a calf to navigate between the taller and thicker scrub, chewing as he pleased and enjoying the meal in the shade, but it was a lot harder for a horse to push through. After an hour the calico-colored bronc had had enough of this foolishness and spied a way out. He suddenly turned toward a large red bush covered with long sharp thorns.

Wasted cried out, "You damn stupid—" Too late. The horse plowed on and Wasted had to slide off the back, quick, or suffer a porcupine fate. Wasted looked around in anger, then as he gauged the task, shrugged with acceptance. He could follow the tracks better this way and Jackrabbit would just eat on the other side of this brush and wait for him. Wasted liked Jack because he was smart and quick. Unfortunately that also meant having a mind of his own at times. Wasted turned his eyes to the hoof tracks on the ground and pushed his way through the thick bluish-gray sagebrush.

Eventually he got to a small clearing with some sunlight on the ground. The calf was sleeping there in a folded pile, safe and full, content in the way cattle live in the moment. She had black spots on white with a touch of red between her eyes and down to her nose. Wasted walked over and gave out a soft moo and reached over to rub the calf's neck. It was startled for a second and raised its head, blinking and blowing dust from its nostrils. By this time Wasted was scratching its head between the ears and softly calling, "Whoa, bossy. Good dogie." The calf rose sleepily on its gangling legs while Wasted gently rubbed his gloved hand over its back and side like a mother would lick her calf awake. Wasted gave it an easy few pats on its flank and walked to an opening in the brush wall. He called over his shoulder to the calf, "Here, dogie," and continued calling it as he stepped through the opening and walked a few yards to stand outside the sagebrush. He looked around in the afternoon light and without a thought, yodeled a bit, letting his voice rise and fall in a smooth enough melodic affection that it surprised him. Little things like this came to Wasted of late when he least expected it. Something in his past dropped loose without a memory of it. Like that night with the wolf. Suddenly Jackrabbit poked his head around the sagebrush, curious as to what the hell his human was caterwauling about. Wasted laughed out loud at the way Jack was eyeballing him.

Then the calf stuck its head out of the brush and mooed as if to say, *hey, I'm the big deal here.*

After Wasted had the calf roped, he walked it and Jackrabbit back around the sagebrush "canyon" to where they came in. As Wasted stepped out into the open he glanced up into the hills and saw three men on horses. He stopped and backed up a few steps to watch without being seen. Two riders faced the one as they conversed. It went on a couple of minutes when the two men turned their horses around and rode off to the outskirts of Ardway's property. The lone rider guided his horse in the opposite direction around the trees. He traveled at a half gallop and turned to ride up along the trail back to the ranch. There was no mistaking the big man. It was Kroeber.

A week later Wasted had thirty-two calves packed in the corral with cows wandering up to feed them. Wilson had sent Kroeber up with a work crew of ten men to fix the dilapidated shack, its roof and grounds. They arrived about eight in the morning. Wasted had been staying out there the entire time so he volunteered to show the men around the property to point out the repairs and get them started. Wasted told Kroeber that he could check it out after they went to work to make sure they were "doing it up to his standards." Kroeber was a little surprised at Wasted's initiative but it sounded too good to turn down. Wasted pointed up a slight rise to two trees with a hammock. "Kroeber, I've been staying up there in a hammock to keep an eye on the corral and calves at night. It's a perfect spot to watch the work and catch anything that needs your attention." Kroeber turned and stared up to the sling bed and the shady trees. He grunted and then without a word he rode up to it. Wasted hustled Bailey and the men around, pointing out the jobs to do and who he thought would best serve each one. After about ten minutes of this Wasted looked up to the hammock. Kroeber was laid out in it with his hat covering his face and outlined against the sky.

"Here's the deal, fellas. I already got the wood measured and cut for the roof, the corral and the pump house. Got the tools, nails and such placed at each work area."

Bailey grinned, "Any booze and girls from Fancy Nancy's?"

Wasted ignored him. "I stuffed a blanket with pine needles and straw up in that hammock. Kroeber will sleep like a rock. We all know our jobs. So get to work but don't be yelling and joking with each other." He winked to them, "Well, least not loud like you always do. I figure in a few hours we'll be just about done as lunchtime nears. Now, Bailey, did you bring the biscuits, ham and honey?"

Bailey looked over at his saddlebags. "Yep. Fresh cooked this morning early."

"Good. So at noon, you'll go up and wake Kroeber and hand him that food. Place it right on his belly as he lays in that hammock. Don't give him a chance to get up."

Jordie, Tom and Nat elbowed and chuckled to each other as the rest of the men grinned.

Wasted smiled slightly to them and back to Bailey, "So as you're telling Kroeber how work is going and he's filling his face with the biscuits, ham and honey, you glance over to that big rock by one of the trees and sort of make a little holler. Walk over and pick up the bottle of whiskey I stashed there." Wasted turned to Tom, "Which, Tom, I found in the shack and you were the last one out here."

Tom acted shocked and innocently said, "I have no recollection of that bottle, Your Honor."

"So Bailey, you tell Kroeber to look and then hand him the bottle. And he'll mouth off and say that this proves I'm a sot and laugh and carry on how stupid I was to leave it up there. Then Bailey you say he was sure mighty right to say so about me and then mention getting back to work so that we'll be done by evening. Then skedaddle back down here before he can think of something to say or do."

Bailey laughed, "Kroeber eats the food. Drinks the booze. In the sleepy-time hammock. And passes out the rest of the day."

Nat looked at Wasted with eyes wide as saucers, "Damn, Wasted. You're a cunning old curly wolf!"

Wasted leaned back, "We finish what little work is left, and clean up and take it easy. We'll probably have to wake Kroeber up to look over the place so we can get back for supper. He'll sign off quick to get back so he can sleep it off in his bunk."

All the crew laughed out loudly. Wasted held his hands up and signaled to keep it down. The men walked away sniggering to each other. Jordie turned to Tom, "That Wasted has sure turned out to be plumb full of surprises."

The day went as planned. The men did the work cheerfully without having to break their backs and most importantly with Kroeber out of their hair. He lay up in the hammock all day, quiet as a mouse except for the snoring. As they packed up, Kroeber was roused and came down to look it all over. And just like Wasted said, he just looked around and nodded, got on his horse and took off fast to get back to his bunk and sleep off his drunk. They rounded up the calves and cattle and drove them back to the ranch, singing a song for Wasted and making up lyrics like "Wasted's a man to be reckoned, watch out, he'll have your girl in a second-ed!" They laughed and made fun of each other and their lyrics while Wasted yodeled a little. It wasn't an opera house voice but it'd do for the cattle at nights.

Hidden off in the trees Wilson watched and nudged his horse to follow them at a distance back to the bunkhouse.

Chapter Eleven:

The Fight

K roeber had risen early to ride around the ranch that morning to check on the various projects. Everything was in perfect order and the crews were on top of things. Kroeber rode back to the stables as if he had the whole world on a string. He smiled big to himself, a fat cat that ate the canary. He thought of how the men had been working hard and fast, like never before. At last they understood who was boss. They even did what he said without mealy-mouthing off. He didn't have to stick around long on the work crews anymore. Yeah, he finally got them whupped into shape. Truth be told he was getting tired of busting jaws and kicking those lunkheads' asses. It was boring. He wasn't a man made for that kind of work. He had a knack for bigger things. Wilson was complimenting him on everything getting done, how the ranch was running smoother at every turn. The head count on the herd was up. He smelled a big bonus coming.

And just in time before the big surprise was about to drop. Kroeber was barely able to keep the lid on it. Soon he'd be living high on the hog. He rode up to the fence and dismounted then worked at loosening the strap to his saddle. He lifted the saddle up off his horse and turned to find Ardway and Wilson riding toward him.

Ardway's hair and beard had grown shaggier with neglect but his eyes were still as cutting as ever. "You done with moving that spring herd?"

Kroeber was taken by surprise from hearing Ardway ask him something direct for a change. For months Ardway had just nodded and let Wilson do the speaking while he sipped from a flask. Kroeber stood there holding the saddle for a few seconds before answering, "The men are...working on it. I came in to...ah, report. Get any new orders."

With a slight annoyance to his eyes Ardway tightened his lips as he considered this. "Who did you leave in charge?"

"Ah...Jordie." Kroeber was irritated at this questioning but hid it.

The rancher arched an eyebrow and glanced over to Wilson, who spoke up immediately, "Broad man. Limps. Broke his leg two years ago."

"That so..." Ardway hung that out in the air. Kroeber was angry and confused. Everything had been going so well. Why did Ardway have to stick his nose in? Ardway quietly gave him an order, "Saddle up a fresh horse, Kroeber. We'll meet you with the herd." He and Wilson turned their horses about and rode off.

Kroeber fumed to himself as he absentmindedly moved around carrying the saddle. Finally he raised it high overhead and angrily tossed the saddle down hard at the ground. Kroeber stared at the saddle while stewing for a few seconds. Suddenly he grabbed the fence's top rail and slung himself over. Kroeber chased after a horse in the corral while cursing Ardway.

A stone bluff above the herd blazed with yellow and pale dried grass in the afternoon sunlight. Huge white clouds stacked in between each other floated lazily against the light blue sky. Their shadows moved in long dappled patterns across the green pasture leading up to the hills.

Up above on an outcrop of rock Ardway and Wilson stared down, observing the men working to drive the herd. Ardway pointed at a man who was riding along the front of the cattle. Kroeber raced his horse up from behind to draw up even with his bosses. Ardway watched the herd, glanced over to Kroeber, "Which one is Jordie?"

Kroeber stared forward without replying. Wilson pointed below. "That's him. Driving the wagon."

Ardway studied the men working without speaking for half a minute. Finally he spoke, "Hell of a way to lead a crew working a herd." He looked over to Kroeber, "From a wagon...at the end."

He turned back to stare closely at how the men worked the herd's movement. Ardway watched one man who constantly rode back and forth along the front line, shouting and whistling out instructions to the cowboys, stopping only to study the changing arc of the herd he moved quick on a calico quarter horse to close any break in the traveling boundary containing the herd. "Who is that lead cowpoke?"

"It's that damn pisshead, Wasted!" Kroeber's voice was strained with hate and embarrassment. "I told him not to—"

Ardway cut him off, "So, he disobeyed you."

Kroeber stared out at Wasted, his blood flush over his face. "Not any longer by damn sure!" Kroeber whipped the reins over his horse and kicked its flanks to charge down the hill toward Wasted.

Wilson and Ardway exchanged knowing glances. As they put their boots to the horses, urging them into a gallop, Wilson yelled to his boss, "Hope you know what you're doing."

∽

Wasted waved his hat, whistled at Bailey as he rode on the left side lead of the herd. Bailey turned his horse and it loped over keeping in front of the cattle to draw alongside of Wasted. Having seen some cattle stray off they both cut across the grass to send them back with the rest.

Bailey noticed something in the distance. He caught Wasted's eye and dipped his hat in that direction.

Kroeber was beelining straight for them at a gallop. Wasted took it in, looked back at the men.

Broke-nosed Tom and the other cowhands gawked and pointed, waving for others to look at the fast-riding Kroeber.

Anxiously stroking his wispy mustache at its ends, Bailey spoke up, "Here it is, Wasted. Kroeber's riding all horns and rattles." He leaned forward and squinted to see Ardway and Wilson coming up fast, "Damn, the big bugs come to watch. I told you this pot was boiling."

Wasted kept his eyes on Kroeber barreling in quick. "Shit, Bailey, why are you always right?"

His friend was calm but drew a deep breath, "Remember—if that big bucket of hog manure don't pull a gun and he starts a fight... Swing, tuck and run." Bailey was feeling anxious at what was coming. "Damn, I wish we had practiced more instead of talking fighting. Okay, so the plan is to run and tire him out. He's big but soft. Go for the gut. If he gets his hands on you..."

Kroeber raced along, getting closer by the moment and growing larger. Wasted could make out his angry dark eyes and scowl. "By ginger, he only needs one punch."

"First chance. Drop a big rock on his head." Bailey glanced over to Wasted, "Don't fool around and wait. Now, Wasted. I mean it. Ain't you tired of his beating on you?"

Wasted turned to his friend. A bit of flint sparked in his eyes.

Bailey nodded, "I knowed you got it in you."

Wasted sucked in a deep breath, then exhaled. He stepped down off Jackrabbit and waited. Without realizing it he spoke low and to himself, "We all come to Jesus in the end..."

Kroeber rode up fast, turning his horse like a doll with his great strength, and leaped off to land on the grass with a rough thud. With a few long strides he stood towering over Wasted. Ardway and Wilson galloped up to draw their horses to a stop and watch a few yards away. Kroeber made all of his height, then bent down to lean into Wasted's face. "Thought you'd pull one over on me, you silly damn bar rag! You took point. Disobeyed my orders."

Wasted tossed a quick glance to Ardway, "The men wanted it. 'Sides, you knew I would. I always do."

"Shut up!" raged Kroeber. The other men rode up, jumping off their horses and crowding around the two. The herd was forgotten. The men's eyes were wide and afraid for Wasted. He couldn't win this fight. He never did before against Kroeber. No one ever did against that big son of a bitch. They had seen ugly fights in town where there wasn't much left when Kroeber got done. Sometimes Sheriff Gammill broke it up in time but hell, those whupped men... A beating like that, something was broke in them forever. And here there was too much bad blood dammed up concerning Wasted. Kroeber was hell bent to kill him.

"I'm the boss here! Not a pissant drunk who don't know his own name. Or if he was squeezed out by a whore or his daddy's asshole."

Bailey and Wasted shared arched eyebrows signaling that was quite the insult.

Kroeber's knuckles cracked loudly as he formed two fists. He hunched over with his big apish arms wide, waiting for Wasted to make a move.

Wasted looked around to his friends. Despite their concern each gave Wasted a nod or wink to say, take that son of a bitch. Wasted handed his hat to Bailey, brought his arms up, hands balling into fists. Wasted turned to stare into the hatred in Kroeber's cold eyes. Resigned, he quietly whispered to no one who could hear, "Guess it's my call...to drop the ball."

He feinted with the left fist. Kroeber's head moved away instantly. And straight into Wasted's other fist in an uppercut punch that rocked Kroeber's jaw back. The big man shook it off while his eyes sprung open wider and red with anger.

Kroeber swung his right fist wide. Wasted ducked, hammered a left to Kroeber's gut, followed fast with a right. Kroeber groaned, part shock and part pain. He reached out to grab Wasted's shirt at the shoulder.

Wasted was spun around in Kroeber's ham-hock grip. He went with it, delivering a roundhouse kick to Kroeber's right knee. The hulking man snarled in pain.

The cowboys hooted and yelled, surprised as much as thrilled to see Wasted get in some good licks.

Ardway's eyes took it in with no show of emotion. It was too early.

Bent low, Kroeber charged with a surprising burst of speed. He head-butted Wasted in the stomach. Wasted staggered back, wheezing for breath. Kroeber swung his huge arm around.

Wasted turned but was struck a glancing blow that sent him spinning.

Kroeber hauled back and kicked Wasted right in the tail, sending him flying face first to the ground. Kroeber moved around Wasted with a quickness that didn't seem possible for so large a man. He brutally kicked Wasted in the ribs, sending him rolling across the dirt.

The cowboys' faces went slack in shock, their mouths open and crying, "Owww." For the first time Ardway's brow knitted with lines of worry.

The huge junior foreman lifted Wasted up to his knees. Kroeber's big fist knocked him back down hard to the ground. Wasted struggled to rise. Kroeber stepped back to deliver a vicious kick to Wasted's head, rolling his entire body with it on his belly.

Bailey and the men turned their gazes, afraid to watch but compelled to do so and jump in if Kroeber went too far.

Kroeber sucked in air with huge gasps, breathing hard. He grinned through the sweat that poured down his face. He bent over and grabbed Wasted's long beard with one huge paw.

Wasted's right hand dropped upon a large rock. Though his head was spinning he felt the sharp rough edges under his fingers. He gripped hold of it and squeezed hard to make his fingers bleed on the stone. He felt the pain and it kept Wasted conscious.

Kroeber jerked at Wasted's beard, rolling him over. His battered face was lined in blood. Wasted eyes were squeezed shut facing up in the light. The sun blazed red against his closed eyelids.

Wasted's friends looked on, sick and alarmed at what was to come. Ardway nudged Wilson, signaling to be on alert. Kroeber was bent over Wasted's face. He raised his arm high, his fist balling up as he prepared to put all his weight into the punch.

Wasted's right arm swung up and out. His fist held the rock, smashing it against the side of Kroeber's head. For a moment the hulking man stood over Wasted in shock with his fist held back, ready to strike. His knees trembled, buckled and he dropped to each. Wasted turned, brought the rock up, smashing it again full into the side of Kroeber's head. Kroeber fell flat as Wasted rolled out of the way to his right.

Bailey's eyes bulged in excitement as Wasted pulled himself up. He stood up, staggered a step as he shook off the dark spots clouding his sight. Wasted straightened his back, took a deep breath and glanced down at Kroeber's back. "Get up." He backed up and gave Kroeber a full-flung kick in the ribs. "Get up, you can of lard!"

Kroeber squinted up at Wasted, the side of his face dripping blood. He painfully managed to get to his knees. Holding on to one leg he pushed himself up to stand.

The circle of men stared in suspense, their jaws hung wide open like fish out of water, hanging on each move Wasted and Kroeber made. The two battered men glared at each other with hate but also exhaustion. The surge of adrenaline spent in the early stage of the fight had been replaced by fatigue and the awareness that their arms and bodies had turned to lead.

Bailey glanced nervously over to Ardway and Wilson, unsure how this could go. He spoke low to himself. "Wasted...It's now or..."

As if sensing what Bailey knew, a flash of fire ignited in Wasted's eyes. His right fist shot out like a piston firing, It smashed into Kroeber's chin, knocking his head back to the left. Kroeber was stunned, caught completely unaware by the powerful blow.

Kroeber wasn't the only one shocked. Wasted looked astonished at his fist as if it had grown from another arm. Bailey saw and yelled, "Wasted! Don't think. Turn it loose!" Something had triggered down deep inside of Wasted. He felt mad, energized, like a bucket of cold water had been tossed into his face. His exhaustion was gone. He felt light as a feather. He turned back to Kroeber. His left fist rocketed out.

The blow snapped Kroeber's head to the right. Smack, the right fist struck Kroeber, knocking the face to the left. Whack! Back to the right. Crack! To the left.

Inside, Wasted's deep self shifted gears. One moment he was on one level, then suddenly he was on some new inner plane. He was awoke in a different way that reached back and understood that he had beaten men with his fists before. It was all there in his arms and hands. Fights. He had engaged in many. Lost and won and learned or been taught to fight with his fists but he felt it all coming back in one seething rush to his mind and body.

Kroeber swayed before him, beaten to a stupor. The men were so shocked at the punches thrown they stood unsure of what was happening. Ardway was the one that spoke up, "Them dogies won't wait forever..."

Wasted glanced at Ardway as he reached out to anchor the unsteady Kroeber by the shoulder. He reached back with his right fist. Bailey and the men leaned forward, swallowing their breaths with anticipation.

Wasted's fist hammered everything he could put into an upper-cut to Kroeber's jaw. Kroeber was knocked up to his full height. He stepped back two small steps unconscious, then toppled over backwards to slam his full six feet, four inches to the ground.

Pandemonium broke out among the cowpokes. Men were screaming and throwing their hats in the sky. Horses were spooked and trotted away as their riders jumped and kicked at the air.

Ardway gave Wilson a deep sigh of relief, both sharing in grateful smiles. Ardway turned away from the celebration to pull out his flask. He took a big guzzle of whiskey. And then another.

The men crowded around Wasted, shaking his hand and slapping his back. It was a good day. That son of a bitch, Kroeber, got his ass handed to him and they all witnessed it. And miracles of miracles, it was the one man none of them thought had the sand to stand up to him. Bailey waited and let Wasted bask in the men's celebration. Finally he made his way through the crowd and put his hand on Wasted's shoulder. They shared a quiet moment, just staring into each other's eyes. Wasted's face was bruised and streaked with blood, but he and Bailey shared the biggest grins. Bailey turned and looked down at the bloodied Kroeber.

Suddenly he yelled out for all to hear, "Look who's WASTED...now!"

The rest of the men laughed and whooped it up around each other. They slapped their hands on Wasted's back and lifted him up over their heads. They carried him over to set him in the saddle on Jackrabbit. Only Jordie remained over by the unconscious Kroeber's prone body. He looked around to make sure no one was staring in his direction. With a swift motion, he delivered a powerful kick to Kroeber's ribs. Kroeber grunted in the dirt. Smiling with satisfaction, Jordie limped back over to join in with the others celebrating Wasted and his triumph.

Kroeber laid spread out on the ground as Wasted rode around his body, his arms upraised in victory as the men cheered and the cattle answered in their deep moos.

Chapter Twelve:

The Benefactors

An enormous black bear reared ferociously on its haunches, clawing the air at a mountain lion that tensed its coiled muscles to spring from a boulder. They snarled in fury at each other, seized by the jolting savagery of the moment before the charge of battle. Each glared eternally from either side of a great stone fireplace twenty feet long and eight feet tall. There had been many drunken nights with grizzled old friends and a roaring fire in that massive hearth with shadows dancing about in Ardway's den that led to boozy exclamations that hell was waiting on the other side for them all. Indian relics of primitive arrows and stone hatchets lined the walls along with old musket rifles, bone-handled knives and ball-and-cap pistols of single-shot and revolver chambers. None of these were bought as souvenirs, each earned or were used to survive the dangers inherent in building a ranch in the wilderness of Wyoming. Drinking whiskey and telling stories of battles, ghosts and tall tales was as natural here as the moonlight through the window casting sinister shadows that made men appear like Wendigo or Teihiihan. As those evenings wore on many stared into the fireplace coals beneath snaking trails of smoke and saw Satan's red eyes greedily leering out about the room looking for sinners.

Somehow through the many changes brought by Burton's wife Patricia, the room was organized into a pleasing symmetry much like her outdoor courtyard. Her unique touch to the den was a great window made of heavy-planed glass in wide frames that provided a stunning view of the property, its buildings and the lands leading into the pristine hills and woods beyond. Ardway's large rustic den was a vivid record of his frontier past. The walls of cedar gave off the fragrance of the woods while the mounted heads of deer, elk, moose and antelope reminded of the wildlife that often was viewed through the windows over the grounds. There were chairs draped in pelts of cattle, deer and buffalo. A great couch of brown leather and covered in rugs looked plush and comfortable. High above the ceiling was covered in hundreds and hundreds of antlers. This world and time and those in it believed there was an endless supply of nature and man would always be dominant. The only dilemma for each generation was how to hold on to it.

Ardway stood lost in thought before one wall. Miss Claudine entered from the hall that led back to the kitchen. Wasted followed behind her, staring around at the house with no pretense of hiding his astonishment. His face was bruised and swollen. He wore the same hand-me down clothes from his friends that he fought Kroeber in earlier, now quickly brushed and still damp from washing. Dried dark bloodstains had been rubbed with lye but were still stubbornly soaked into the shirt's collar.

Ardway turned from the wall, surprised at not hearing them come in. He nodded to Claudine and she turned and walked back into the hall. Ardway trained his eyes on Wasted who stood straight but was nervous. Maybe more so than before the fight. Ardway smiled which relieved Wasted. "The men let you rest yet?"

"Nope. They all gave me cuts of their cake at dinner. I couldn't turn them down 'cause they were so blasted happy about it. I'm stuffed full as a tick."

The older man smiled. He liked to hear his men were pleased in this kind of way. "Good of 'em. I like that. Wilson says they respect you. Listen to you. And you listen to them and mean what you say. He thinks you're our best worker."

"Naaaaa. Wilson's your best worker. Smartest, too, except for Miss Claudine." Ardway gestured to the bar, "I'm offering a drink to my best hand."

Wasted stared at the bar's shelves, filled bottles of brandy, whiskey, Scotch, sherries, ports and rye. Ardway prided himself on having one of the best loaded bars in the state. His wife had enjoyed wines and he had a basement room devoted just to such. Now the wines were only used by Miss Claudine for cooking and serving with food.

A bittersweet smile crossed Wasted's lips as he turned back to Ardway, "Thanks, no. I hope you understand. It feels good to look at a bottle and walk away." He nodded to a sliver tray with an elegant pot and china cups set on a small table by the couch. "That hot coffee?"

"It is." Ardway walked over and poured a steaming cup. Wasted followed him to the table. Ardway handed the cup to Wasted on a saucer. He gestured to the sugar cubes in a dish and a cream server. Wasted waved both off. Ardway walked back to the brandy and poured himself more in a crystal glass. The delight he took hinted that he had poured a few already. He motioned for Wasted to sit at the couch.

"Sit down. Let's jaw and see where it goes."

Wasted sat carefully, holding to the cup and saucer with both hands. His back straight and with a prim manner he lifted the cup, leaving the saucer on one knee. He sipped the coffee and raised his eyebrows in surprise. "Hmm, licorice?"

Ardway carried his glass and the decanter of brandy over and sat in a big chair that was made of steer horns and leather. He faced Wasted as he set the brandy on a small table next to him and smiled, "Yes. Claudine made it special. Said she guessed you to be a licorice man."

Wasted was pleased and a little embarrassed at such attention. "Please tell Miss Claudine it's the best coffee I ever tasted." He enjoyed drinking the coffee while glancing about the room, grinning big at each trophy or memento. The den's grandeur seemed beyond anything he had ever known. Ardway studied him while swallowing his brandy.

Wasted spoke, "This room feels good. Lived in...Proud."

Ardway nodded, pleased. He glanced around, enjoyed experiencing his past through Wasted's eyes. He turned to Wasted, "We still calling you, Wasted?"

"Yeah. Funny, it's kinda' growed on me. Keeps me thankful."

"That's a smart way to look at it."

Wasted looked directly at Ardway then his eyes raised up to stare behind him. There on the wall was a large formal painting of a shaven, clean-cut Ardway, his beautiful brunette wife, Patricia, and their twelve-year-old son, Burton Junior. Despite the formal nature of their dress and poise there was a warmth to their eyes and lips that suggested each was on the verge of bursting out laughing. This was a happy moment captured for all time, which made it all the sadder that its truth had died and been lost.

Ardway noticed Wasted eyeballing the painting. He turned to it and then back. "My family."

"I heard your wife was...pretty. But I don't think I have ever seen such a stunner."

Ardway made a pained smile, "I think so."

"No guessing who the boy is. Spitting image of you. He still favor you?"

Ardway paused a moment before answering, "I...suppose."

Wasted saw that Ardway had grown uncomfortable. "I'm sorry to stare. Just...it makes me wonder what I'm missing...not knowing about my past...and my family."

The rancher considered this. His eyes shrugged with an old ache.

"You might be lucky." He downed his brandy and poured some more. "Let's speak of more current events. I fired a shifty range boss this afternoon and need a new one. You interested?"

Wasted had just sipped coffee from the cup. He coughed and looked around, not sure he heard Ardway right. "You...you're joshing me!"

Chuckling out loud, Ardway got a kick out of watching Wasted's reaction. "No, no. Wilson and the boys talked it over. You're the man we want."

For a few seconds the gobsmacked Wasted had to wait as it sank in. He suddenly jumped up, spilling the coffee. He crossed over to the tray to set the cup and saucer down, wiping his wet hands up and down on his shirt. His face was beaming as he excitedly walked over to Ardway with his hand held out.

"Oh, thank you, Mr. Ardway. I'm...pleased to oblige." Standing, Ardway took Wasted's hand. They shook. "You're welcome, son."

Wasted continued shaking Ardway's hand, looking around the room with his sudden happiness. "I...I sure was needing this. I prayed for something. Some sign...that...that I was somebody. And this...is sure it!"

He realized he was still shaking Ardway's hand and stopped. He let go and smiled at how silly he looked. "This job. It's a start. No matter who I used to be."

Relishing Wasted's enthusiasm, Ardway peered into his face. "Is that important? I mean, who you were before?"

Wasted's eyes lost their excitement, "Well. I must have been a...a terrible bad man once. For God to wipe it all away."

Ardway studied Wasted, looking deeper than before.

"You ever get any recollections? A face? A home?"

The younger man's expression became serious. "Sometimes, I dream. Of a woman."

The rancher's eyes turned up in a knowing mirth while making a hollow laugh, "Ain't there always a woman..."

He looked Wasted up and down, thinking to himself for a moment, then making a decision. Ardway nodded his head in a direction for Wasted to follow him. He started for a hall leading to the stairs.

"Wasted, I can't help with your past. But maybe I got something. Something that might help...with starting new."

A few minutes later the two stood in the darkness at the end of a hall on the second floor. A door creaked open as Ardway turned his head back to Wasted and said, "In here..."

A match was struck, casting its flare to expose a lamp attached to a wall. Ardway leaned in and pulled the glass cover up. He ignited its kerosene wick then turned the flow key. The light bloomed and filled the room with its soft gold to reveal a boy's world on a ranch.

Wasted looked about at its walls and furniture. A shelf was filled with books and above that was a large set of white steer horns with sharp black tips. A framed map of the Wyoming Territory hung above a bed in a corner. Flintstone arrowheads on a blanket spread out from around it in lines, arranged like sun rays. There was an old and elegant wooden desk and wooden chair of natural red color opposite the bed, an heirloom from Patricia's side of the family. It had a window above with drawn curtains. A sturdy-looking wooden wardrobe and clothes drawer finished lining the walls. In a corner was a basket that held the folded small clothing of a baby and a young child.

Nailed above the desk window on the wall was a pair of rusty old spurs shaped like stars and fastened to tattered leather straps. Over this was a set of carved wood pegs that held a fishing rod and reel. Two mounted fish at forty five degree angles "jumped" out at each end of the wall.

Ardway stepped to the center of the room where a large trunk was placed upon a great red Indian rug with white and yellow stripes. Ardway regarded the trunk with a gentleness in his son's room that was unlike the hellish ride to the ranch. He softly placed his hand on the lid and its memories from another time filled his face. Ardway smiled but it could not hide the sadness or longing in his eyes. Shrugging it off he lifted a key that was lying on the curved lid and inserted it into the brass lock. He turned it and raised the lid. Wasted watched as Ardway stared into, hesitated, and then tenderly reached into the trunk.

Wasted thought back and how completely opposite this behavior was from that awful night that Ardway knocked him about Rouget's Mill in a rage and tossed him into the wagon with this very trunk. Whatever was happening in this moment he realized that Ardway was dealing with something bigger than himself and a worthless drunk that he snatched away to his ranch. Wasted felt small and meaningless for having no memories. Was he ever going to find out why his past escaped his knowing? And why was Ardway tormented by his own past in every living moment? Maybe Ardway was right in saying that it was better not to know.

A long Bowie knife in a rough leather sheaf was pulled from the trunk. Ardway held on to it like treasure and carefully set it aside on the rug.

Next Ardway took extra care as he lifted up a handsome, tooled leather, two-holstered gun belt. Inside it were two shiny .45 Colt pistols with ivory inlay handles. It looked like it was just taken from a shelf in an expensive gun shop. The light glittered and danced on the barrel and frame's engraved metal. Wasted was struck by the image and thought of light sparkling on a lake at sunset. Ardway extended the guns and belt to Wasted. "Here. Take 'em."

Wasted took a step back, unprepared for this lavish gesture.

"On, no. I...Them guns are special. I'm not worth the—"

A bittersweet smile crossed Ardway's face. "You can't be my range boss without pistols. Go on. Take them."

He thrust the gift into Wasted's hands. His eyes lingered a long moment on the guns before he let go.

Ardway watched while Wasted marveled over the guns like discovering a precious stone.

"They were never fired. You'll need to shoot them. Get 'em to set right for you. Ah, you'll...keep 'em clean?"

Wasted's eyes turned from the guns to earnestly regard Ardway. "Oh. Yes, sir! I will! I'll give them the best care. You can inspect them anytime you wish."

"I trust you." Ardway smiled, delighted and sad at the same time. He glanced back at the trunk.

"There's some clothes that might fit you. I sent them and...and they were returned. I'll have Claudine go through them. Send 'em over to your new bunk. You got a wardrobe now. A bed closer to the fire, too."

Wasted took a deep breath, overcome with his good fortune. He tried to speak but could only manage to shake his head gratefully as he smiled. Ardway looked him over, weighing whether to ask a question. Finally he decided to speak up.

"Wasted, I was wondering. The first couple of months you was here. Did you ever...want to kill me?"

Wasted swallowed. He gathered himself up then sheepishly grinned. "Every dang-blasted minute."

Ardway nodded silently. "Well...I do that to people."

He led Wasted to the door and let him out. He turned the lamp key and the flame died. Ardway closed the door and put his memories away. They walked down the dark hallway to the stairs and the light coming up from below. Wasted's voice sounded in the blackness.

"I'm really glad now."

"Why?"

"That I didn't kill you."

Silence. After a few steps Ardway started laughing as they reached the stairs. Ardway's voice grew louder and the guffaws more boisterous as they walked down to the bottom floor. Even Wasted joined in.

∾

In Spirits Bend at that late moment the town was settling in for the night. Except for the saloons no light graced the streets nor people walked down them. Above in the sky a half moon shone faintly through the drifting gray clouds. Down at the end of the main street off from the shops and stores was the two-story Fendris Feed Store. The Ardway Hotel was taller but this was the longest building in two hundred miles. It started out much smaller as a feed store but Fendris decided to add this and that to suit his mood. The store now sold a bit of everything. The clouds parted and moonlight shone on the establishment's blue trim and white paint to make those features stand out along with the big sign over the front door that declared "FENDRIS" in large red letters.

Inside in a rustic back room were rough-cut wooden shelves filled with supplies. Barrels and boxes were stacked tightly in rows on the shelves. In a far corner was a closed-off office. Through the thin walls the sounds of snoring rattled its wood.

In the room's deep shadows the heavy breathing and grunting of a large man added to the snoring. Now and then he groaned in pain and shifted how he lay in the bed.

A match exploded with sulfurous burning light. As it settled, it touched a candle's wick to form a rippling spire of yellow flame. Emerging into view a candle stood in a faint circle of soft gold, placed on a small table at the foot of a bed. Someone tossed the lit match to land on the sleeper's face. Kroeber twitched around, slapping at his face then pulling a pistol from under his pillow. He swiftly cocked the hammer, pointing the gun at the candle's flame.

Fendris sat in a chair next to the table with the candle. He was half in and half out of the flame's glow. One pale blue eye stared at Kroeber in the bed. "You look like shit."

Kroeber's face was puffed up and bruised. A cloth bandage wrapped around his head to cover the wound on the side. He grunted and un-cocked the gun, sliding it back under his pillow. "That drunk looks worse."

Fendris looked on, tired and bored.

"So." He paused. "My inside man with Ardway...is now on the outside...of nothing."

Kroeber's tone was irked, "That pisshead did it! Hit me with a rock."

Fendris wearily and quietly said, "Don't speak."

Like a specter materializing out of the dark Jurant appeared by Fendris. He leaned in and whispered into his ear. Fendris's eyes looked up, he nodded back. Jurant turned and disappeared again.

Kroeber glanced about, spooked at how Jurant came and went without a sound. Fendris turned back to Kroeber with that calm but weary manner. "Kroeber. I didn't come down here...at this hour...to hear you whine about Ardway's charity case."

He leaned forward into the pale sphere of soft light. Both of his blue eyes bored into Kroeber. He spoke as to a child. "Kroeber. You...were a part of my plans. My plans to draw Ardway...out."

Kroeber started to object, "But, I—"

Fendris's cold blue eyes narrowed, cutting off Kroeber's protest.

"Now that you're the one...out...it would look...bad...if I took you in. Improper. My plans require that everything must look...proper."

The large man's voice rose in panic. "I still know how Ardway runs things. His goings. Schedules and—"

Fendris shouted, "Kroeber!" His eyes raged at Kroeber a few seconds before settling back to a calm state. "What I need...is an angle. To keep you around...without much suspicion." He thought to himself for a few seconds. "I need something that plays to my side." Fendris turned to the darkness on the left of Kroeber's bed, "Right, Pete?"

A tall ugly man with a shaggy red mustache stepped into the light by the bed. "Yes, boss."

Kroeber whipped around to stare uneasily up at Pete. Pete nodded quietly at him. Slowly Kroeber slid his hand under the pillow, searching for the gun. He couldn't find it. Panicked, he frantically dug around looking for the gun.

Click. A gun hammer cocked in the dark on the other side of the bed. Leaning into the candle's glow a short, stout Mexican pointed Kroeber's gun at his frightened face.

"Right, Benito?" spoke Fendris.

"Si, Señor Fendris."

These two had been asleep in the back of Fendris's wagon that day with Ardway at the train station. They were not drunk or hungover this time.

Fendris leaned back in the chair. "Boys. Burt has his charity case. We should have one." An idea lit up in those cold blue eyes. "Like... like the poor bastard...that was beat...to within...an inch of his life... by that mean drunk...out at Ardway's place."

His men caught on, nodding with tightly coiled smiles at Fendris. "Beaten so ugly...that people will feel a...terrible pity for him."

Kroeber's eyes grew wide, realizing what Fendris meant. He looked to the Mexican and then to Pete, trying to gauge if they understood. They did. Kroeber turned to Fendris with his lower lip trembling and eyes wild.

"Please...Mr. Fendris——"

Fendris cut him off, "Shhhhhhh..." He looked at his men. "Boys..."

The loud racket at the start of Kroeber's violent beating bounced off the walls of the room as Fendris watched. His head moved slightly forward as his eyes grew eager at the sickening noise of each pounding slap and punch against Kroeber's face and head.

Kroeber tried not to yell at first and live up to his reputation of a big man. A tough man. Pete and Benito spoke only with their fists or their gun barrels splitting Kroeber's flesh. Fendris watched, his tongue wetting his lips.

Kroeber began to yell. Then he cried. Nothing he did stopped the pounding. Kroeber wailed in harsh gasps and barking huffs under the blows, unable to yell because it was all coming so fast.

Fendris watched. His pale blue irises widened in the candle's yellow light, shiny and moist. Reflected in both of Fendris's eyes was Kroeber's torn bloody face.

Kroeber finally managed to squeeze out a desperate scream like an animal bellowing against dying. The two men stopped, shocked at how primal and wretched Kroeber sounded. They had worked up a sweat and were huffing to catch their breath. Kroeber managed to mumble through his mashed lips, "Phhuuleashe..."

The three men erupted with laughter. Pete and Benito roared as they started the beating again. Fendris grinned wide with his coffee-yellow teeth gleaming in the candlelight.

Chapter Thirteen:

A Stirring

———

Wasted's desolated eyes had grown wide. A stricken look of horror filled his face. In his clenched hands were two pistols. The barrels leaked blue smoke that floated slowly up and curled around his face like a halo. There was no beard or long hair. He stared off to the right at something terrible in the dark. Two quick gunshots roared in the dark.

Wasted jolted up in bed, wide awake. Despite his beard and long hair he was covered in sweat. His eyes darted around the room, unsure where he was. He had been visited by the woman and the gunshots as usual in his deepest sleep. His past was always waiting for him there. And even with waking it clung to him and he drifted within that feeling, trying to make sense of it.

Loud snoring and deep breathing brought him back to the bunkhouse. In the gloom he saw the stacked beds and men sleeping. Wasted glanced around adjusting his eyes to the shadows. There were six small windows in the quarters, three on each side of the walls. Moonlight streamed through a middle window striking the floor in a pale white shaft. The curtains were drawn on the other windows. The light cast around the room was faint and gave a slender silver edge to objects.

He saw the beautiful raven-haired woman sitting by a table. But was that a man by the door? His eyes became more accustomed to the bunkhouse shadows. The woman faded into clothing tossed over a chair. There was no man. Feeling some relief Wasted leaned against a wall. Something caught his eye. It glittered with a small spark. As he turned to the light it became brighter. Wasted rose out of his bed and walked to the flickering shine.

The moonlight was glistening playfully off the metal of the guns from Ardway, as if beckoning him to come closer. They hung in their shiny polished leather belt hooked over a peg on his new wardrobe. Wasted stepped lightly across the floor to not wake the others. He stood before the guns, sparkling in the moonlight and hanging directly at his eye level. For a long moment he stared, unsure what he was looking at—the silver moonlight or the guns. Wasted imagined that the guns stared back, wondering about...him. A dread filled Wasted, was he dreaming and awake at the same time? These guns. The gunshots in his dreams. The woman. Wasted began to feel afraid, like he should run from the guns. For the first time since the lodge he felt like drinking whiskey, lots of whiskey, escaping, drunk and forgetting everything and curling up with a bottle and hiding forever.

The guns created a push and tug sensation within Wasted. The hand-carved engraving lines ran twisted and coiled about the shiny metal with no apparent conclusion. Hypnotic and spiraling without an end or start. Wasted stared as one gun grew larger, racing along its engravings, its light glinting in multiple helixes of iridescence. The ivory inlay handles had the carved wings of an eagle or maybe it was a fallen Icarus. Wasted closed his eyes and tried to think of something else. He saw the beautiful lady that haunted him and she laughed to his face and wouldn't stop. He opened his eyes and tried to avoid gazing at the guns and their push/pull feeling. Wasted couldn't resist the guns, with a shudder of delight and fear he gave in.

Wasted reached out and grabbed one Colt by its handle. He gripped it tightly and immediately felt...grateful. The pistol seemed thankful, too, just waiting for his touch. His fingers gripped the butt tighter, feeling the wings on the ivory pressing against his palm. He was sure in this state that the wings grew, extending out of his wrist. Carefully and slowly Wasted pulled the pistol free from its oiled leather holster. Even this action gave off a feeling like taking a deep easy breath. Natural and comfortable. He cradled the gun in both of his hands. The weight felt light but solid. Wasted took hold again in his right hand. It was not a gun anymore, it had become an extension of his body flowing through his life's energy and spirit. That thought came with an image of the old Sioux from the lodge and the head of the wolf lashed to the corral gate. The voice of the Native American whispered, "Šung'manitu Tanka..."

He spun the chamber with his left hand, the sound rattling like a poisonous snake. Wasted raised the gun to stare down the the top of the barrel at its sight. His eye trained the sight across the room to focus on the sleeping face of Bailey. Inside a feeling ignited. He cocked the hammer back with his thumb, aware that he had done this action a thousand times before. The gun sight loomed larger in Wasted's vision to target on Bailey's nose. Wasted's finger closed on the trigger and—

His hand snapped the gun barrel up. Wasted stared at the ceiling where the Colt was pointed. He breathed in, careful and measured. Slowly he lowered the gun to stare at its polished metal. It was a handsome gun for sure but what made holding it seem like he was drinking the smoothest whiskey ever made, his brain tingling for more? Wasted's old dread had returned, the compelling feeling that the gun was too powerful. A warning? He gazed absently out into the dark until he realized he was staring straight down the inside bore of the gun, its barrel pointed directly between his eyes.

~

The others lay in deep slumber on their bunks, the only sounds those of soft breathing along with snoring. The shaft of moonlight on the bunkhouse floor had passed on, melting into the pale light turning black to gray at four o'clock in the morning. What was left of the night was that gentle quiet before dawn.

A loud gunshot jolted the ranch hands awake. They slapped and kicked out at walls and beds in confusion. Each fell out of their bunks, stumbling into the other while tossing their clothes on. Bailey grabbed his Army Colt in one hand and stumbled toward the gun's echo out the back door, holding his pants up with the other hand. The other men tottered into each other as they followed after him.

The sleepy men rushed out of the bunkhouse, piling into a confused logjam behind Bailey who squinted out in the semidarkness.

Lined up on top of fence rails, bottles exploded one by one with the rapid sound of gunfire, erupting glass shards about in the air. Tin cans atop the fence posts blasted up into the sky to fly across the yard. Bullets hammered the large white skull of a steer, hurling bone fragments out like a bomb went off. The men threw their hands up over their ears at the racket.

Wasted stood thirty yards away, firing both Colts with a calm grace. He stopped. Wasted pulled bullets from his belt, emptied his pistol of the spent shells and inserted the new cartridges. He expertly whip-tossed his guns into their leather holsters strapped to his thighs.

Bailey and his friends blinked and squinted, not sure if if they were still in bed dreaming. Bailey found his voice and yelled, "Wasted! What the hellfire blazes are—"

Wasted's arms blurred, fast-drawing the pistols. A bean can was popped, ricocheting it high up into the air. Wasted kept firing, hitting the can repeatedly and keeping it bouncing about the atmosphere like it was jerked on an invisible string. Mouths opened wide in astonishment, Wasted's friends gawked at his speed and marksmanship.

The booming fusillade stopped with the can landing on the grass, bouncing and rolling to a stop at Bailey's feet. Several punctured bullet holes dotted about the can. Stunned by this unexpected display, Bailey fumbled the grip on his gun and pants, the pants dropping to his knees. Bailey blurted out, finishing his earlier thought, "—you doing?"

Wasted slowly held the pistols out before him, touching the barrels together as blue smoke drifted up out of their bores, twisting and circling the other like in a dance. Wasted watched the fumes dissipate, thinking of death and souls leaving this world. He drifted back and turned to Bailey, his eyes heavy with a grim awareness.

"Doing? I'm remembering..."

~

The stables building was old but the best-maintained on the property. Ardway reasoned that cattle can live out in the weather but a good range horse was like gold and needed a substantial place to keep it groomed and protected. He and his friends built it while he was still sleeping under a tarp with two log walls built into the side of a hill. He ordered it be kept spotless, mopped and swept three times a day. And to prove its cleanliness he once ate breakfast off the clay tile floor which he added ten years after it was built. Ardway couldn't help but love it out of his respect for horses and it being the first place erected on the property. He had added stalls to it over the years and put a new slate roof on two years ago. It not only kept the rain and snow out but the red and bluish colors of the shale plates were distinctive from anything else in over five hundred miles. Patricia had pushed him to do it before she left. Ardway put a slate roof over his own house the next year, hoping it might entice Patricia to consider coming back. It didn't, but Ardway liked how it reminded him of loving her.

Ardway walked into this personal sanctuary wearing his old red leather slicker. He peered around the room to see if anyone was there. His horse, Big Black, and others had been taken outside with the sun rising. Cautiously he walked past the stalls over to the tack room. His eyes scanned about as he paused and listened. Satisfied that he was alone Ardway moved to the wall and reached for a board positioned at eye level. Tugging at its corner, he pulled it free. Behind it was a hidden compartment between the framing.

Ardway reached inside his slicker and pulled something out that only his long coat could disguise, bundled up in brown leather. He carefully pulled the long Sheffield Bowie knife out of its sheath, the one he removed from his son's trunk. Nine inches long and two inches wide of sharp steel glinted silver in the light against a pallid yellow handle of bone. For a few moments Ardway regarded the intimidating weapon with obvious affection, his eyes moist and with a tenderness that stared through the years. Breathing a deep sigh filled with memories he replaced the knife in its cover. Looking at the compartment Ardway brushed his fingers upon letters carved there, "BURT and BURT Jr.". He set the long knife inside and replaced the board to secure it in the grooves that held it. He backed away to stare at the wall, reliving the moments that resided behind it with the Bowie knife. Ardway had wanted a Bowie knife so badly as a child growing up and being enthralled by the legend of the Vidalia Sandbar Fight. Jim Bowie fought a heroic battle with five attackers and received two bullet wounds, seven stab wounds and a pistol broken over his head. Ardway had told Junior the story many times. Junior wanted a Bowie knife but Patricia wouldn't have it. So this was their shared secret. This and more filled Ardway's mind.

"Mr. Ardway?" A hint of Perique tobacco filled the room.

He swung his head around, irritated at being interrupted here in this special place.

A tall man stood in the shadow of the doorway, the morning sunlight burning white at the edges surrounding him. He snuffed out a pipe with a rag.

"Yes? Who the blazes are you?"

The man stepped forward. His eyes had a blackness that sucked the light out of the room. Ardway thought of two holes in a mine shaft, the kind you throw rocks down and can't hear them hit bottom.

"Name's Jurant. Benton Jurant. The black lady at the house said I'd find you here."

Ardway didn't remember Jurant from the train station or at the hotel after visiting Haben. But his voice couldn't hide his annoyance.

"Well? State your business!"

He walked over to stand before a worn saddle propped up in place on a holding stand and gave Jurant his back. Ardway worked with thin woven cord and needle, re-stitching the seams around its padding.

Jurant watched Ardway ignore him with his back. Only a few had ever done that and to their regret.

"I heard in town you lost your range boss. Thought you might be hiring."

Ardway whipped the cord around and pulled its needle through the hole and tightened it in a practiced if testy manner. He repeated this threading over and over without looking up. "Job's filled. You wasted your time riding out here, Jurant."

Jurant was the one irritated now.

"Too bad. I could have used the work. I'm a pretty good hand." Ardway snorted over his shoulder.

"At what? Wearing out your welcome?"

Jurant stewed on this a few seconds.

"I can't change your mind? I'd work a week for fr—"

"Said we ain't hiring. Don't let the door hit you in the ass, Jurant."

Jurant wasn't expecting this. A few moments passed as he considered his next move. Fendris expected him to get a job, and who the hell did Ardway get to replace Kroeber so quickly? He felt the heat rising behind his eyes watching the rancher, so arrogant and dismissive. Impulsively he quietly pulled one of his pistols and pointed it at the back of Ardway's head. He sighted the gun on Ardway's hat, thinking how it would be so easy to do. He looked around, noticed the stable was exceptionally well built. It would hide the sound of the shot. Jurant could slip away and be gone before anyone knew.

His finger curled around the trigger.

Ardway was lost in the stitching work, focusing his anger at the task over having his privacy interrupted. He reached into his slicker and brought out a flask to take a drink. Then another.

Seeing this Jurant cocked his arm, raised the gun up. A knowing smile parted his lips. He softly lowered the gun back in its holster, careful to not make a sound. Jurant quietly turned and walked out the door. As he stepped along he looked back over his shoulder. He could see Ardway through the door, taking another sip at the flask.

Jurant nodded, speaking low to himself, "Buvez, Monsieur. Your health." He had grown up watching how this behavior turned out with the rich and powerful. Jurant laughed softly as he walked along. He turned the corner of the stables and ran smack-dab into Wasted, hurrying on his way to the corral. Both stopped abruptly, backs drawn up and hands on their guns. Jurant stared at the wild black hair and beard, then his eyes darted to Wasted's hands on his Colts.

"You gonna use those?" He nodded down to the guns.

Wasted looked to Jurant's hands on his own guns. He relaxed and opened his hands and withdrew them from the pistols. He held each up in surrender.

"Sorry, Mister. I didn't see you until the last second around that corner." Jurant's hands came off his guns while he stepped back to look Wasted over.

"Damn, boy, I was sure a bear had me!" He laughed as he looked around the property and up in the hills. "Nothing like this where I come from down in New Orleans." He looked back at Wasted. "Pretty fast hands. Thought you were gonna cut me down."

Wasted smiled uneasily. He wasn't used to talk like this. And only his ranch friends teased him about his hair. This business of having the guns was new and Wasted felt conflicted and confused about it. Living at the ranch and dealing with how his life was changing was different but it was to be expected. But this particular stranger brought a sense of danger to it all. Damn those dark eyes, too! Wasted wanted to change the subject, "No flies on your hands either, Mister."

Ardway appeared. He stood beside Wasted like a real bear, pissed at this disturbance in his territory and with his clan. "Jurant! You still here? If this is how you work, holding up my men from carrying out their duties? No wonder you offered to loaf for free."

Jurant's face lost its color, firming up like a white brick. Ardway had already pushed him to his limit. His pitch-black eyes somehow grew even darker while his mind raced with possibilities. He would take the furry hick out first...and then Ardway.

Wilson and some of the men nearby heard their boss yelling and came trotting from their work about the grounds. Jurant noticed twenty or so closing in. Within seconds there was a crowd shoulder-to-shoulder around him. He knew only drunks started gunfights in a mob. And they usually got stomped to death for the effort.

Suddenly Wasted spoke up, "Mister Ardway. This man Jurant was leaving when we met head-on coming 'round the corner here. It was me that held him up."

Ardway frowned but accepted the excuse. He spat his order at Jurant, "Well, git then!"

Jurant looked around at the men with those piercing black eyes. His face had an angry grimace, like a venomous snake wound up about to strike. He moved to leave and a few men parted some space to let him go. Ardway and the men watched with a growing outrage as Jurant walked toward the house and to his horse. Feeling their eyes and anger on his back Jurant turned and held his arms out wide while walking backwards and yelled, "Thanks for the hospitality, Ardway! I hope to return it someday." He turned about and disappeared into the shadows among the Ponderosa pines and bur oaks surrounding the house.

Wilson turned as he spoke to the men, "Back to work, boys. Unless anybody else wants to cross Mister Ardway." He gave Ardway a crooked smile that caused Ardway to almost laugh in spite of himself. He gruffly turned to Wasted.

"Where was you headed?"

Wasted spoke up, "Ah, to the corral. Need to get Jack saddled."

"I'll walk with you."

Wasted wasn't sure why Ardway would do this but it sounded like he was about to get a chewing out.

They walked over to the corral and Wasted bent and slipped between the fence's poles that were rough cut from young trees. He walked over to Jackrabbit between the other horses. With his secret ritual of hiding the Bowie knife accomplished Ardway took the red slicker off and threw it over a post top. He leaned on the rails to watch Wasted approach Jack.

Jackrabbit played hard to get, stayed a little ahead of Wasted as he approached him. He dodged and cut in-between other horses to put some distance to Wasted. But Wasted knew his games. He went over to another horse and started talking to it. Softly calling it sweet names. "Here, Red. Yeah, Red. That's a good gal, Red. Yes, you are prettier than Jack." Jack watched and started edging closer to Wasted.

Ardway observed and his irritated frown over Jurant began to fade.

Jack was at Wasted's back now as he continued looking only into Red's eyes and speaking softly. Jack nudged Wasted's shoulder. He turned and acted surprised, "Oh, hey, Jack. Where you been?" He turned back to Red and stroked her neck. Jack moved closer, putting his nose over Wasted's shoulder to nuzzle Red on the snout.

Wasted turned and looked into Jack's eyes. He spoke in a quiet whisper, "Jack, Jack, Jack...Are you glad to see me?"

The horse's snout pushed Wasted's hat back on his head. Jack rubbed its muzzle gently against Wasted's forehead to answer. Wasted reached up and petted him under his cheek. "I'm happy to see you, boy." And with that he brought the bridle up with the other hand and slipped it over Jack's head with no fuss. Wasted turned and gave Red an affectionate slap on her haunch, then led Jackrabbit back to the fence where his saddle and gear were hung over the top rail. Wasted put a blanket on Jack and then slung his saddle up and on his back.

As Wasted tightened the cinches and breast collar and checked the latigo straps, Ardway entered the corral and walked over to them.

He ran his hands over Jack's shoulders, flanks and hips in knowing approval. Jack swung his tail freely, whipping it across Ardway's face. Ardway laughed and came around to stare up into the horse's soft eyes. Ardway pulled a carrot from his pants back pocket and held it up. Jack crunched it up with his teeth, swallowed, and gave a slight puff of breath and a purr of restlessness.

"Jack's ready to get going." Ardway looked to Wasted, "How about you?"

Wasted pulled the cinch knot down firmly and checked around the saddle. It all looked tight and secure. He turned to Ardway.

"Well, I'd be pulling Bocephus's tail if I said I knew everything I'm supposed to about range bossing."

"Wilson stands for you and that's good enough. 'Sides you just handled Jack like a twenty-year horse man. You couldn't have learned that in the short time here."

Wasted looked at the horses around the corral. "I was a tenderfoot when Bailey and Nat got hold of me. Horses knew it, too. But I got over that quick. I've got a powerful endearment for critters that is pure natural. Don't know if it's 'cause of my upbringing but I suspect it's true."

Ardway watched the other horses play and trot about the corral. "That Jurant had me so pissed I could bite myself. But being around these horses and watching you with Jack has put me in another place. I wish I could go out with you but..."

"You got a ranch to run." Wasted smiled and put his foot in the stirrup, grabbed the swell and the horn, pulling himself up in the saddle. "'Fore I go, you got any advice to a new junior foreman?"

The rancher looked down at his boots in the light brown dust and thought a few seconds. Ardway looked up, his sharp eyes focused on Wasted. "One big rule. Don't let the men buffalo you. You're more than a friend now. You're their boss. And they'll test you. Always do. That's just how things go. So you'll have to let them know, with some grit and a kick, who's running things. When things get rough, as they always do, they'll need a strong man to lead 'em through it. Get me?"

Wasted let it sink in. Ardway walked over and opened the gate and Wasted rode Jack over in a slow trot. Ardway nodded up to the high ground.

Wasted stared out the gate. With an excited kick and a yell, Wasted raced Jack straight up the path to the hills. Ardway stared after him remembering the first time he rode out in that direction. Everything was new back then and the future was wide open.

Somebody yelled from the barn, "Mister Ardway! Can you come look at this damn wagon?"

Ardway closed and locked the gate. He pulled the flask out of his red slicker and took a drink and put it back. Ardway stared over his shoulder at Wasted while digging his hands in the back pockets of his pants. With a sigh of resignation, he turned and walked toward the barn, kicking at stones along the way.

Chapter Fourteen:

The New Range Boss

The next two weeks of Wasted's life were filled with jobs that never seemed to finish themselves as completely as when he was just a ranch hand. "Was it enough?" was his constant nagging companion. Being the boss on jobs away from the ranch house grounds gave him an independence to do as he liked as long as it worked out. Sometimes it did. But lots of times a simple task became a nightmare in execution. A rainstorm blew out of the East his third day on the job, interrupting the work and scattering the cattle being herded to a pasture on the South Range. Afterward it caused Wasted to deal with mud and pools of water that tired out the herd and slowed the progress of horses and crew slogging through it. But that wasn't the worst of it. The water brought more than the usual infestation of flies and mosquitoes, biting about the critters and men something terrible. The bandanas came out immediately. Nat wore two, wrapping them around the top and bottom halves of his head leaving just slits for his eyes. Jordie and Bailey tried to do this but their bandanas kept slipping all over their faces. Every now and then a man would let out a scream but it was mostly for a person's release and the goddamn frustration of it all.

After the rain Mother Nature and her elements decided to have their own sweet time with everyone. At the end of the rainstorm a blinding lightning bolt cracked a huge Ponderosa pine, blasting the tree into giant splintered logs. Heavy limbs fell from the air to rain over the men and cows. The brilliance streaked the landscape ghostly white and wiped out its shadows for a brief few seconds that felt like years. Tom claimed it felt like falling in and out of heaven. Bailey said the same thing but cussed that it was more like being kicked in and out of hell. What was left of the tree tumbled with a crashing roar to slam into the earth. This was followed by an explosive concussion of thunder that shook through both human and animal like nothing in life before. Then came an electrical charge that sizzled the atmosphere with the eerie sounds of pops and crackling. The hairs shot up on everyone's bodies and heads, including the critters, in freakish ways. That one-two-three combination spooked the cattle for miles, along with the men and horses. For a long moment man and critter thought it was the end of the world. No one moved for a full minute, afraid that doing so would set off some other calamity. This weird state of things probably prevented a stampede. When the cattle and horses realized things were safe enough to breathe again they had to slowly trudge through the deep mud and sand to find the flooded creeks washed out by the rains. What was a day's job turned into five days' worth. Wasted wearily learned that for the boss nothing went as easily as planned. And if it miraculously did go as intended it was followed with getting the orders to jump quickly on another job as to beat whatever catastrophe was barreling down the road next. Times like this Wasted wondered why he took the job.

His friends worked hard for Wasted during this ordeal. No one bitched or moaned about the work. Well, no more than usual because a cowboy's life was always marked by complaining about the long hard hours. Most of the boys were set for this existence by now. They had grown up with the requirements of the ranch hand's life or they found it a satisfying way to escape a dead-end job, a crime of youth in a different part of the world, or perhaps the loss of a woman for a million reasons. Still, the troubles with this South Range herd movement were vexing them. It pulled Ardway and Wilson out from the ranch house to pitch in for a couple of days because it was just what cowboys do, even the Big Bugs.

Everyone slept out around the restless cattle in case of stampede until the job of moving them to the high range pasture was done. Despite the work no one slept well what with the cold, scattered rains and winds. Lightning and thunder played across the fields here and there night and day to let them know who was really running things in this open part of the world. When the herd was finally moved to its destination and was grazing in relative safety, the sun broke through the clouds and the weather turned steaming hot like working around a furnace with two hundred percent humidity. The cattle took it as a relief after the trip, the boys thought God hated them.

Wasted found out he had one last responsibility that no one had told him about on the way back home. He rode among the exhausted men on their horses, shaking sleepers awake before they pitched off and broke their necks. It got so he used a rope tied with a knot to slap their legs or backs with more than a little extra pain because he was too tired to reach over with his arm. A man would jerk up and cuss before he realized it was for his own good, "Oh! You son of a—...Ah, thank you, Wasted." On the last mile to the bunkhouse Wasted was whacking himself with the rope.

Once they finally got back to the ranch the men stumbled slowly about and struggled to find the strength to brush down their horses after putting up their saddles. Then they dragged themselves to make sure that the horses were fed well. The horses responded with soft neighs and puffed at each other, happy to be back with good feed and clean water.

The hungry men groaned and cussed about aching backs and shoulders as they stretched and hobbled over to the mess hall. This grousing ebbed away as the boys lapped up a spicy beef stew with the chunks chopped small and easy to swallow. Hot biscuits with butter and honey reinforced that they were home again and the worst was over. Yet they almost cried tears when Miss Claudine's famous red bean pie was brought out for a surprise. When each man took his first bite, eyes rolled back as big smiles took over with a moaning that Bailey joked was like being at Fancy Nancy's. The taste was so wonderful, slightly sweet, subtly spiced and custardy. Kind of like a sweet potato pie with a slightly nutty flavor and a crispy crust on the soft, sweet filling. A fine reward for their extraordinary work, Ardway had asked Claudine to make it special to assure each man that ehe understood they had passed the hat for the ranch and herd.

～

Entering the bunkhouse afterward, the fed and tired men slipped off their clothes to trail over the floor, staggering with throbbing backs and legs to their bunks. Sleep, blessed sleep was the only thought in their weary minds. Wasted had beaten them all there. A bowl of stew was half-eaten on his bunk. He lay half in and out of his bed with his pants pulled down but one boot still on as he slept unmoving like a dead man. Bailey and Jordie pulled off his boot and pants before they collapsed in their bunks. It was the least they could do. Their new range foreman had been baptized in a patch of hell with no men dead and only two cows missing.

There was still daylight in the sky when Claudine entered the bunkhouse with more cuts of red bean pie. Not a man was awake, their snoring practically blowing the roof off. She covered the large tray with a cloth and left it. At the the door she turned and spoke, "God bless these good men, Lord, who toil in honest hard work and serve you with it. Amen." Claudine turned the key on the front door lamp, extinguishing its glow and walked back to the house.

After a weekend of doing nothing but resting the men were back with the herd on the South Range. It was a lush green valley, sun-kissed with the start of the yellow and light brown tones coloring the grass under the warmer rays of a new summer. Rolling hills led up to the distant mountains that were painted in faint gray and teal in the sky's distant haze.

In this stunning setting, taken for granted like most are in their time, the Ardway and Son Ranch cowboys rode fast with their hooped ropes raised high and arms swirling them round and round in fast circles. At the right moment they tossed them to land about the necks of the confused young calves. These were culled from the herd and led away under a bright blue sky with enormous white clouds that cast flat shadows for miles, shifting and stretching over the men and cattle.

The roped calves were driven or dragged to a makeshift "pen" created from the lucky congruence of the weathered landscape. It was a shallow gully that was too steep for the calves to climb out. Nat had pounded in a few posts and strung wire at the opening and created a square wood-framed gate, also hung with wire. Nothing permanent but it would do for the day's task of branding the calves. The wiry Nat was sweating while working the gate, letting calves in and out.

Jordie had a rope on a calf and pulled it by the ear from the pen toward the branding fire. Other riders brought calves to the pen behind him as Nat kept it under control. Everyone worked fast in the kicked-up dust that littered brown spots sticking to the dampness about their clothes and faces. Jordie's broad shoulders bunched as he reached down and jerked the calf's legs out from under her. It fell on its side and bawled in shock. Two other men latched on to her limbs and kept her to the ground as Jordie kept his boot on her neck.

Bailey was pumping a bellows rigged up to a portable iron frame that was set to blast air over the hot coals and burning wood. He stopped and reached over with his thick gloves to stir the branding iron's long handle. Its end was raked deep inside the bed of the red embers, causing specks of hot debris to fly into the air. Bailey raised the iron symbol of Ardway's brand out of the fire. The *A* glowed red, a ribbon of pale blue steam flung off its scorching metal against the humidity in the air.

He brought the branding iron over the calf's hip and pressed it down onto the animal's skin, sending a puff of singed hair and the odor of burnt hide and smoke into the air. The calf cried out as Bailey removed the hot iron, leaving the pinkish white *A* brand of Ardway with a slight hook curved outward at the bottom right leg of the letter. The men let go of the calf and it jumped up to run back to the herd, shaking its back leg with the new brand above it.

Bailey and Jordie smiled to each other and the rest. This was mild hot work but didn't test your grit like that last week of pain and misery. The crew almost felt relaxed going about these chores with just their honed instincts and nothing out of the ordinary to worry about. Time for some fun. A sense of mischief was brewing in the air.

Wasted rode in on Jack and dismounted by the others' horses that were circled about a small tree and tied to its branches. He bound Jack to the tree while keeping his eyes darting about the area for things to shore up. He walked over to Nat while whistling and yelling at the others bringing in the calves. "Hey, Barnes! Hold up!"

He looked to Ware, "Nat, slow the count coming in. Pen's getting too full."

Nat playfully responded, "Yes, sir, Mis-ter Wasted!"

Wasted shot the rascal a crooked grin.

Tom finished tying a calf's legs to ready it for branding. He looked up at hearing Nat's teasing with Wasted, scratched at his long black sideburns and winked to Bailey. "Mis-ter Wasted! Tell these here dogies to lay down! I'm tired of roping 'em!"

Red-faced Bailey, with sweat pouring down his cheeks, slipped a slight grin at Tom. He held up the branding iron and called out with a high-pitched whine, "Oh, Mis-ter Wasted! Make this here fire a mite cooler. I'm getting ho-o-ot!"

Wasted stewed on this as he glanced silently about at the men, who laughed and pointed at him.

Jordie carried a large armload of kindling to dump on the fire, scattering ashes into the air. He raised one boot and shook it, then the other.

"Oh, please, Mis-ter Was-ted! Tickle my toes real gentle-like. My beetle crushers is a' killin' me!"

Wasted's lip was held tight, holding his comments in.

Somewhere close a cowboy on a horse yelled out, "Oh-oh! My ass hurts from sitting in this saddle all morning, Mis-ter Was-ted!"

Wasted's eyes narrowed, darted around to each man as they laughed.

One of the men held a calf down with one arm and rubbed his own butt in mock pain with the other hand.

"Oooowww! Can you bring me a corn cob, Mis-ter Was-ted? There's no outhouse for miles and I need a wiping bad!"

The men roared at this, laughing and slapping at each other and pointing over at Wasted.

Wasted didn't allow himself to smile. His hands clung on his hips while inside he simmered and waited. This only drove the men to more howling and hysterical fits. The work had stopped to make fun of Wasted. A chorus of voices called from all directions, "Mis-ter Was-ted! Help!"

Wasted's eyes suddenly blazed red and it wasn't because of the fire's reflection. His Colt pistols blurred from their holsters. Wasted took aim and shot at targets about the branding area.

A bullet shattered the wood lever on the pen.

Nat leapt back in shock, fell on his butt and stumbled over to his knees. Calves escaped to bolt about the area, colliding into the men.

Jordie's hat caught an expertly-put bullet and flew off his bald head. His wide eyes looked up in shock.

"Jesus and Mary!"

Tom's rope was sliced in two by a zinging bullet, freeing the calf under him to jump up and kick his shin. He sailed up into the air and on his back. Gasping helplessly out of breath, Tom looked like a turtle flipped on its shell, waving his arms and legs uselessly.

A bullet nicked the branding iron, *ka-ping!*, causing it to fly out of Bailey's hand. It flipped across the fire to toss the coals and ashes high into the air. These rained down on Bailey, dropping between his shirt and into his pants. With a wild scream Bailey jumped and writhed about while trying to shake the hot coals loose. Faster than a scalded cat he stripped off his smoldering clothes.

The pen and branding area turned dead quiet. Even the cattle stopped bellowing. The men gaped with open mouths and large white eyes at Wasted, his guns up and ready.

"Listen up, you shave tails! I can do this all day. So get this damn work done and quick. After supper you can call me a ring-tailed monkey all night. Until then, quit this shoaling, or I'll..."

He fired two shots behind the naked Bailey's boot heels, throwing up a spray of sand and dust.

Bailey jumped up in the air. He dropped in a run with his pants down to the bellows and pumped it furiously, the coals firing up red and sparks flying.

The other men broke into fast sprints back to their assorted jobs. Nat was chasing calves back to the pen as if his life depended on it. Others hopped on their horses and furiously herded the young cows. Jordie chopped wood for the fire like a machine. Tom had an alarmed calf by the leg and was trying to take him to the ground with not much luck. Finally he grabbed it by the neck and both of them went down. Tom scrambled to stay on top.

Wasted watched the men rush about while holding his guns on them. Gradually the work slowed appropriately and took on its natural rhythm again. Satisfied with getting the men back on schedule, Wasted holstered his guns and walked over to Jack and mounted.

His eyes fell on Bailey raking the coals with the iron, still naked. "Bailey, put some clothes on...before you catch cold."

Bailey peeked over his shoulder as Wasted rode off. He stopped stirring the coals and blew out a deep breath of relief. Looking down at his naked body Bailey chuckled to himself and pulled up his pants.

"Yes, sir...Mister Wasted."

Chapter Fifteen:

Fendris

——————

Rouget was wiping spilled whiskey and stale beer off a barrel top that doubled as a table when Fendris walked into his bar. It was a Thursday around midnight which surprised him because Fendris usually dropped in on weekends around three in the morning and whittled senseless. But even more unusual was that his two egg-sucking wheel-horses, Pete and Benito, weren't with him. Rouget's only two patrons were passed out in different corners. One was a saddletramp stranger. The other was Jacob "Jake" Altenhofen, a giant ignorant muleskinner.

The bartender quickly strode over and greeted one of the richest men in the territory, who came with a powerful thirst when the urge hit him.

"Mister Fendris! Good to see you. A whiskey bottle and a beer?"

Fendris grinned wide and stared closely at Rouget without speaking, making Rouget a little nervous. He glanced to the doorway to see if Fendris was really alone. Fendris noticed Rouget's eye movements and smiled even wider.

"Rouget, I'm afraid I'm not drunk enough tonight to partake of your fine line of spirits."

Rouget grimaced a smile for Fendris out of his disappointment because he was always good for a month's worth of business on one evening. This wasn't lost on Fendris either and he pulled out a big coin purse that jingled with silver dollars. Rouget's demeanor brightened considerably. "But I would like to buy several rounds of drinks," he looked around the dark room with the passed out men, "for your, eh, regular partakers." He tossed ten dollars of silver on the warped board that served as a bar counter.

Rouget's pupils dilated at seeing this. He quickly scooped the coins up and said, "I'll make sure your generosity is appreciated." Then it was his turn to look closely at Fendris. "If you're not drinking tonight, Mister Fendris, what can I do to make your visit a more pleasant one?"

Fendris laughed loudly at Rouget, then glanced around to make sure the drunks were asleep. "Rouget, you're on top of things. Something I had not realized before due to my being as drunk as a blind dog with a bone in your bar." Rouget perked up knowing Fendris was after something.

"Rouget, you remember that last time ol' Burton Ardway was in here?"

Rouget's face and mood darkened, "Hard to forget that night. Mister Ardway was on a bender and throwed away the brakes."

Fendris leaned in, "Yes, it was quite a tear. Ah, wasn't there some other drunk in here?"

"Oh. That stupid jasper. I've seen jinglers in my time but he took the cake. He couldn't remember his name or anything before the last bottle. His mind was broke, he said. Ha. That's right. And a bottle almost killed him."

Fendris leaned closer, wanting Rouget to continue.

"See, this ol' sot tried to steal a bottle, and out of Mister Ardway's hands! Even though he was sleeping and tighter than a tick on a dog's ass you might as well poke a bear with a knife while it's taking a nap."

Fendris chuckled at this because he knew it was true. "I'm surprised Burton didn't kill him."

"Believe me, Mister Fendris, he was going to!" He looked to the bar at the spot it happened. "Mister Ardway woke up and shot the bottle out of the saphead's hand, not trying to, just jostled awake. It's a miracle that sot wasn't killed. So Mister Ardway starts swinging and tossing him around the place, knocking him over barrels and chairs and into the walls." Rouget got more excited with the telling and from seeing how interested Fendris was about it. "Finally he threw the spooney out the door and into the street. Mister Ardway pulled his Colt and I thought it was curtains for sure for that hairy son of a bitch."

Fendris straightened up, looked perplexed, "Well, what stopped him?"

The bartender smiled, "I did."

"You? How?" Fendris's face couldn't hide his surprise.

"I don't know what came over me. I put my hand on Mister Ardway's shoulder and asked him for, 'mercy.' I guess I've seen so many boozers killed in my time over...the smallest things. Such a waste. But also for Mister Ardway. God judges our mistakes as well as our kind actions."

The expression on Fendris's face was a blank to Rouget. He thought Fendris was thinking over God's judgments. Maybe reconsidering his own mistakes over a long life. Rouget knew that Ash Fendris had come to Spirits Bend around the same time as Burton Ardway. That they had fought with and against each other at one time or another. Fendris lost a son once and—

Fendris's laughter roared around the small room, threatening to wake the whole town, not just those passed out in the room. Rouget recoiled, unsure and confused at this.

His face twisted up in consternation at Fendris who tried to control himself. After almost a minute Fendris stopped, though still chuckling and giggling.

In a corner of the bar one of the sleeping drunks stirred.

"I'm sorry, Rouget. I...I am shamed for my outburst. Ah, what did Burton do after your appeal to his better nature?"

"He cracked the drunk over the head with his gun barrel and threw him in the wagon with that trunk. Then Mister Ardway drove the wagon out of town to his ranch like it was on fire."

Fendris considered this, "Did Burton say anything?"

"He said he would show this man mercy by taking him out to his ranch. That it would either make him a man...or God would kill him."

The tall rancher's face turned cold sober while staring past Rouget. His vision turned inside himself while muttering, "Me and ol' Burton..."

The huge German muleskinner Jake Altenhofen staggered from his corner to scream, "Fendris!" as he slammed a huge fist upside Ash's head.

Rouget jumped, falling backwards over a chair to whack his head on the wall. He lay on his back seeing stars as Jake lined up on Fendris. Jake drew a large knife in one hand, his other hand balled into a fist for the knockout punch. Altenhofen's deep voice quaked with emotion. He spat out the words in his heavy German accent, "My sister! You never get a girl pregnant again, after I cut your balls off."

Fendris wagged his head about like a dog shaking off water. His vision cleared enough to see Jake's fist closing on him like a boulder down a hill. Fendris reacted instantly. His head dodged fast to the right. Jake immediately stabbed the knife to the left. Fendris's head snapped away, two inches from the blade.

There was no panic in the way Fendris was moving. A lifetime of survival in murderous battles was boiled down into Fendris's instinct and flowed naturally through his body. He anticipated each of Jake's punches and knife thrusts, dodging and weaving while the man-mountain grew frustrated and winded. Jake was used to ending his fights with one or two punches, not having to put in a lot of work. He was tiring. Fendris counted on that.

Fendris ducked his head down to dodge another of Jake's huffing knife thrusts. He had an eye on a thick warped board leaning between two barrels and this move had led him to it. He brought the distorted board up to smash its two by eight inches of wood squarely under Jake's wide chin.

Jake's head shot back as Fendris whipped around and slammed the edge of the wood into the right side flesh of his neck. Jake cried out in pain. Fendris spun around and chopped the left side of his neck with all his strength.

A hot blaze shot like lightning through Jake's long neck to his bucket head. The knife began jittering about in his trembling fingers then dropped to the floor. A searing light inside his skull forced him to squeeze his lids shut. Jake stood helpless with his hands clenched before his face. He fought through his agony to stutter, "S-ss-stop..."

But Fendris wasn't having that. He smashed the board against the back of Jake's skull, causing the giant to topple forward to his knees. Fendris didn't have to reach up now, having Jake's head and neck level with his chest. Ash brought the heavy board back and swung it full force to the back of the muleskinner's neck. Crack went a sound in his neck as Jake fell face down in the sticky sawdust covering the dirt floor.

Fendris danced around Altenhofen's body and howled with a fury like he was possessed. He swung the board's edge like a machete to slam it down on Jake's spine and head. Ribs and bone were snapped. And still Fendris beat on the giant like a wild ape.

Rouget stood up and held onto a barrel to steady himself. He managed to look over and was horrified to see Fendris in his blood rage. He stumbled over and put his hand on Fendris's arm. "Mister Fendris! Please! Mercy..."

Fendris stared out from his red haze and recognized Rouget. Irritated, he hoarsely spat out, "Mercy?" He chortled as his wild eyes hinted at something broken deep inside. "Goddamn, this skinner tried to kill me! No man dares to..."

Fendris saw the panic breaking out over Rouget's face. He knew it meant he was going too far but..."I ain't Burt Ardway you're crying to. Now get out! Before I start on you, fat man!"

Rouget backed up. He glanced about, then ran out the door. Rouget didn't stop running until he had locked the door inside his own shack. He lay awake in bed that night, jumping at every sound while hugging his shotgun. The next morning Rouget avoided going to his bar. He checked to make sure Sheriff Gammill was in town before he shuffled over to the bar in the late afternoon. Timidly he glanced around the front door expecting to find a mutilated pile of bones and guts. Inside, the room was tidy and proper with no sign that there had been any trouble. Even the sawdust had been raked clean. No one ever heard of Jake Altenhofen after that but no one liked him much to begin with. In the days to come and over the many years thereafter Rouget got angry when Altenhofen's name came up. He swore to the whole bar that he never knew the bastard and threw out anyone that tried to make a conversation wondering what happened to him.

Chapter Sixteen:

Ardway

A month later the men worked a section over by the northeast-
ern side of the property, pitching camp for the night beside the
black surface of a large lake. It was dark after a demanding twelve
hours and the moon had swollen to a huge silver balloon against the
night sky. Scattered stars winked and sparkled around it, drawn like
fireflies in summer.

Amongst the stars real fireflies appeared. They dipped and
bobbed about this heaven. A fish sprung forth from a luminous universe, catching a firefly in its mouth before splashing back beneath
the dark water. The moon and stars mirrored in the lake's surface
shimmered in expanding and colliding rings of black and silver.

Trees marked the far edges of the lake. The moonlight dusted
their tops white above shadowed thickets which rose beyond and
into the hills.

A large campfire blazed a bright amber glow near the lake's
edge. Two covered wagons stood out black against its flames and
light. A man in silhouette walked around it, picking up gear to pack
away for the evening.

Tired men lay sleeping under their blankets scattered about the
area, their weak fires fading like their thoughts into dreams or just
lost in the dark.

On a hill above, Wasted watched as he rode Jack alongside Bailey
and his horse, Sally. Bailey drooped, looking like a half sack of potatoes

in his saddle, barely aware of what he was doing. "Wasted." He paused for several seconds. "Ah...Are we going...to look over...the bottom?"

"We just got done riding the bottom," replied Wasted.

"Oh. ...So. ...Do we still...got to check it out?"

Wasted looked over at his exhausted friend and smiled. "Who's on bobtail guard?"

Bailey thought a bit, "Aaaaa...Nat. Nat Ware." He chuckled lightly. "He don't care...he's Nat Ware. He wrestled a bear...With no hair..."

"Go to your bedroll, you curly wolf." Wasted leaned over and lightly slapped Sally's rump, sending her with Bailey trotting off to his camp spot twenty yards away. Wasted watched to make sure they arrived. Bailey climbed down and worked by rote to pull the saddle off.

He gave Sally a fast rubdown while laying his head on her shoulders and singing nonsense to her, "Nat Ware...no hair...ate a bear... Ha!" Bailey tied her to a log with a pail of water, collapsed by his saddle, resting his head on it, and passed out immediately.

Wasted rode away in the other direction near a line of trees. He inhaled a deep whiff of the pines and cedar and heaved a contented sigh while stretching his arms out. He yawned and looked over the camp. It was quiet in that late night outdoors way with only a few owl hoots and even they sounded sleepy. He couldn't find any reason not to go to bed. The range boss was always the last to sleep.

Branches snapped loudly from the woods nearby. Suddenly alert, Wasted nudged Jackrabbit over in its direction. Stopping at the trees, Wasted peered deep into their dark shadows. His head moved at a clamor that sounded to his right. Someone made a groan and thrashed about in the brush. A horse whinnied and trotted out of the trees. A large saddle horse mare came over and nuzzled against Jack's nose. "Big Black?" Wasted turned back to stare into the woods, "Where's your—"

Inside the trees' dark shadows a voice called out. "Goddamn it, Big Black! Where are you, you fool horse?" There was more thrashing and struggling among the bushes.

Wasted recognized the voice that went with this horse and called out, "She's with me, Mister Ardway."

A drunken Ardway tottered backwards out of the thicket and spun around to Wasted. Winded from the effort he reached out and held to a tree to steady himself. Seeing his horse with Jack and Wasted he looked up and yelled, "Wasted! Hell, you lost?" He laughed at his joke and lost his grip on the tree, stumbling forward to fall flat on his face.

Wasted quickly swung down off Jack and went to Ardway, helping to lift him to his feet. Ardway's tipsy eyes stared close into Wasted's face. "This being your cattle work so far from the ranch and everything, well, I decided to come out and see if you needed any help."

"All I can get. Come on. Let's get you over to my fire."

Wasted pulled the reins of the horses and led them and Ardway along. Ardway teetered unsteadily, his body going up and down and then left to right and back. He must have been drinking the entire twelve hour trip. Wasted watched his erratic movements, reaching out now impulsively here and there, ready to catch Ardway if he fell. "Say, Mister Ardway. Would you wanna' sit and rest a bit?"

Ardway comically straightened himself up, moving his feet outward in exaggerated overly-careful steps. He gruffly replied, "Hell, I'll walk around the whole damn lake! Wear your legs off!"

They made it to Wasted's camp spot on the hill. It was barely lit by a bed of pinkish gray coals inside a circle of soot-stained large rocks. A coffee pot and cup were stored by it with a cloth sack and a coiled-up bedroll.

"Here we are. Kick your feet out and I'll get the fire going again."

Ardway squinted at the campground and then peered up around it. Satisfied, he plopped down in the dirt by the fire.

Wasted bent down and squatted by the coals and stirred at them with kindling, causing each to ignite into a blaze. He added some chopped wood. The flames rose higher. The area took on a flickering yellow glow with the heat scattered out in a wider loop. Wasted placed the pot on some flat stones arranged in a circle in the center. "This'll be hot in two shakes," said Wasted. The rocks were already warm from the coals and the pot was boiling in a few minutes.

In the flickering light the lines on Ardway's face appeared deeper and there were more of them then before when he abducted Wasted. His hair had grown longer along with a bushy beard. Both showed more gray. None of this was lost on Wasted.

"You picked a good spot here, to keep your eyes on things." Ardway grinned as he stared out at the lake. "I camped here for years. In the early days."

"I wondered who whistled up this spot and those campfire rocks. You?" Ardway nodded, pleased that Wasted figured out to use this particular place.

"I appreciate you coming all the way out here to help. I think things is pretty much under control. 'Course you might find something—"

Ardway cut him off, "I was lying." He flashed a devilish grin like a kid. "Hell, I...just wanted an excuse...to get away from the ranch." They shared a knowing look. Then Ardway turned away. "Claudine's gone on a goddamn temperance campaign. I can't even take a short drink without her praying to save my soul...or something else as foolish." Remembering, he pulled a flask out of his vest and offered it to Wasted. "Care for a nip?"

Wasted gave a slight smile of surprise. He shook his head, no.

Ardway realized his mistake and sheepishly drew back the flask. "Sorry. I forgot." He raised it respectfully to Wasted. "Well, here's to dancing with prancing women!" He tilted it to his lips and drained the container. Finished, he licked his lips with his eyes closed, enjoying the whiskey's warmth and its sweet taste of vanilla and oak. Wasted watched, knowing too well that Ardway was struggling inside.

With the flask emptied, Ardway got up and staggered over to Big Black. He removed the saddle bags and his bedroll then pulled off the saddle with some effort. Wasted stood up. Ardway saw and quipped, "I got it." He heaved the saddle over a log. Next he rolled out his blanket and flopped down on it. Finally he reached into his saddle bag and pulled out a whiskey bottle. He lifted the bottle to his teeth, pulled the cork out and spit it away. Ardway's speech was slurred as he wheezed, "Whew! Must be feeling the ride. It's as cold as a witch's teat." He took a heavy swig from the bottle. His head shook reflexively at the liquor's kick.

Wasted reached over the fire with a folded rag to grab the coffee pot's hot metal handle. He poured two cups and handed one to Ardway.

"Here. This'll warm your innards."

Ardway sat up and peered a mite suspect at the cup. He shrugged and took it. As he sipped, his eyes widened as the hot coffee went down. "Uh. That'll make a dead cat dance." He took a deeper sniff of the steam rising from the cup. "Umph. A cup of belly wash smells twice as good out here."

Wasted was pleased. "Coffee. Food. Just breathing. It's all better out here..." He raised his cup and sipped while enjoying the moment. His eyes stared up at the stars, "...under a big open sky."

The men sat quietly before the fire, staring out at the lake and the heavens as this splendor washed over them. A shooting star streaked through the sky leaving a brief trail of sparks that was reflected across the water below.

Wasted and Ardway's expressions were calm and relaxed, each feeling a kinship with the natural world that called to them with unspoken words. Being here away from city life in places untouched by man was the key to that understanding. All men or women that loved this cowboy's life couldn't describe what they felt so deep in their blood, their bones, hearts and minds. That sacred kinship brought down their guards and opened lips to speak with no reason but to let secrets out in the honesty felt among the wilds.

Ardway was floating somewhere between the lake and stars with his memories when a deep sigh blew from his nose, much like a horse. "Peaceful here...as a thumb in a baby's mouth." Ardway chuckled, "Junior used to live for coming out here. Just us. We'd act like Sioux Injuns. Swim. Fish. Chase each other. Shoot off guns at rocks." A memory made Ardway laugh loudly. "Throwed knifes, sticking 'em in logs..."

He grinned over at Wasted, his bleary eyes lit up at the thought. "I gave him a Bowie knife. 'Course we couldn't let Patricia see it, 'cause she would have raised holy hell. So we hid it in the tack shed. It was our 'Men's Secret.'"

Ardway stared through the lake and sky to the time of that memory. Wasted watched him while enjoying the smell of his coffee and the coolness of the woods down to the water. Ardway glanced back to Wasted, his words slurred from the liquor. The touched emotions added a tremble to their sound. "We came here. To get in one last wingding 'fore Junior left. Five years ago..." He looked out seeing the world as it was then. "Ha! He had me whooping and running..." Ardway unconsciously raised his hand out in the night to touch the thought. "...like I was a wild boy again. Nothing to worry or think about except the fun we were having..." He breathed deeply with a heavy feeling of regret. "Cut our palms with his Bowie knife. We shook red hands on it..." Ardway closed his extended hand, reliving that moment. "Said we was...blood brothers..." He made a fist in the air, then squeezed it tight with his pain. "...forever."

Wasted felt Ardway's suffering as he watched him lower his clenched fist like holding a knot in his heart. They sat there in silence for a long time. Ardway drank from his bottle as Wasted sipped his coffee. Fish could be heard leaping and splashing about the lake. The owls called for mates in the distant woods. Sleeping, the cattle were quiet except for an occasional calf mooing up at the stars glittering in the sky.

Wasted cleared his throat. "I...I can't remember a thing about my father. Or my mother neither. But..." His eyes turned to Ardway. "I'm sure your son holds on to that time and that trip."

Ardway's head moved to lock his devastated eyes with Wasted. "You...really think so?"

"Yeah. Like it was gold."

Ardway dropped his coffee cup to clutch at his bottle. He lifted its lip to pour the liquor down his throat. Wasted turned away. He was sitting on his blanket, knees up and rocking slightly on his heels. He turned back to Ardway when he heard him stop sucking the bottle to catch a breath.

Ardway's eyes were red and shiny as he wiped the tears away with his coat sleeve, "He wrote me a letter. Came with his trunk that day...you and me...met. Sent back his guns. And that knife." Ardway took another long drink. He looked up, his vision swirling and lost in the liquor. "He wrote. ...Said his mother..." Each word was like a bullet in his soul. "...Told him...why she left. She said, '...your father...tore a hole in my heart!'" Ardway gasped, choking for breath. "Oh, God! What have I done?"

Wasted stood up. He started for Ardway, hesitated, as Ardway broke down sobbing uncontrollably, all his guards down. It was as raw as a man could get in front of another. Wasted saw and knew that out here in the woods in the dark of night was the best way to let Ardway lance out some of that poison he was holding inside. He looked out to the lake. The men were asleep. The drone of the crickets and cacophony of mating calls from the frogs mixed over Ardway's tormented wailing. And so Wasted waited.

After several minutes Ardway's frantic sobs grew softer, his breathing slowed and he passed out. Wasted got his blanket and draped it over him. He carefully tucked it in to keep out the cooler night's temperature. Ardway's fingers were clutched around the bottle of whiskey just like...

Wasted lingered over Ardway while staring at the bottle. His own memories reached up and seized him. That fateful night in Rouget's. The black-haired beauty. The laughter. The gunshots. He remembered the many times of his begging, of crying, for a drink. Stealing bottles from other drunks. Drinking from glasses left behind by customers. Licking up the spilled liquor on tables and bar counters when no one was looking. But he knew that was a sham. He didn't care that people saw him lap that liquor up like a thirsty mongrel. He remembered their faces turned up with disgust or laughter at him. Ardway had a reason to drink. What was Wasted's excuse? He thought back to how bad his guts felt without getting some liquor in them. How his brain felt that it was going to rip out of his skull and devour his body if he didn't get a drink. What was the reason that made him like that? Why did that night with the wolf trigger his walk away from those feelings? And his awakening about his skills with his fists and the guns? What was so terrible to make his life's memory abandon him for the liquor and with it all of his self-respect?

He was still looking at the bottle in Ardway's hands. He reached down and slipped it loose from his fingers. Ardway grunted and his fingers fell on the blanket and pulled it to him tighter. Wasted stood up straight, holding the bottle over the fire. Wasted stared at the bottle as if it had the answers he desperately yearned for. Gradually he began to feel the old craving, the desire to taste the burn on his tongue and throat from the whiskey. He peered closely at the bottle and the whiskey inside. Its liquor glowed bright in the fire's glow like that night at the lodge. Wasted's vision focused in on how it sparkled gold in the light. He could see Ardway sleeping below through its honey-colored liquor. The closer he looked at the image of Ardway the more it blurred until Wasted saw a new face, his own reflection, staring out of the bottle at him.

Startled, Wasted spun on his feet and raised the bottle over his shoulder. With a wild toss he threw the bottle deep into the woods. Its shattering of glass was muffled by the trees and brush. Wasted turned and reached for Ardway's saddlebags. He yanked out the three whiskey bottles and spun around to throw each in the air. Deep inside the dark woodland the tinkling sounds of the bottles shattering against the trees were muffled, the pieces dropping to the leafy cover of the ground.

Hearing the glass breaking, the rage in Wasted's eyes slowly passed. He glanced over at Ardway, sleeping soundly. A log on the fire sizzled, making a loud pop as the heated sap inside ruptured the outer charred bark. Wasted turned to this blazing eruption, following its bright gold and crimson sparks as they floated up to mix and disappear against the stars. Then he stared down to the heavenly world mirrored across the dark waters. His thoughts felt like reflections with no idea of what was up or down. An ancient owl that was startled earlier from the crashing bottles near its roosting tree trained its sharp eyes on the solitary Wasted. Perhaps the nocturnal predator sensed something akin in this man, calling out with Wasted's own thoughts, "Who...?"

Ardway snored in the early gray light, deep in sleep with his head covered under a big blanket. His nose twitched slightly. His breathing changed as his lungs sucked in more of the air. An odor was causing a pleasant reaction. Ardway's eyes fluttered ever so slightly. He turned to the satisfying fragrance as his eyes opened. His head drew back in surprise at seeing the blanket about him. He turned to the lake.

The purple night sky was losing the early dawn's battle with streaks of red edging through it. Ardway's men were gathered at the wagons, sleepy-eyed and waiting in line to receive breakfast. Many drank from cups of steaming coffee. Ardway looked over to find two riders out with the herd.

He rolled back onto his blanket. The smell of coffee brewing drew his gaze to the pot on the fire. He wondered how many times coffee had saved his life. Wasted was bent over a fire with its smoke drifting in a blue ring around his back. Ardway's stomach growled like it was going to attack.

Wasted turned with a hot skillet to Ardway. Inside four trout fillets were cooking in boiling bacon fat.

"We better feed that bear afore it eats the herd."

Stretching his arms and legs, Ardway slowly sat up. He reached over and groggily poured himself a cup of coffee. He sipped carefully as it was still practically boiling. It made him feel a little better after his rough night. Wasted handed him a tin plate with two trout and biscuits. With heavy lids, he nodded thanks to Wasted and dug in with his hands.

A few minutes later, a wide-eyed Ardway wiped his biscuit about the plate of bones to get at every crumb. He set his plate aside while licking his fingers before he raised the coffee cup to his lips, its temperature tolerable now. He took a long drink. With a gasp of appreciation he spoke, "Lordie, that trout was the best I've ever eaten. Thank you, Wasted, from the bottom of my stomach." He grabbed the pot and poured himself a second cup of coffee. "Oh, and this Arbuckle's is just the way I like it. Strong enough to walk over and slap you."

Wasted smiled as he finished eating his food. He enjoyed Ardway like this. Genuine and happy. "Thank Bailey for getting up early to catch the fish."

"I will, I will! You and Bailey get back to the ranch, I'm telling Claudine to stuff you both. Her fried chicken's so good it'll make you hit your grandma."

Ardway stared down at the men finishing breakfast with a sunny approval. Some were already on their horses riding out to the herd. A few moments from last night began to pop into his mind. His eyes shifted uneasily to Wasted. "Guess I was, ah...roostered up pretty good last night."

Wasted gathered up the plates. He poured himself a refill of coffee, his eyes on the men and the herd below. "Corned as full as full can be."

Ardway's eyes darted around. He tried to look unconcerned. "Yeah. I don't remember too good after getting here." He paused then asked, "Did I go on 'bout anything?"

Wasted drank his thick dark coffee, eyes below on the men. "Oh. Just ranch talk. Cattle. Horses."

Ardway chuckled nervously, "Yeah, yeah. Can't shut me up."

Wasted's eyes darted about, weighing whether to speak up. He finally looked over at Ardway. "You talked in your sleep."

Ardway was genuinely shocked. "Huh? I did? Ah, like...about what?"

Wasted offered the pot to him for more coffee. Ardway shook his head, no. Wasted poured it into his own cup without answering. With a slight hint of irritation, Ardway spoke up, "Well?"

"It was a...a woman. Mentioned her name."

"My wife? Patricia?"

"No. It was another name. Called her—"

Ardway cut him off. "Stop." His cheeks turned a slight red. "Forget it."

Without another word Ardway stood up. He rolled up his bedding then walked over and dropped it by his saddle. He worked silently to saddle up Big Black. Finally he picked up the saddle bags and noticed they were light. Ardway lifted up the flaps. Seeing no bottles he turned to look at Wasted.

Wasted stared back unsure what to do or say.

Stepping into the stirrup Ardway swung up into the saddle and grabbed the reins. "You're doing a fine job, Wasted. Thanks for the hospitality." With a slap on the reins at Big Black, Ardway turned the horse and trotted into the woods.

Wasted watched him disappear into the green before finishing his reply. "You said...Ruby."

Chapter Seventeen:

Gammill

———

The little church in Spirits Bend was resurrected from an old wagon wheel shop which had been originally operated by a man named Clute Jackson. Jackson also did wagon repairs but the blacksmith grabbed most of his trade over ten years. After Jackson decided to call it quits and move to Cheyenne, a few enterprising whores took over the empty shack. The gals weren't selling wheels but a man could get a quick roll among the ladies' hills and valleys. They secretly worked their trade on the discreet side from their jobs at Fancy Nancy's. That was until Nancy discovered their competition. She threatened to horsewhip the women until the sheriff got wind of it. Gammill made a deal to shut them down and send them back to Nancy with a cut in pay until they made up for the whorehouse's lost profits. Such was venture capitalism in the Wyoming Territory. Gammill then figured that the best plan to keep the shop off the black market was to make it into a church.

The shop wasn't fancy, basically a large wooden box-like hut with four windows like a lot of stores in the town. Two windows at the front, two along the north wall. The south side wall divided the room with the Hick's Harness and Bridle Goods Store next door. There was a wall in the back that was sectioned off as a narrow storage room to hang wheels on pegs along with tools. Now it held wide-planked boards and such for outdoor church picnics and city social events. Gammill had a door opening sawed out of the back wall as an escape exit. The pastor, acknowledging his sheriff's nature, laughed and said, "You never know when the devil might visit and we got to make a run for it."

An old but sturdy pot belly stove was set in the middle of the room. Fendris donated the stove just to dig at Ardway. Burt would have to see it every time he attended the church or acknowledge it when he soaked up its heat during a cold winter's spell. There were fourteen simple wooden pews, seven and seven lining the two halves of the room. A podium made of black walnut was at the back from where Pastor John Gammill stood and preached. In the corner was a desk where Gammill worked on sermons and church business. Next to that was a small table for holiday services like Easter and Christmas which required the usual liturgical items. A Bible rested on a small pinewood stand facing the congregation with its pages always open—a simple but nice touch suggested by Miss Claudine.

It was a Wednesday night at seven o'clock and Gammill stood silently by the podium studying his notes and a Bible. A lantern was hung from the ceiling and spilled its amber light toward the darker side of the room. The summer light was still bright at this time coming in the windows. Twenty or so people sat chatting quietly in the pews close to the podium with their faces partially divided in blue from the window's light and a yellow glow from the lantern.

Midweek worship was always dictated by the Sheriff's changing schedule. Sometimes it went a month or two without a gathering and that went for a few Sundays too. A small number of good hearts tried to fill in for the pastor but none had his gift for speaking The Word with such stirring and absolute conviction. Eighteen years ago when Gammill took the unpopular job of sheriff he shot it out and roughed it up with desperate outlaws and murderous lowlifes who made it well known that they would never see the inside of a jail nor hang from a rope. Scheduled preaching had always been hit or miss ever since. Those kinds of yellowbelly snakes were still around but now Gammill was the government's only servant in an area with growing commerce and a new railroad and two hundred miles to cover. Gammill still chased no-goods but was also serving legal notices, writs and such for that part of the territory. Statehood was merely a matter of time. Perhaps then some money for paying deputies could give the pastor more time to preach. Gammill prayed to God for such good fortune every time he lowered his brow in silent prayer.

Many new members asked what made a man as rough, big and smart as Gammill to become a preacher. It sure wasn't the money nor the shack they prayed in. Gammill told them that his mother was a slave and had been given a Bible from their master's wife. She taught his mother how to read it under the pretext of picking up goods from different lists when she was sent to town for shopping. The state of Georgia had a law against teaching slaves to read and write but it was considered an allowance for such slave chores. Little John Gammill was taught to read and write by his mother at night under candlelight. Thinking back Gammill would smile and say, "It was the first and best book I ever read and changed my life." Of course he never mentioned the time running wild with Burton Ardway and mixing in with owlhoots' troubles before they both went through a prison stretch in Arizona. There was no stockade back then. Just tents out in that godforsaken desert. Gammill told himself if God pulled him through that hell, he would pay it back by spreading the Good Word.

The gathered group of Christians were excited to hear Gammill get wound up with the Savior's Word and also to have the excuse to gather and gossip with friends outside their circle or just to break free for an hour or so from the tedium of their hard work. Spirits Bend had no opera house where they could be shocked and entertained by actors, singers and musicians. There was a sewing circle. A fire brigade. A temperance league. The school had some kids plays like "Buster's Lost Dog" (the dog part was the coveted role) and choir soirees. Fancy Nancy's had a piano player. So did Molly's. But only men attended those places. Older men and decent ladies were just out of luck for a good time in Spirits Bend.

Pastor Gammill's face rose up from the Bible, satisfied he had the sermon right in his mind. He looked up and around the room. Widow Jenkins was there as always. Bill Stokes, the postal delivery agent, smiled at him. The small crowd stopped talking and the room became quiet. Each face was open and pleasant, their eyes attentive and expectant. Gammill felt their warmth and acknowledged it with a wide smile. He was a massive man, six feet, six inches and built like a buffalo, wide and muscled. The later years had hung some extra pounds on him but you would never call Gammill fat. Folks would exclaim that he was awful big—big as life!

"Howdy, friends and Christians."

All loudly answered back in unison, "Howdy, Pastor John!"

It was a fond opening ritual that always began their gatherings.

"Let's bend our heads for a silent prayer." Gammill bowed his head while his large hands gripped the squared edges of the podium. The others turned their faces to the old and warped wood planks in the floor. The room was still and quiet except for the slight murmur of breathing. After about two minutes of communing with the Lord, Gammill looked up, raised his arms and exclaimed, "Amen."

Immediately the people rose and began singing a hymn, "Shall We Gather At The River." It wasn't a choir performance but a joy was there in those voices that made it genuine and affecting. The townspeople looked around as they sang, listening to their friends and seeing a soft Christian spirit in their faces unlike on the street or at work.

Gammill sang loudest and his face beamed exultation at each of his flock. Everyone was caught up in the moment and felt a warm grace descending upon their circle.

"Soon we'll reach the shining river
Soon our pilgrimage will cease
Soon our happy hearts will quiver
With the melody of peace..."

Gammill stepped out in front of the podium and his voice punched louder, exhorting the others to join him, "This last verse is for the whole town to know what they are missing!" They all grinned at each other and sang the last verse with full lungs and hearts and voices to match.

"Yes, we'll gather at the river
The beautiful, the beautiful riv-ver
Farther with the saints at the river
That flows by the throne of God"

The Pastor energetically lowered and cautioned with his hands, signaling to remain quiet. Everyone knew to wait. Suddenly a dog began barking in a fit. A man's voice while coming out of a house, shouted, "Shut that racket up, Butch! You fool dog it's just that damn church shooting their mouths off. Now come here!" They heard the sound of a dog yelping as it was dragged around a house. That faded and on Gammill's nod, everyone had a good laugh around the room, including Gammill.

"Poor Butch. I keep waiting for him to drag ol' Mister Faerber down here to sing." Gammill drew in a deep breath and guffawed along with the others recovering from that closing verse.

Gammill stepped back behind the podium as the church members gathered themselves to settle in for the evening's messages and sermon. He pulled some spectacles from his jacket and placed them on his nose. He looked at his notes a second and then gazed out at his congregation as he drew a deep breath.

"God has a plan for all of us."

The members smiled. It wasn't going to be one of Pastor Gammill's fire and brimstone sermons on drinking or gambling.

"God loves us all and when we realize that we can do mighty things. Because no matter what you do in life or if you're well off or just have a pot and a tent, He knows everything about you and that you have a place in His plan. Rejoice! You matter. He has work for you to do! It may seem common and ordinary but it's actually part of a greater plan."

His eyes searched about the room and Gammill was pleased that each person was leaning forward and hanging on each word. Sometimes people were sleepy from dinner and he had to walk around to keep them awake. Or, at least that was what he liked to think, that their sleepy faces were from full bellies and not because of some slack preaching on his part.

"Worshippers such as you may be kind and generous when others are cold and withholding. Giving out food to the needy in times of want or offering such respite from the heat or the cold of this hard world makes your place in Heaven. Your warmhearted nature will guide others to follow God. Your act of forgiveness can help turn a wayward soul around. Jesus was a kind man who taught we must be tolerant of each other's weakness. It is the Lord's guidance that teaches you to forgive a man's sins if he repents. Not everyone is a heroic David or Saul. Most of us are of the sweet likes of Mary, the mother of Jesus, and of the reformed nature of Mary Magdalene. We try to live by the Lord Jesus's words along with the world's laws that allow us to help people be their better selves in trying times—"

Four pistol shots echoed loudly outside in the street. All turned to the front windows and open door. There was angry shouting coming from the direction of Molly's Saloon. Now the congregation turned their eyes to Gammill. His body shifted from a cheerful pastor to the mountain bear attitude of a sheriff—a grim sheriff focused on listening closely and gauging the important details of the danger. The shouting had stopped and the streets sounded quiet again. He was about to go on with the sermon when two more gunshots rang out. Letting out a deep exhale of breath, Gammill announced, "Sorry for the interruption, folks." He looked to Stokes, "Bill, will you read a few chapters from the Good Book while I am gone?"

"Sure thing, Sheriff—I mean, Pastor."

Gammill walked to his table. He removed his spectacles, slid them into his jacket pocket, grabbed up the holsters with their pistols from a hat rack and strapped the leather on. He strode over to the doorway. Standing in the opening, Gammill peered carefully up and then down the street, gauging and calculating the time of day, the receding light and the unseen men with guns. He reached into his shirt pocket and pulled out the star-shaped brass badge that Ardway gave him when he accepted the job two decades ago. It was scuffed in places from scrapes over the years but he still polished the star every Thursday to shine on the weekends. The setting sun's rays caught the symbol's brass and tossed up its reflection, a yellow star, across Gammill's face. He pinned the badge on his jacket and stepped outside.

～

Gammill pulled his guns and checked each one over as he walked to Molly's. He knew they were clean and proper but wanted to double-check that each was fully loaded. Satisfied, he slipped them easily back into their holsters. Unconsciously he ran his fingers around his cartridge belt and found no bullets were missing. He measured the sky's coming darkness, became acutely aware of his surroundings. Some men walking toward him became mindful that Gammill had on his fierce "stone eyes" appearance. Reacting quickly, they instinctively lunged into the closest door or alley to get the hell out of the way of the trouble that the Sheriff was going to meet.

At Molly's two men stood on the wooden sidewalk outside the barroom's two front swinging doors. They were drunk and harassing people coming in and out of the saloon. They knocked a man's stylish "gambler hat" off and kicked it down the street. One pulled his gun and shot the hat as the man reached for it. The hat flipped and tumbled down the street. The man was caught unsure whether to chase his hat or duck into a doorway. He ran into an alley as a shot chipped wood off the building's corner above him.

Gammill stepped fast and silently along the sidewalk on the other side of the street while sticking to the shadows. The big man got to a closed store directly across the street without being seen. He reached up and pulled a key from behind a sign that let him unlock the door and he slid unseen into its darkness. The light on the street had slipped away fast. Gammill left the door open. Molly's was lit up inside and light spilled out through its windows and swinging doors around its front entrance. He watched clearly out the doorway at the men in front of Molly's but they only saw the twilight's shadows he was draped in on his side of the street. It was Pete Winchell and Benito Ayala but no Fendris, which was odd. Come to think of it, Gammill hadn't seen much of Fendris lately. Fendris usually kept these two on a short leash. This kind of drunk behavior was just common fooling around but this was not regular corned-up cowboys blowing off steam. These two vicious criminals took care of Fendris's dirty problems and left no tracks. Gammill had warned them last month about shooting off guns while drunk. A line had been drawn.

Pete nudged Benito as two cowboys walked across the street toward the saloon. They were laughing about something when they stepped up on the boardwalk to Molly's. Pete greeted them with a flourish, bending forward and waving his arms to enter. The men laughed and started in when Benito stepped up and demanded,

"Two dollars, amigos." The men thought this was hilarious until Pete sneaked behind them and stole their guns from their holsters. Benito stuck his pistols into their faces. Pete leaned over between and spoke softly into their ears. "Two dollars to get in, boys. Or two dollars to leave. What's it gonna be?"

Gammill had left his viewing spot and trotted carefully while silently across the street when Benito first spoke to the men. Both of Fendris's men were too busy running their play to notice Gammill closing on them with both guns drawn. The creaking of the walk's boards as Gammill stepped up caused Pete to turn. All he saw was one of Gammill's gun barrels flash before his face combined with a thud sound, then stars and then blackness. It happened so fast that Benito only saw Pete slump behind the two men like a tossed sack of laundry. Suddenly a gun barrel was poking in his eye while another jabbed his ribs. He could only cry, "Sheriff!"

"Benito, don't make me kill you over acting like a mule. Put the gun down. Now!"

Benito kept the gun pointed at the two men who held their hands up like they were being robbed. Their faces had lost all blood and were as white as the moon rising in the sky. "Sheriff, I don't like—"

Gammill shot the gun pointed at Benito's eye, but had turned the angle of the barrel up. The bullet grazed Benito's forehead with a loud blast. Gammill used the other gun in Benito's ribs to strike at his wrist with the hand holding the pistol. It went off into the walkway. One of the cowboys grabbed Benito's wrist and the gun as Gammill cracked his pistol over the Mexican's skull. With a moan Benito dropped to lie next to Pete. Both of their faces were drenched in blood.

The cowboy that held Benito's gun was shaking and for a moment it looked like he was going to use it. Gammill shoved one of his guns in its holster and placed his free hand on the man's arm. "He ain't worth the waste of lead, son." The cowboy stared into Gammill's eyes for a time, the shock and anger draining out of his face. Finally the cowboy heaved a heavy sigh and handed Benito's gun to Gammill. A crowd of drinkers and Molly's staff had gathered at the door. Gammill smiled to the man, "Go inside. They'll buy you and your pard drinks all night to hear you tell it." At this the fellow looked to his companion. Both their eyes lit up. The two men pushed through the doors followed by the excited crowd.

The Sheriff looked at Pete and Benito lying in a pile. He rolled them over checking for guns, removing three and finding two knives. He dumped these with Benito's other gun in a horse trough. Gammill gave his big boot a swinging kick right in Benito's tail bone causing him to squirm and yell. He repeated the same on Pete. Both groaned and fussed to push themselves up to sit. Benito placed his hands over his ears, "Ooow. My ears are ringing...como cien la iglesias."

They wiped the blood from their eyes to blink and focused to see. Pete wailed, "Hell's bells, Sheriff! We's just having some fun and—"

Gammill kicked Pete in the head, knocking him to the sidewalk. "Shut your traps! If I hear another word between here and the jail I'll bust your heads open and let all that black stuff run out. Now, get up! Don't make me kick you again."

The battered drunks stood unsteadily, pitched and weaved as they staggered toward the jail with Gammill behind. Spirits Bend's first jail was a beautiful and elegant log building that was the oldest erected building in town. The citizenry took great pride in having the only jail for one hundred miles. But eight years before, a prisoner who murdered his grandfather over money accidentally set his straw mattress on fire when he fell asleep smoking. The tobacco had been passed to him by a friend through a barred window but no one ever fessed up to the crime. The resulting inferno burned through the old wooden structure like it was seasoned firewood, cremating the prisoner with it. Many told stories of seeing him on fire, his hair blazing and arms peeling flesh while he tried to wrench the bars out of the window, screaming for God to save him. They said it must have been what Hell was like. Gammill used the story time and again for emphasis in church. So from then on no one was allowed to smoke in the jail even though it was rebuilt with cut sandstone, which made being thrown in jail an even worse punishment for the smokers — which was everybody that got thrown in jail. This rule probably stopped many shootings and knifings over the years since. Hot situations cooled when someone shouted, "Hey, remember! Jail ain't got no smoking."

When they got to the front of the brown sandstone jail, Gammill called out, "Grab that bucket there by the trough. Fill it with water and wash the blood off. Don't get any blood in the trough or I'll make you bleed some more." They washed up while shooting angry looks at Gammill. He unlocked the dark jail and led them in while striking a match to light a lantern. Three cells with heavy iron slats crisscrossed for walls and fronts appeared out of the gloom. Gammill opened a cell door and Pete and Benito walked in without saying a word. The Sheriff closed the cell door and locked it with a key he kept in his desk drawer. Pete crawled into the bottom of two tiered bunks. Benito make a feeble attempt at climbing up to the top bunk, then looked around and sank to the floor to stretch out. In minutes both of the drunk men were deep asleep and snorting like moose rutting in the woods. Gammill frowned, turned and went out the front door, locking it, before quickly heading back toward the church.

~

Gammill slipped in unseen through the church door as Bill was reading from Corinthians. "'Love is patient and kind; love does not envy or boast; it is not arrogant or rude. It does not insist on its own way; it is not irritable or resentful; it does not rejoice at wrongdoing, but rejoices with the truth.'"

Gammill walked past the pews and up to the podium. He quickly removed his guns as Bill stepped away to take his seat. Back to being a pastor, Gammill smiled at Bill. "Thank you, Bill." He glanced to the members, "Sorry for the interruption, brothers and sisters."

"You was pretty quick. Glad you're back safe and sound," said Bill.

"I'm glad to be back quick and I appreciate walking in and hearing you speaking the words of first Corinthians, chapter thirteen, verse four. Love. It's sure hard to accept that notion sometimes. The power of what love can do." Gammill thought back on what he had to do to handle the black-souled Pete and Benito. There was no love in that. So many hard men in this world demanded Gammill to act harder. And yet, he longed for a world with the love of Jesus like his mother taught him about. Or maybe he lamented for the love of his mother who wanted that. Gammill doubted that he would ever see such a world but still, it was a beautiful place to hope for. "Who knows some other passages about love in the Bible?"

Widow Jenkins raised her hand. Gammill nodded to her. She said, "My command is this: 'love each other as I have loved you.'"

A young mother, Cassidy Leavel, spoke up: "'Luke, chapter six, verse thirty one: do to others as you would have them do onto you.' I...I think you have to love others to believe in this."

Pastor John nodded cheerfully in agreement.

Abner Bryer stood up. Gammill nodded at him. Abner looked down at his wife Helen and smiled. "Corinthians, chapter sixteen, verse fourteen: 'Do everything in love.'" Helen blushed and reached for Abner's hand as he sat down.

Old Peter Saalwaechter stood up after some effort but with a wide grin, said "I learned this as a young boy in Germany. Proverbs, chapter seventeen, verse seventeen: 'A friend loves at all times, and a brother is born for adversity.'"

Gammill was feeling better. His fellow Christians brought him back from that hard place he often visited to carry out his duties for protecting Spirits Bend. He wasn't alone. His mother was right to teach him to read and love the Bible and God. Embracing God and thereby Jesus's teachings had led John Gammill to a better place beyond that hard existence that immoral people reveled in. He would enforce the law but strive to be God's servant to those in need. This belief gave him solace that the hard world could change. Someday...

While the church members enjoyed the Bible's thoughts on love with each other, a dark man had very quietly separated from the night outside and entered the church, moving to a black corner of the room. The day's glow had gone, leaving only darkness where he stood, away from the feeble light of the lantern illuminating the church on its far side. The man watched and listened unseen by the congregation and its pastor.

Gammill held to his podium and spoke from his heart. "'Flee the evil desires of youth and pursue righteousness, faith, love and peace, along with those who call on the Lord out of a pure heart.' Second Timothy, chapter two, verse twenty-two."

The man in the dark corner stepped out like a plume of smoke trickling into the light. The members stared ahead, focused on their Pastor John, at first unaware of the man walking between the pews. A scent of fruit and strong tobacco floated through the air. Gammill sensed his presence before he came into view. Out of instinct Gammill's hands dropped to his sides, reaching for his guns that were not there.

Jurant stared to each side of the room, taking a mental account of those who came to the church. There was something unnerving in his stoic cold expression. An inhuman pride possessed him. A belief only in himself. Jurant was on a mission that night. And it wasn't from God.

Jurant stopped three pews back from the podium to face Gammill. Each man sized the other up the way dangerous men do, studying each other's hands and gauging their physiques and finally staring into each other's eyes. The eyes revealed how far a person was prepared to go. Gammill had seen Jurant hanging out with Fendris about the town, usually late in the evening as Jurant whispered in his ear. With a nod from Fendris, Jurant would turn and disappear into the night. This was the first time Gammill had seen Jurant's face clearly and up close. He stared into those cruel, dark eyes, black as pitch, with no reflection of light.

"Sorry to interrupt your church meeting, Sheriff. But Mister Fendris has learned you have some of his friends in your jail and would like them released. He is willing to pay whatever bail you think is appropriate." The words were spoken with a Cajun accent that hinted more of the swamp than the city streets of New Orleans.

Gammill was worried. Not for himself but for his church members. Their faces began to draw up in concern and fear. This was not a church calling by Jurant. They sensed something darker.

"Fendris's friends are sleeping off their earlier bad judgments," said Gammill. "They'll be up for release tomorrow at noon. Bail ten dollars each."

Jurant's eyes never left Gammill's. "Mister Fendris won't like waiting."

"Fendris doesn't like a lot of things. You're new here, Mister...?"

"Jurant. Formerly of New Orleans. You might have heard of me."

Gammill had heard of the deadly gunslinger. But his face never showed it. He shook his head. "No. New Orleans is a far piece from

Spirits Bend, Mister Jurant. Come by the jail at noon for your friends and I'll accommodate you then."

Jurant bristled a moment, setting his jaw. He held out his arms to show off the guns strapped to his hips. "Perhaps we could reach an accommodation right now."

The church members quickly slid away to the far ends of the pews.

Gammill looked to Jurant's guns. "I'm sorry but we don't allow guns in the church." He stepped out from behind the podium to hold his arms out and revealed that he had no holsters with guns on him.

Jurant's lips drew tight in irritation. He looked around at the frightened faces about the room. This was not what he had hoped for, nor what Fendris had in his plans. Killing an unarmed sheriff with lots of witnesses would draw too much attention. The time was not right for that. A thought struck him and caused an obscene smile.

"Well, it is regrettable that I cannot help Mister Fendris and his friends. I guess the only thing appropriate...is to quote a Bible passage. Judges, Chapter two, verse nineteen: 'But when the judge died, the people returned to ways even more corrupt than those of their ancestors, following other gods and serving and worshipping them. They refused to give up their evil practices and stubborn ways.'"

Jurant turned to leave. He was at the door when Gammill called after him, "Job, chapter four, verse eight, Mister Jurant." Jurant stopped with his back to Gammill. "'As I have observed, those who plow evil and those who sow trouble...reap it.'"

Jurant waited a tense moment in the doorframe...like he was going to turn around and plow some evil. Instead, he continued out the door and down the street.

The church members sighed with relief and looked back to Pastor John. Gammill stared into the darkness of the doorway. "Let's amen it for tonight's gathering, brothers and sisters." Gammill turned to them. "I will see you back here, Sunday. God go with you."

The members quickly said their muted "amens" while nodding their goodbyes. Then they scurried out the door to their homes and fast to bed where they lay in the dark with eyes squeezed shut to sleep. But there was no sleep for hours, only dread and fear.

With the congregation dispersed, Gammill stepped outside and stared into the darkness down the street to the Fendris Feed & Goods

Store. There was a light shining from the window in Fendris's office up on the second floor. Gammill thought about Jurant. Those black eyes. Him coming all the way up here to Wyoming from New Orleans. Burt was right to worry about Fendris. Something evil was in the making. Gammill's mood turned into melancholy as he thought of how people were going to die because...the Devil had come to Spirits Bend.

Chapter Eighteen:

Miss Claudine

Two days later on a sunny Friday morning an exuberant crowd of slicked up cowboys, boots shined, hair greased and parted, laughed and teased each other in the front yard of Ardway's ranch. They were busting at the seams to leave for town with two wagons full of men and some on horses. From the porch Ardway sat in a rocking chair and enjoyed watching his men shout and carry on. His uncut hair and beard showed its gray making him appear like a grandpa in that chair but no one would dare tell him that except Miss Claudine. A glass was half-filled with whiskey on a table. A bottle of whiskey was set underneath the table top and within easy reach. To all but Ardway it was apparent that he wasn't trying very hard anymore to hide his drinking.

Bailey stood up in a wagon and shouted toward the bunkhouse.

"Hurry up, Wasted! My money's setting my pants on fire. We gotta' get to town fast so Lucy can work my firehose and put it out!"

The men yelled and howled at Bailey. They also hooted playful insults at each other while winking outrageously to their friends. This was natural for these man-children as they had not been into town in almost two months. Each had pockets bulging with cash to throw around and an inclination to follow Bailey's enthusiasm to spend it fast and loose. Some of the older men sacked a few dollars away each week but the youngsters let it run through their fingers like water in a rain storm. And once a few drinks had been knocked back they all became men of the world whom none could besmirch. Card games. New clothes.

Women. Food. A room at the hotel (though this was prudently shared with friends to cut costs). Control was for Sunday, not Friday and Saturday. They would sleep off the all-nighters when riding back in the wagon. It was a glorious feeling to buy a shot of whiskey or a new hat or better yet ride the rodeo with one of Fancy Nancy's fillies and with no guilt or reason to it. To be in town with your wheel-horses and game for a wild time, seeking pleasures instead of wrestling a steer under a boiling sun or splitting logs in a frigid winter, made a man lose all sense of decorum and time. The stories would be told later of the victories, and the failures, and repeated to become epic memories in a world where the boasting was just as important as the events themselves.

Miss Claudine walked out of the bunkhouse while putting some scissors back in a big snap-buckled satchel. There was a peculiar glint in her eyes as she walked over to stand at the entrance to the courtyard. She looked over at the men with anticipation and a secret smile.

Abruptly the men's chatter trailed off into silence while a few birds chirped high up in the trees. The men stared to the bunkhouse with their mouths agape and eyes wide and blinking. Wasted had walked out fast and was headed directly for Bailey's wagon, his eyes staring straight ahead and avoiding any contact with the men. He knew what was coming.

Wasted's beard and hair had been cut by half in length. He wore Junior's shiny new clothes, sewn to fit him to a tee by Miss Claudine. She also had barbered his hair with more flair than the usual cowboy's extreme trim that seemed whacked off by a sheep's shear and a dull razor. Wasted wore a gray vest, black pants with a Spanish boot cut, white shirt, string tie and black boots with Spanish heels. A black Reno hat like gamblers wore topped it all off with a band of elegant silver threaded embroidery. His appearance was so striking that the cowhands could not believe what they were witnessing. In lowered voices they whispered their astonishment to each other. "Is that Wasted?"

"Naa, can't be Wasted!"

"Hells bells, it IS Wasted!"

Ardway saw Wasted in his son's clothes and almost jumped. His mind was immediately flooded with thoughts and emotions while the whiskey packed a jerk to his heart. Wasted continued to walk fast for the wagon but caught Ardway's shocked expression. He barely squinted a hint of a smile to Ardway. In that moment Ardway felt a bittersweet release and gave Wasted a slight smile back despite the sadness he felt.

"Woowee!" shouted Bailey as Wasted stopped before the wagon and fidgeted, knowing that the teasing was about to commence. "Boys, we might as well get off the wagon and stay here in our bunks at the ranch. All the fillies in town are gonna' be birddogging Wasted everywhere we go. We ain't got a chance with the ladies now that he's all combed and groomed up like a...a breeding stallion!"

Wasted sighed and shook his head before climbing up in the wagon. The men began to roar and howl. Tom gave a teasing wolf-whistle. The cowboys reached over and affectionately tugged and pushed while ragging on him.

"That Wasted's a purty boy Jim Dandy, he is!!"

"Look out girls. Mister Belvidere is a-coming."

"Why, he's as handsome as a new stake rope on a thirty-dollar pony!"

Bailey was sitting by Wasted and watched him stew under the good-natured kidding from his friends. He leaned in and solemnly whispered, "Remember, Wasted—you shoot all of us, Ardway is gonna' make you do all the work."

Wasted gave a mock-shocked expression to his best friend in the world. He stood up and shouted to the rest while trying not to laugh, "You boys... You... You better watch your step or...or..." He collapsed into a laughing fit at Bailey, who had pulled his lip up in comic mockery.

His crew shouted in unison, "Yes sir, Mister Wasted!"

The wagons began rolling down the gate road trailing loud laughter.

Ardway stood up and shouted, "Stay outta the hoosegow until I get there. See you slickers tonight!"

The men waved and continued joshing amongst themselves while the wagons and horsemen disappeared down the road.

A couple of hours later the sun was high in the sky and the air was warm and still. Most of the men in the wagon were lying about the floorboard, hats over their faces and snoozing. Wasted and Bailey sat in the back with their legs hanging off the end looking back at the road. Bailey was doing most of the talking, planning his weekend out for visiting Lucy and eating at Sticks. Wasted listened and nodded as he always did. Bailey caught himself and turned to his friend. "Wasted. Tell me—what's going on behind that dumb doggie face of yours?"

Wasted looked from Bailey and out among the trees along the road and thought a moment. "Hellfire, Bailey. I'm just thinking about...how to stay out of trouble."

Bailey leaned over laughing. "Are you crazy? We need to get into some trouble, boy! Shake that trail dust off our rumps and act like something that don't know what cow patties smell like."

Wasted smiled but with an uneasy turn to his eyes. "That's alright for you. But I'm afraid if I get too wild I might..." He let the sentence trail off, then continued somberly, "I 'spect there was probably an awful reason I didn't have recollections before coming to the ranch. What I do remember is—"

Bailey cut him off, "Oh, for Pete's sake, Wasted! I been riding with you for months and I know you ain't got a mean bone in your body. You can shoot like a Wild Bill Hickok but you don't even like to shoot game for dinner. You're lucky. Me, I wish I couldn't remember half the things I've messed up."

Wasted thought back on this. He was worried he might start liking the killing, even for food. And from game animals to..."Look. You don't understand what it's like to have a feeling, a little voice that talks right and wrong, but no memory to back it up. It is not a pleasant thing either way to be ashamed of something you can't even remember."

Bailey stared at his friend and put his arm around Wasted's neck. "Put this in your bank. No matter what you remember or not, I'm not going anywhere. We're on the other side of that bridge, Wasted. It don't matter to me."

Wasted felt a knot in his throat and smiled gratefully to Bailey. Bailey shook his head. "Lordie. We gotta' get you laid."

~

It was a few hours later after the men had left when Wilson drove the black carriage with the sun roof up to the front of the house. Ardway and Miss Claudine walked out as Wilson stepped down from the coach. He reached to hold Claudine's hand and helped her up into the buggy. Claudine sat in the seat, saying. "Thank you, Jedidiah."

Ardway stepped up and sat down next to her, picking up the reins. "You got the next trip," he said to Wilson. "Don't sleep all weekend with it being so quiet here with a little ghost crew."

"I'll try. I hope both of you enjoy getting away to town. I don't know how I'll survive without Miss Claudine's coffee."

Claudine swatted playfully at Wilson's shoulder. "I left you some cinnamon rolls in the oven."

Ardway spoke up, "You did?"

Claudine leaned over and whispered in Wilson's ear. He smiled. "Thank you, Miss Claudine."

"I guess we better get going so I can get into town and buy some cinnamon rolls at the bakery because I can't get none at my home." Ardway winked at Wilson as Claudine shook her head.

Wilson waved as Ardway flicked the reins and the two horses began pulling the buggy away. "Make sure the boys bring back some wagon grease from Schmidt. Not from Tolly. His grease is watered down."

Ardway nodded over his shoulder to Wilson, "Yes, boss!"

Wilson and Ardway shared a knowing smile as the carriage grew smaller down the road. It was a joke between them for the last few years as Ardway gave up more of running the ranch to Wilson. A strong trust had been built between them.

Over two hours later Claudine Hawkins discreetly studied Ardway in his silence as he watched the road and drove the horses. She had seen that smile he shared with Wilson and the confidence it signified many times before as they embarked on these trips to town. Jedidiah was the best thing that had happened to the ranch, especially when it was apparent that Patricia was not going to come back and taking Junior with her for his schooling. Burton was a mess after that. But the hope of Junior returning drew him back from drink and despair. He worked even harder at building the ranch and

Wilson was a big part of that. They cleared land. Built wells. Moved cattle back and forth for grass and water. Fought the elements. And created bigger herds and more cattle for market. With the ranch's success Burton took a greater interest in Spirits Bend. He wanted a town Patricia could marvel over if she ever came back. Junior was the key to that thinking. When Junior returned. And Junior was running the ranch. And a railroad made it easier to come back and the town had a hotel and...

But Claudine knew that even the best plans get laid on roads that get washed out in unforeseen storms. She thought of her beautiful enslaved mother from New Orleans, Diana, who was traded to the Cheyenne and how Claudine had grown up for ten years the daughter of the nation's chief along with a younger sister, Wilma. Her father Minninnewah, or "Wild Wind," discovered gold in South Dakota and with her mother's help secured the papers for the land rights. With this new wealth she was shipped off back east to school to make something of herself. And that it did because she learned that she was as out of place in that world as...a white crow in the forest. Six years of hell afterwards her father got the insane notion that he could trust and drink with the white man. White bankers had led him to this mistaken thinking and they swindled the gold mine away. Soon after, her mother died of smallpox, followed by her father. And Claudine Hawkfeather aka Hawkins was alone with no known whereabouts of her sister Wilma.

It was a horrible shock to lose one's parents but the worst of circumstances was that Claudine was set adrift as an intelligent and educated woman with a fierce degree of personal integrity including that of a Cheyenne warrior's code of honor. She was both black and native who didn't fit in anywhere, what people called a "handsome woman" in their world of prejudice and deceit. Luckily Claudine was a disciplined person who embraced work unlike most of her pampered white classmates at school. Her Cheyenne upbringing had taught her that to live was an act of defiance. One of her favorite teachers at school was obsessed with French cooking and Claudine became so, too. She had thrown herself into learning it out of a love for its art and taste. The kitchen became Claudine's domain and delicious food was a great equalizer for its chef. When the bottom fell out this ability to make chicken confit, French onion soup, bouillabaisse, salmon en papillote, Quiche Lorraine, croque monsieur, boeuf bourguignon and lamb shank navarin put her to work immediately. On steam-powered river boats going up and down the Mississippi River Claudine created meals for five years that delighted the wealthiest passengers. She was hired away from this life at great expense and was constantly in rotation among many "elite" families who would pay her higher and higher salaries and with it very exclusive personal perks. She was the exotic toast of Philadelphia's high society who employed her mother's New Orleans French accent and learned knowledge of the language to charm the elite as the mysterious Miss Claudine. She liked to let them think she was a Paris negress of some African royal background while the City of Brotherly Love's working class lynched and killed blacks and immigrants in the street. Claudine had carefully saved her abundant income and invested it successfully through the help of her many well-connected employers. But while her life was prosperous it lacked for intimate companionship and closeness. She had secret affairs with white businessmen who wanted a mistress, not a wife. The same for black men that were wealthy foreign dignitaries but would never marry an American. Lacking marriage she pleaded to become these men's business partners but that was laughed upon. Her affairs became boring dreams lived again and again.

At fifty years old Claudine longed for something like the early life she grew up in. Simple. With love and affection and a place in the wilds outside of Eastern cities. She had been searching for her sister Wilma for years in South Dakota while posting notices in the papers there and in surrounding states. Wilma was contacted by a friend in South Dakota about reading the advertisement and she wrote Claudine a letter from Wyoming. Overjoyed, Claudine gave notice to her shocked and grieving employer, packed up and moved to Spirits Bend where Wilma was living with her daughter, Winona, which was Cheyenne for "first daughter." Wilma's husband had run out on them twenty years before and she was working for a tanner and was known to be able to outwork any man at all the foul-smelling stages of the leather's preparatory and finished work.

Being reunited with her sister and niece was a great triumph for Claudine until it wore out after ten months. It seemed the sisters were both headstrong and unable to live with together no matter how much they loved each other. Claudine had bought them a new house. She bought out the tanner and Wilma was running the business and very well. Too well. Their egos clashed often and devolved into Cheyenne insults. Later they would laugh over how the "old talk" bubbled up when they got mad. Something had to be done.

Claudine knew a well-to-do couple she met on the stage while coming to Spirits Bend. Patricia and Burton Ardway. Patricia and Claudine talked foods and recipes the whole trip. Later Patricia admitted she knew of Claudine from Philadelphia and how her family could never meet her price. Claudine was not so choosy now and she wanted something like her old life without all the fuss and bother. And that is how she came to live with the Ardways. She was required to cook the family meals and soon became a great friend of the family, being of both the frontier and of Philadelphia which pleased Burton and Patricia to no end. Not satisfied with just cooking at the house, she worked with the bunkhouse cook to elevate his culinary fare and was soon revered by the ranch hands. The ranch life in the wilderness gave her the joys of her early life. She adored Junior. And she could visit Wilma on a weekend once a month which was just short enough time that both actually enjoyed being together. They became even closer when Winona died of symptoms of consumption. They had become Christians in John Gammill's church after John delivered a moving funeral service for Winona.

Yes, plans were silly things to count on when God had other ideas. Claudine wondered how Burton would come out of this—or, out of his despair over losing Junior. She had given up on trying to keep him from drinking but she still she prayed for him, first thing in the morning and the last thing before bed at night.

The carriage slowed as Ardway pulled it over to a shaded spot they always used for a stretch and bladder break at the halfway mark to Spirits Bend. He walked over to a nearby creek and brought back a bucket of water for the horses to drink. They grazed at the grass on the side of the beaten road. Because of Patricia and Junior, Ardway had mandated that an outhouse was built off behind some trees so unaware travelers would not see it. It was maintained monthly and cleaned by his men. Claudine availed herself of it as Ardway went to a large tree he favored close by. It was also a chance to drink from the flask he carried without Claudine giving him hell. When they returned to the carriage, Claudine reached in a wicker basket and brought out a plate with cornbread pieces. On another plate slender cuts of ham had been fried up in a skillet to be eaten with the cornbread. Ardway gave her a crooked smile as she handed him some on a napkin. He raised it up to his lips and took a big bite and spoke with his mouth full of food.

"Thank you, Claudine."

She smiled back, amused, "You're welcome, Burton."

They sat in the noonday shade and enjoyed the simple but delicious meal. The pork was glazed with honey in the frying. The golden brown cornbread looked like small corn cobs and had a crispy buttery coating from being baked in a special iron skillet with the cob molds. When they finished, she put the plate and napkins away and brought out an elegant glass bottle with a hooked ceramic cap and poured them sweet black tea into china cups. As he sipped the tea and looked down the road, Ardway felt a serenity and calm that surprised him. Like the old days. Claudine's cooking could do that. But something else was easing his mind. The trip. Being between places. Nothing but the ride to think about and with an old friend. He looked over at Claudine. She was about ten years older than him but seemed ten years younger in looks. Claudine took his empty cup with hers and tucked it back in the basket. He grabbed the reins and asked, "Ready?" She nodded. He gave the leather a little flip and the horses rolled the carriage back onto the road and into the sunlight.

Down the road a bit Ardway turned to Claudine, "You're quiet."

"You don't want me talking as you know what I'll say. Let's enjoy the ride. Lots of memories along this old road."

Ardway glanced up the road and to the woods on its left and right. "Are you saying I'm old? Again?"

Claudine gave him a sour look and they both broke out laughing.

"Guess I might be getting along," he said, "Since I built this road out of nothing. We use it enough now to keep the weeds from taking over. But they aren't ever going away."

Claudine shifted and stuck her legs out to stretch under her blue dress. "A lot of deep ruts after Spring. You're going to have to lay down some gravel."

"Gravel? Horses don't like gravel," he sniffed at her.

"You can run one of those big iron rolling pins over it. I've seen it done. Presses the rocks down into the ground so tight they stay put. Horses will thank you later. And anybody else using this 'old' road. Your legacy will be laying a paved road in ten years so you might as well make it easy for them then."

"Paved road..." Ardway stared down the way, gave the reins a little whip. The horses picked the stride up but not much. They knew the route as well as Ardway.

"The way things are going, what makes you think I'll have a 'legacy'?"

There was no sarcasm or bitterness in Ardway's voice. His eyes showed a need to hear his friend's thoughts.

Claudine straightened up, pulling her legs up to sit. She loved Ardway and his family. His home was her home now, a precious tie to her Indian past and the outdoors. His ranch and its men were her family. She knew she would die someday either in bed at the Ardway ranch or in the kitchen. Maybe it would be while walking up the hill to her favorite spot where she grew roses and the pink Indian Paint- brush. That clearing was where she figured to be the first buried on it. Claudine had declared the ranch cemetery would be started there for the beautiful view at dawn and sunset. It served no purpose oth- er than that and was left to her solitude and attention. Ardway was quite fine with her pronouncement as he didn't like to think about such things.

"Wilson is your legacy and that includes the girl he has his eye on. I think that poor boy, Wasted, could be your legacy but you'll have to work that out. The men that till the land and keep your cattle are your legacy," she paused to look around at the pine trees and rolling hills. "Your son, Burton Junior, is your legacy. And don't forget, I'm your legacy. So you and me and everyone else has got to keep building it. It's unknown who'll end up with it but we sure as Hades, pardon my Greek, can't give up. 'Sides, I know you too well. You'll never give up on this ranch until your last breath."

Ardway stared into Claudine's dark eyes for a long moment. He saw her unyielding faith and the truth as she knew it. He turned back to the road and the horses.

"You're a lot of trouble sometimes, Miss Claudine," he shrugged, "but you're the best decision Patricia ever crossed me with."

They rode the rest of the way in silence. Not out of anger or having nothing to say, but the way friends do who just want to enjoy the trip with each other and that's enough.

The main street of Spirits Bend was losing its light at the end of the day. Pale yellow streaks of brightness leaked out of the saloons, hotel and eateries to paint at the shadows that grew darker with each moment. Ardway's men were scattered here and there, filing raucously in and out of one bar or another. The laughter and cussing flowed while trailing them.

Town residents in work or their dress clothes mingled among the rowdy cowboys, enjoying their spectacle or cursing it under their breath. A woman's voice sang "Mustang Gray." It drifted faintly from some saloon on the summer's breeze.

"But he'll go no more a-ranging
The savage to affright;
He's heard his last war whoop
And fought his last fight."

Ardway and Claudine pulled up to the hotel. He stepped down first while lending a hand to Claudine. "Thank you, Burton. You have the shopping list to drop off at Seeley's. I'll see you on Sunday." She added, "In church. Not the jail."

Gammill was walking down the street and saw them. He waved and stepped across to greet them. He wore a simple gray wool suit that fit his large frame well. On his lapel was the worn brass badge, shined up for the weekend.

"Well, lookee here, Claudine. Here's the jail and the church both come to meet us!" exclaimed Ardway.

Claudine gave Gammill a warm smile which he returned as he lifted his hat to her.

"Pastor Gammill," she said. "So good to see you. Now, I'm counting on you to keep a Christian eye on Burt."

This was an obvious well-worn ritual between the two.

"Yes, Ma'am, Miss Claudine. I'll toss him in jail later tonight just to make sure I can do that."

Ardway rolled his eyes at both of them, "You two worry about me all you want. I'm the one that's got wild chuckleheads to watch over in town who ain't got the good sense that God gave a goose." He tipped his hat to Claudine. "Tell Sister Wilma I said hello and thank her for taking—"

"Me off your hands." Claudine gave Ardway a frustrated sigh. She smiled up at him and Gammill in resignation, "Goodnight, gentlemen." She turned and stepped away in an elegant genteel manner despite the rough planks of the walkway.

The two men watched attentively as she continued down the block. Miss Claudine turned around to look back. Gammill and Ardway waved and smiled cheerfully to her. She pivoted and disappeared around the corner.

Satisfied they were freed up for the night, Ardway turned back to his oldest friend with a mock-serious expression that Gammill mirrored.

"Well, we better get to seeing what kind of trouble is a-dancing with my tanglefoots."

"Not much trouble that you don't know about," said Gammill.

"Ha! Said the kettle to the pot."

They crossed the street to stand before Molly's Saloon. Ardway stopped and gave Gammill a sly grin.

"I was talking to Claudine on the trip and she told me preachers ain't supposed to drink beer."

Gammill drew back, "On, no! It's not a hard spirit. Beer is like wine. For communion and such things. Besides it's good for you."

Ardway gave Gammill a sideways glance.

"That in the Bible?"

Gammill glanced left and right impishly, "I hope so. I've been preaching it for years."

Chapter Nineteen:

Wilson

———

Jedidiah Wilson had worked for twelve years at the ranch, the last seven as the head foreman. No push or pull to it, following Ardway's orders. Wilson read his boss well enough to keep Ardway satisfied and without much talk about it. Ardway liked Wilson because of their shared synchronicity for running the ranch. He could be tough when the going required it but Wilson was not a hard man. The cowhands liked Wilson as fair and curious, unafraid to admit when he didn't know something and had to seek another's opinion. Ardway and Wilson had been both willing to give Kroeber a chance. And Kroeber delivered for a year. Then his ego turned him into pig squat. Unfortunately a common story when a man was handed responsibility over others without having any empathy. Not so for Wilson. He proved time and again to make good choices in light of slim options.

Ardway planned to surprise Wilson at the first of next year with having a cabin built for him over by the Big Elk Spring about a mile from the main house—a reward for Wilson's good work in helping to build the ranch. But it was also a reason for Jedidiah to stick around. Wilson had a sweetheart, Junnifay "June" Crawford, that he was taken with enough to talk about marrying her. She was a widow at twenty-five with two kids after her husband Carson caught pneumonia and passed away two years ago. June worked long hours at the bakery but still had a bright natural smile which lit up like the sun when Wilson came in the door.

The bakery owner allowed her and the kids to stay in a shack behind the shop, rent free, hoping to keep a good worker tied to his business. This new cabin would keep Wilson from taking a job in town and June happy to stay out at the ranch. And besides, Ardway had taken more than a shine to her boy and girl, Clement and Abigail. They called him, Mister Burt, and thought he was the greatest man that ever lived with all the guns, Indian weapons and animal trophies around his "giant" house. There was no gruff drunk rancher to be found when they came to visit. Miss Claudine bribed them to come out as often as possible with honey berry sheet cake. June laughed, "I don't need such enticements to see Jed. But the young'uns would shoot me if I refused them Miss Claudine's cake." Wilson had become like family to Ardway and he meant to do right by him and his.

After Ardway and Claudine left for town, Wilson rode around the ranch checking his skeleton work crew going about the jobs. There wasn't much to do but clean the grounds along with the regular maintenance. From the chicken coop to the barn and bunkhouse the men were sweeping or raking and scooping up whatever dirt and debris there was, tossing it in a wheelbarrow to take and dump in a big long wash crater from the last rain. Later he'd have the men bring in some dirt in wagons to finish it off and use mules to drag a grader over it. He had a man painting on a shed and one spot-painting any structure with a little peeling paint or blemishes. Two men worked on the corral gate, fixing the worn out wood handle on its lock. The squeaky wood hinges would have to wait until Ardway returned with that grease.

There were four riders out checking the four herds. All were young and good with a rifle. They could shoot the eye out of a squirrel at a hundred or more yards. They got a bonus for staying at the ranch over the weekend and patrolling, keeping coyotes and wild dogs away. It wasn't until autumn and winter when food got scarce that they saw the worst problems with wolves and mountain cats. Bears were more apt to kill a calf in the late fall before they went into hibernation or early spring when they woke up. But with a smaller crew of men and horses covering the area and the cattle it gave the lazier meat eaters cause to consider pulling down a sick cow or smaller calf. The rifle boys knew to fire off some shots at anything eyeing the cattle. Better to shoot a few bold toothy animals stupid enough to be seen before they killed anything. Scare the hell out of 'em to stick to the bush or up in the hills. Even if a bullet missed it would tear into a tree or rock with an awful noise and the hungry beasts got the message: chase a deer or young moose, eat a rabbit or insects but stay far away from the herd of cows.

It was about seven o'clock and the light was turning the purple color of young plums. The sun had already set, its glare cut early by the tall mountains and hills around the ranch.

The men ate well. Reid, the mess hall cook, had less mouths to feed and more time to prepare and rustle up the meals. Chicken dumplings with baked turnips had the cowboys singing Reid's praises but then he surprised everyone with a slice of buckwheat cake served with a thick huckleberry compote. With only a fourth of the mouths to fill as usual, everyone had all they could eat.

At a little before eight o'clock the men were patting their full bellies while they lit up cigarettes and casually sipped coffee. No one felt like speaking, choosing to enjoy the last of a good day quietly before moving on to the bunkhouse. The room grew pleasantly darker like the view out the open door and windows. The lamps had been lit, casting a soft glow in the tobacco smoke as the eight men and Wilson sat with their legs up on chairs and their arms on the tables.

The sounds of scrubbing dishes with splashing water came from the kitchen. Reid was softly cooing a yodel tune while he washed plates and his young helper, Seth, sloshed water out of a bucket rinsing the dishes clean to put on a rack.

Two scruffy characters melted into view from out of the shadows in the doorway. The two men pointed their rifles on the men in the mess hall. Wilson noticed them first and sat up, dropping his boots lightly to the floor.

Jurant stepped into the light from behind the men and shouted, "Don't move! Keep your hands on the tables."

The cowboys sat straight up in their chairs, their eyes darting pensively to each other. No one put their hands on the tables.

Jurant's men stepped out in a wider circle to keep their guns pinned on Wilson and his men. The two moved with quick nervous motions. Each was unkempt and filthy, unlike Jurant's spit and polished appearance. Jurant had no rifle, just his holstered pistols. His calm, assured manner implied that it was more than enough.

Jurant looked around and zeroed in on Wilson. "You. The ramrod...Wilson. Tell 'em to get their—"

Seth rushed out of the kitchen dressed in his greasy apron and waving an old Colt Walker revolver. The big pistol was heavy to his hands and shook as Seth pointed it.

In a blur Jurant drew his own Colt Single Shot Action and shot Seth in the chest. Blood detonated out like a red firework explosion. The scrawny young boy was slammed backwards by the .45 caliber bullet leaving a red trail after him into the kitchen. His pistol clattered upon the floor where he'd been standing.

Jurant's two nervous men dropped low with eyes on their rifle sights while drawing beads on the ranch boys.

With a cat-like spin, Jurant pulled his second gun and pointed both at Wilson. "Next one gets noble in here, Wilson gets the first bullet." He yelled at the kitchen, "You hear that Cookie?"

A few seconds later an anxious Reid stuck his head out from behind the door frame. He stepped out with his trembling hands held up and showing no weapons on him.

Jurant tilted his chin at Reid, then jerked it toward the tables.

Reid looked back at Seth's crumpled body as he trod carefully around him. He walked with a furious expression to the table, sat down and put his hands out on top.

The two men with Jurant giggled to each other. Abner was tall and had a knotty raw-boned look, like a gnarled tree from the desert. "Bean" was short and burly with the hard unblinking eyes of a mongrel that fought in alleys for scraps among the trash. Both had wooly unshorn beards lining the bottom halves of their oily, dirty faces. They looked unwashed, perhaps since getting tossed out of their families for not contributing money for the old man's whiskey and tobacco. They had hooked up back East in the army and deserted together. "Go West, young man," was a grave matter of the law to these two rather than friendly guidance from Horace Greeley.

Wilson furiously studied each of the men while sitting with his hands down on the table. His thoughts raced to Jurant. He recognized him as the man that pissed off Ardway and just about drew on Wasted here at the ranch. He must have been looking to get on here to kill Ardway. Wilson's stomach tightened, he knew this wasn't going to end without blood. He could only stall for time until he figured out some kind of distraction. Poor Seth. If he could possibly get that kind of diversion again, Wilson would go for Jurant and hope his men took the two saddle tramps before they could shoot him. He drew in a heavy breath. It would be awful close...

June's face illuminated Wilson's thoughts. He fought to push her out. He'd have to, to get through this. But try as Wilson might June continued to stare at him with that bright sweet smile. He spoke up, "We don't have much money here."

"Ardway's our money. Where is he?"

Wilson's heart lightened a tiny bit. "In town. Watching over the crew on their time off."

Jurant shook his head and groaned with disgust. "Shit!...Second time I rode out here for nothing." He fumed to himself as he thought it over and lowered his guns to his sides. He looked over at his men and gave a bitter chuckle. "Ha...And we wasted time taking the back country trails so as to not be seen."

"We missed 'em?" asked Bean.

Abner gave him an angry scowl, "Dammit, Bean, they was on the main road."

Bean's brow knotted up. "What's Mister Fendris gonna' say?"

Fendris, thought Wilson. The cat's out of the bag now. Wilson glanced with a spark in his eyes at his men around the room. They had been waiting for his signal.

Wilson's elbows rose as his hands reached for his guns. The ranch men did the same.

Jurant's men were still wondering what to do. Not Jurant. Both his Colts were up and firing as if he had never lowered the one.

Bean finally blinked, his mongrel eyes disbelieving Jurant's inhuman speed.

The bullets ripped into Wilson, then immediately through the other cowboys across the dining room. Bean saw it all like one image. Men reaching for guns. Bullets hitting bodies. The blood erupted like blooms of red flowers, flinging petals into the air.

Wilson was blown back into the chair, his blood and guts splattered across the table. Eight other Ardway men fell dead about the room, knocking over chairs and collapsing upon the upturned furniture to the floor.

Wilson's life flowed out of his body, the blood pressure going, his form shrinking into itself as if a balloon had popped.

Jurant's black eyes reflected no emotion. Death was his constant companion, more real than life to him. He held his smoking guns, waiting for some revolt among the dying. His face relaxed. His guns were expertly flipped back into their holsters.

Abner and Bean gaped in awe at the scene and then to Jurant. Bean whooped, "Woooooweee!"

He rushed over to Wilson and began checking through his pockets. Abner followed him immediately and bent to search the pockets of the dead men on the floor surrounding Wilson.

Wilson's eyelids were held at halfway over their pupils by sheer will as his inner light was dying. A slight wheeze sounded as his punctured lungs sucked desperately to pull at air. He watched Bean pull a locket from his vest and open it, then grin obscenely back at him with those round dog eyes. The locket held a picture of a woman with a sunny smile. With a supreme effort just a half-second before the call of the grave Wilson silently mouthed the word, "June."

Wilson's gun barrel trembled on the table and whipped up to Bean's face. Wilson's finger squeezed a hair more on the trigger of the gun. The barrel roared, sending a bullet through Bean's eye. The slug blew out the back of his skull and covered Abner with a fishnet splash of red gore. The cadaver was flung to the floor like a bloody rag tossed at a hog killing.

What had been Wilson's mortal form collapsed into itself. The skin shrunk, sagging under his clothes to became a deflated meat puppet. Jurant carefully walked over and held his gun out. With the barrel he pushed aside Wilson's dead hand holding the gun. He returned his pistol back into the holster. Jurant knew the signs. Wilson was gone.

Abner lay on the floor in shock, wiping frantically at the blood and brains covering his face and body. Jurant stared down at Wilson's dead body with a surprised expression of respect. "Goddamn. There's always one tough son of a bitch that'll make you work for it." He yawned and looked to the kitchen, "I'm grabbing some grub before sleeping. Head back in the morning."

Abner stood up and fumbled with his rifle. The blood and gray pieces of Bean's brain that covered his face made the whites of his round eyes shine with the wildness of an enraged animal. He finally got a grip on the rifle and aimed it at Wilson's body.

A gun blast rang out loud in the room. Abner stared in horror with those white eyes in his red mask at Jurant, who had shot him straight through the heart. He coughed blood and gasped, "Wh—why...?"

Jurant's black eyes stared down at the dying Abner. "Fendris wanted you two to take the blame for the killings. But I shot you... for Wilson, you worthless trash. Even dead he was more man than you ever was."

With disgust Jurant loosed a stream of spit to strike Abner's forehead. Its white foam rolled down over the blood. It slid down between Abner's lifeless wide eyes that stared out in horror with that last memory for all of eternity.

Jurant walked to the kitchen leaving the room of the dead bathed in the golden glow of the lantern. Wilson's head had sagged to his chest, his eyes half-open, staring at his death-gripped pistol with his blood flowing slowly down its barrel, sparkling in the light. It dripped to fall into a dark red pool spreading slowly across the floor and melding with the blood of the others. Blood brothers forever but not by choice and no Bowie Knife ceremony, but a Bowie Vidalia Sandbar Fight was surely coming...

Chapter Twenty:

Molly's Saloon

When a person passed through Molly's swinging doors they were greeted by the largest and most ornate saloon within two hundred miles. It was one that was well-acquainted to most men in that part of the territory. Molly's was one of the only establishments in town not financed with some help by Ardway or Fendris. Like many such ventures the owners made a bundle of money in one town and when things played out, they moved on with the cash and started a new place. Ardway and Fendris were warned by knowing friends who had tried before that running a saloon took a lot of time, arduous efforts and all the workers stole from you. Both men were happy to have a saloon in Spirits Bend without the aggravation and gave it their blessings. Same reasoning for their steering clear of getting in the whorehouse business though they were both offered a bottom floor shared interest in Fancy Nancy's Palace. John had convinced Burton to put his money elsewhere for reasons of his soul and, more importantly, that a decent woman would not marry a man who owned a whorehouse. Fendris had already gotten married to a Swedish woman, Gunilda, and though he partook in Nancy's wares during the marriage he kept it discreet with arranged meetings in the storage room of his feed store. Being ranchers and growing their herds was more than enough for both men at the time.

A visit to Molly's or Fancy Nancy's was considered an honorable tradition for the working men employed by either of the largest ranches in that part of the territory. Since it was Wasted's second time (he was run out before on account of his slovenly appearance and strong smell) he was particularly impressed with all its wonders. Which included in no specific order...

A sour-faced piano player named Kenton who plunked the keys to tunes such as "My Dear Old Mother" which accompanied that Friday night's many moments. Each musical number was decorated with many artistic and dramatic flourishes of keyboard skill by Kenton that pleased the crowd or, as Kenton was wont to say, "Gave them their money's worth."

The music played throughout the saloon which was decorated in dark red and bright gold wallpaper. It was highly dramatic and impressive to the many who lived within walls made of logs and mud. It had a regal effect on the patrons until the alcohol's effects took hold. This often led to bullet holes which could be seen high up on the walls or in the ceiling. Holes that were closer to earth were covered in tin stars painted in gold paint.

The shiny varnished floor lain with grooved wood planks was unheard of in the area. Despite being admired for its luster there was a practical reason for its expense—it was easy to mop up the spilled beer and liquor along with sweeping up the tossed cigar and cigarette butts, and pipe ash that was dropped everywhere with nary a thought. Indeed, the owners did know a thing or two about running saloons.

One of the charms of visiting a saloon such as Molly's was that the help brought you drinks in all places that you positioned yourself. No lines like in some bigger saloons. Bartenders, the saloon girls and bar workers moved quickly to drop off drinks, pick up empty glasses and wipe down spilled liquor during the night's carousing. A customer with an empty mug or shot glass meant a fish with his money waiting to be hooked. Better to chase it than let it wait until the next round. One thing about Wyoming's working class men, they burned through their money faster than a wildfire in a windstorm. Saving money was fine for talking high-minded about with friends and associates during the week, but this was forgiven after one had experienced a few drinks. Molly's staff was expressly dedicated to giving its customers the chance to follow up a consumed drink seconds later with another full glass. Drinks were served even before some men were finished with an earlier one, which was hard to resist staring at for long with a month or week's pay blazing in your pocket.

Since the soothing pleasure of smoking along with the pull of nicotine addiction gave men that heightened jolt to drink more, Molly's had a dedicated tobacco counter at a front corner of the bar close to the entrance. Smoking and chewing tobacco, papers and clay pipes were sold briskly along with matches, playing cards, sweet tasting mouthwashes and strong cologne. Also on display for sale were glass bottles of "Canton's Chewing Tobacco Stain Remover."

In this atmosphere a heavy fog of blue tobacco smoke rose early in the evening over the enthusiastic crowd. Everyone smoked or chewed or was a partaker of both. And not genteelly but with wild vigor. Sometimes it was hard to see about the room for the thick clouds of smoke, especially in the winter months with the closed doors. The floor was constantly covered in spent butts and dumped ashes along with burnt matches despite the ongoing sweeping. No one thought a moment about tossing this smelly residue on the floor. It was like being outside, except when outside people were more fearful of starting grass fires and stomped their discarded matches and butts out in the dirt.

Chewed tobacco was spit into buckets and spittoons. Only when a spitter caught an unacquainted man's trouser leg was there cause for outrage. This was settled in a manly way of shoving and pushing until someone calmed them down or by appeasement with the buying of a drink for the marked man. Most took the drink.

In the back a small stage was painted in white and adorned with kerosene floor lamps. It stood empty with green velvet curtains drawn to the side until some kind of singing or dancing entertainment presented itself. This was never planned as much as accompanying Kenton when someone felt the urge.

Next to the stage resided the piano and Kenton. He always began with a few slow songs but would progress to livelier fare later when the crowd was in the mood. On this night a sturdy and well-endowed "showgirl" stepped over to join Kenton by the piano. She started to sing "My Dear Old Mother" with a strong and pleasing voice that was always welcome among the local crowd. She drank whiskey out of a beer mug as she sang...

WASTED

While this soiled dove warbled to the men, drinks were scattered askew down a shiny bar-top as men picked them up to consume or set them aside to tell a serious or humorous story, laughing loudly or cussing in anger.

Several tables would have men in various stages of solemn card playing at games such as faro, Brag and three-card monte. Dice games of chuck-a-luck and grand hazard went on in a corner. There were Molly's girls who were off work sitting at the tables playing with the men. Two Chinese men from the laundry played cards with two local merchants at one table while cussing in Cantonese. Gambling was a great equalizer among the men in Wyoming.

At one table four scuzzy and shit-faced cowpokes drunkenly murdered a rendition of "Camptown Races." An inebriated man lay face down on a table directly across from the singers. He was stirred awake from his hibernation by the noise. With some effort he pushed himself up by his arms to rise, his face squinched up like hearing a sick cat yowl. But alas his legs gave out and the man spilled like a dead snake off his chair to the floor where he passed out again.

An hour went by as the customers in the saloon drank and smoked and went about their roostered-up celebrations. The showgirl had been walking around singing to the crowd with the men buying her drinks. She returned more than a little tipsy and leaned on the piano where Kenton switched his furious playing of fast tunes to accommodate her slower cadence and dramatic voice which raised itself to be heard over the crowd's noise.

*And kept to my children's toys
Oh, my dear mother...
Tried to save me from this ruin..."*

Her voice trailed off as she tried to remember the words. Failing that she abruptly forced a wide toothy grin under her bleary mascara-blackened eyes, appearing like a grotesque mask at Halloween. She nodded numbly to scattered clapping from the tired men around the room.

On the stage, boots slammed loudly upon the boards. The men and the saloon's staff turned to the sounds. Nat's drunken fuse was lit and he was burning a muscular stomping dance across the stage while humming out a familiar song. Two saloon girls in the middle of the room laughed and rushed on stage to join him. They tried to keep up with the wild Nat and began singing a spirited "Camptown Races." The drunken cowpokes at the table that couldn't sing on key screamed and stood up only to fall over each other. The rest of the room lit up from the energy and whooped and whistled approval. Kenton had taken a break from the piano and sat smoking a cigar with a tip soaked in a shot glass of cognac. He looked about at the room and the excited men catching their next wind. Then he turned and attacked the piano keys to pump up the tune and send it flying along.

While the manic frenzy of this outburst played out, over in a corner Wasted was engaged in a solemn game of poker with three very grim men. He silently and sternly drank water in a mug while they sipped whiskey and beer. The center of the table held their money. A pile of silver dollars was stacked high before Wasted. Around the table the other players were down to a few coins. While Nat and the girls danced and the piano roared in the background this table was oblivious to the world around it. It was at that time of evening when a player could take all the night's money in a win. And each of these serious men played with all their resources for that big win.

Wasted looked up from his cards. "Hate to disappoint you boys. My call...to drop the ball." He laid down a queen high, straight flush of hearts.

The men around the table threw their cards down. A horse-faced man named Bowers made a disgusted nod of his chin. Jack

Turner shook his bald fat head while his desperate face squinched up with pain. A spiffy looking gent, "Boston," pushed his green bowler hat up in frustration as Wasted cupped the winnings to slide over to his pile. While Wasted counted and stacked the dollars Boston's large shoulder muscles and biceps shifted restlessly under his fine Eastern clothes.

His pear-shaped little friend, Worley, sat at the next table and studied Wasted closely but glanced over to Boston when he angrily flung his big arms out to let loose their pent-up energy. A bead of sweat rolled down Worley's cheek. Something was not right here and he worried Boston was going to make it worse. Worley was Boston's card man. He studied the players and let Boston know their tells for holding a winning or losing hand. Wasted didn't show a tell. His face or body never betrayed his thoughts.

And that wasn't the only strange thing. Worley was sure that he had seen Wasted play before. But to his silent consternation he couldn't shake that old memory loose.

Alice, who Wasted knew from her ranch visit, poured water into his glass from a pitcher held in one hand. She also topped off the other men's beers with a pitcher from her other hand. The pitchers were made of heavy glass but Alice handled them easily like they were full milk pails back on the farm.

More games were played in groups about the saloon. Up on the stage Nat had worn himself out while the night rushed past him and he sank to his knees and collapsed there. His sleeping body was carried off by a couple of men. They were directed to take Nat over to the hotel by Ardway who slipped the men some coin. He and Gammill shared a laugh as they turned back to watch who was left from Ardway's crew.

The hours passed as the showgirl sat uneasily on a stool by the piano. Her head drooped, but when she started to fall she would jerk herself straight up. Through a drunken slurring she continued to sing, for herself as much as the crowd.

"I slapped him on his manly face
So much it turned him red..."

The woman laughed in a hollow way.

"He spanked me on my sweet round rump..."

Remembering something, the showgirl's face looked like she had been slapped. Recovering she gave a lonely smile.

"Then he kissed me off to bed!
Oh...my...dear old mother..."

Across the room three "painted ladies" in low-cut dresses strolled about the room smiling and trying to charm the last of the liquored men to take a walk. A pie-eyed Tom grinned blankly from his seat at a table. He was feeling his oats and nothing else. As the ladies passed Tom made a clumsy grab at one. The "lady" snarled at him, wrenching free of his grasp. He stood up unsteadily and she punched Tom square in the face. He fell backwards and onto the lap of a seated cowboy.

The cowboy flipped Tom over with his momentum to land hard to the floor. The cowboy turned back to his drinking buddy as if nothing had happened and they continued to sip their whiskey and converse.

Tom lay on the floor passed out as a few men stepped over him with no heed. Ardway and Gammill appeared. With the help of Jordie they roused Tom to stand and got him to stumble out with Jordie and Ardway holding him up.

Along the way they passed two middle-aged locals in worn bowler hats who sat stewed. One cried desperately as the other solemn friend nodded and patted his hand.

The evening slipped on into the night carried by smoke and drinks. The room began to empty until only a few customers and some tired staff either moping and cleaning or bored at their stations were left. The showgirl draped her arm around Kenton and sang sadly with heavy breaths and a stilted wavering voice. She sang for herself with her back turned to the room.

"Now I drink...a bit too much
And spend...the night...boohoo-ing
I wish I'd...listened to...mother
Oh, my dear...old...mother...tried
To save me...from this ruin..."

For a brief moment the grief consumed her. Her body sagged, she slipped and almost fell. The piano player hugged her close to keep her from falling. The showgirl reacted by pulling away in anger. She slapped Kenton and stormed away. A couple of drunks laughed at them. Kenton watched her leave with a sottish twist to his face. Then hearing the laughter he turned back to the men and threw up his hands with a "what you gonna do" gesture. Kenton turned to the piano and played a few notes, then stopped in mid-note. Suddenly he leapt up and hurried to follow after the showgirl.

Ardway and Gammill were slouched against the bar. They watched the piano player disappear down a hall after the woman. Gammill winked at Ardway. "Well, Burt. What's it going to be? Jail or the hotel?"

Ardway stood up straight, stretched his back with a tired sigh. "What's closer?"

He flipped some gold coins on the bar counter. The bartender's sleepy eyes widened with some grateful pep. "Thank you! Thank you for your company, Mister Ardway." He nodded to Gammill. "A pleasure, Sheriff." Both smiled back to him and walked to the front doors.

In through the swinging doors stepped a large man. He and Ardway stopped and stood starring into each other's eyes.

Kroeber's face was a broken and stitched nightmare. Scars over mottled flesh stretched around eyes that shone with an ever-greater horror. He scowled wickedly.

Shocked, Ardway blurted out, "Kroeber?" Kroeber started to lunge at Ardway. Gammill stepped between them.

The man-monster halted while he clenched his big fists.

Ardway's sickened face didn't hide his honest revulsion and distress.

Kroeber saw. Like he had seen over a hundred times since that night. This was a reminder of how terrible a price he had paid for his betrayal. He whipped around and slammed through the swinging doors which continued to rattle until Gammill placed his hand on the doors to stop.

Ardway stared after Kroeber, unable to speak.

Gammill coughed, "He showed up a while back. Beat to hell. Said your man Wasted did it."

Ardway's lips parted, trying to find the words. Finally his anger took hold.

"Like fire he did! Wasted ended up on top but hells bells, John, Wasted was the one that got the worst of it. I paid Kroeber his wages afterwards and he was mostly just nicked. Claudine saw him, too. So did all the men."

"I believe you," said Gammill. "But a lot of folks in town only heard Kroeber's story."

Ardway's eyes darted back and forth as he raced through his thoughts. "A face that broke..." His head snapped up at the answer. "Fendris."

"Fendris hired him on. Said he felt sorry for Kroeber. Blamed you for—" Gammill was struck with a thought. "Haben was shot. Killed right after he told you about Green getting shot." Gammill searched his thoughts. "That's when Kroeber showed up, his face all beat to hell. Spreading his stories about Wasted...while working for Fendris."

"Blazes, John! This is it. Fendris is coming for me and my men. I can feel it. And I aim to—"

"Hold on, Burt. Not tonight. We're going. You can sleep on it..." Ardway shook his head, started to protest. John nodded, no.

"And do it right. This time of night your men are liquored up, romping all over the place, probably at Nancy's or sleeping it off somewheres." Gammill stared hard at Ardway. "You gonna take on Ash and his gang all by yourself? Blazes, they're as drunk and holed up and sleeping it off as your boys."

With a sigh Ardway considered this. He shrugged while moving to the doors. "Somctimes...you make too much sense."

"You're sleeping at the jail tonight. No backtalk."

Ardway wearily shook his head in defeat. The two walked out, leaving the doors swinging back and forth.

Chapter Twenty-One:

Who the Hell is Swifty Bill Odem?

An hour later at 2 a.m. Molly's had lost most of its customers to the night. A few patrons milled about the room. Most of the staff was gone. The heavy fog of the evening's smoking had lifted, allowing a harsher yellow light. The sad intoxicated showgirl had returned but without Kenton. She sat alone, slumped against the piano. She plunked at the keys producing disconnected notes that echoed the incoherence of the hour while mumbling senseless lyrics to herself.

Wasted and the men continued their game. They stared at their cards with the same intensity but the long playing and drinking had taken its toll. Shoulders were hunched over the table, elbows holding each man up, except Wasted who sat up straight and drank his water. The others had glasses that were empty or half-full of beer. Boston poured a shot of whiskey from his bottle and tossed it back. He leaned forward and hungrily eyed the large pile of money in the middle of the table.

Worley was at his spot at the next table, nursing a beer. He watched Wasted as before but with a clear note of deep concern that pulled at his brows, crowding his cautious eyes. He flicked his gaze over to Boston and recognized potential trouble inching up by the anxious way his muscles flexed under his suit.

Six other men sat alone from each other, scattered about the room, and quietly stared into their drinks. They appeared to be proper men with decent paying jobs. Respectable men compelled to haunt a saloon alone rather than to go home until forced out.

Alice was still there, watching the game but with her eyes trained on Wasted. She set the pitchers of water and beer on Worley's table. Leaning against a chair, she recalled the evening and her surprise at seeing Wasted walk in with his friends. Wasted had bought rounds of drinks for all the players just to be hospitable and not because he was winning most of the hands. He had tipped her well. And yet he had stuck with drinking water except for two scandalous bottles of sarsaparilla and a cup of coffee. Alice had never known a cowboy that didn't drink, especially with liquor in plain sight.

And Wasted didn't cuss. Well, not in front of her. But he joked in a quiet way that the humor snuck up on you. She liked that. Wasted's dark beard and hair still needed cutting to her liking but it was much nicer for being shorter and trimmed up well than the last time she saw him. And gosh Almighty, didn't Wasted wear the best looking clothes that night that she had ever seen? At least, on a man. And most of all he didn't have any conceited airs about wearing those clothes. She listened to herself and blushed a deep crimson, covering her freckles. Alice quickly stepped over to the bar to hide it while refilling the pitchers.

She came back to the table once the red left her cheeks. Wasted was reaching for his glass and noticed it was empty. Alice appeared and bent close to refill it. Wasted watched and realized she had been here the whole evening. He smiled up at her.

"Thank you, Alice. I appreciate the kind attention."

"It was my pleasure, Wasted. Since you got all spruced up to see me."

He grinned at her flirting. Nice to have an attractive woman smile instead of spitting at him. "Aw, it was the least I could do, Alice, for my thunder pot wrangler."

Wasted tossed her a silver dollar on the table with a slight lingering look that Alice returned. He suddenly wanted to quit the card game and ask Alice to a late supper or a stroll. But the game was important. Wasted wanted to see if he could lose or win without getting too crazy. But, of course, the real test was to see if he could play and not feel any thirst for liquor. It had no pull on him so far but now he felt another kind of pull. Alice's smile.

Across the table Boston anxiously and with irritation stared at Wasted and Alice. With an edge to his voice he said, "Your call, Mister. If you can spare the time."

Wasted drew himself back from his thoughts to his cards, then to the others at the table. "My call...to drop the ball."

Worley had been holding back all night but at this he blurted out, "You always say that, Mister? I mean, at cards? Knew a man once. Said the same thing."

Wasted turned to him, surprised at the question. "Ah. Yes. I guess so. Maybe it's my lucky saying."

"I don't give a damn about your luck or your sayings. Just what your cards show!" snarled Boston, clearly annoyed with his own luck at this late hour.

Wasted stared coolly at Boston, feeling a sense of déjà vu. He'd felt that sensation often since he found out what he could do with the pistols. Why did he feel it now? He quietly said, "I'll hold."

Old Horse Face with the red hair coughed with some excitement and spread an ace of diamonds, two jacks and a six and seven of mixed colors. Turner sighed with tired disgust and tossed his cards face down. He stood up and bowed silently to the table and walked to the front doors and out of the saloon.

Boston grinned wide. He laid down two aces and two kings. Wasted made no sound or show of emotion. Boston stretched his arms wide to gather the large pile of money.

Wasted's eyes observed this and grew troubled. Alice saw and made a worried frown. Wasted gave her a little wink. She stifled a chuckle.

Wasted lay down his cards. Ace. King. Queen. Jack. All in spades. Boston's eyebrows rose in surprise. Wasted turned his last card over. A ten of spades. A royal flush. Alice's lips spread wide in a grin. Wasted caught her look of joy and gave her another wink.

Boston was not as happy. He fumed and pounded the table with his fists. "Lucky. Too damn lucky!"

Boston reached for his side pistol. Wasted reacted without thinking. One of his Colts appeared like a magician conjured it, pointed at a surprised Boston. Worley reached out and grabbed Boston by the wrist of his gun hand. Alice let out a clipped yelp.

"Don't!" exclaimed Worley in an excited whisper. "That's Swifty Bill Odem."

Boston looked down at his friend. The fear was genuine in Worley's eyes. Then he looked at Wasted's gun pointed at him. He replayed how fast it had appeared. Boston slowly holstered his gun. Worley exhaled a deep breath and let go of Boston's arm. "My pardon. Been a long night." said Boston as he returned his weapon.

Wasted nodded and slid his gun back into its holster. The large man turned and walked away, followed by Worley. Wasted stood up and looked at Alice. She suddenly remembered to breathe and let out a full inhale of air. "Ho. That sucked the spit out of me." Alice grabbed Wasted's glass and drank with a large gulp. She coughed it out in surprise, spraying the floor. "Oh. Forgot. It's water."

While walking away Boston slowed his pace. Worley tried to hurry him along, pulling at his sleeve. Boston's face grew angrier at each step. "He cheated me."

"Forget it, Boston. Swifty's too damn fast."

"Odem's dead. Over three years now."

Worley talked fast and continued to pull at Boston's arm. "That hair. And beard. Tells me Odem's been hiding. Fendris will pay to know. A lot more than you lost."

"But he stole my money!"

The little man with the large ass and small head whispered at his friend, "Better'n your life." Boston glared down at Worley and made his decision. Worley saw, his face lost its blood and went pasty white. Boston whipped around while drawing his gun.

Wasted had been watching Boston leave. He reached out and shoved Alice to the floor, knocking over his glass of water. It happened so fast that Alice was only aware of a falling glass, its water spreading about in the air. Wasted stepped in front of Alice.

Boston aimed. Wasted's two guns appeared in a blur, both fired as one. The two slugs hammered into Boston, spinning him around fast like a weather vane reversed in a storm. He faced the bar and involuntarily squeezed off a wild shot, splintering the front of the counter. The shocked bartender behind it fell over on his back, kicking to get away. From the floor Alice watched the glass shatter while the blast of Boston's gunshot rang out, confusing her for a moment thinking the bullet caught the glass.

The "respectable" drunks nursing their drinks around the room suddenly jolted to life, their heads jerking around to watch Boston stagger two paces. Boston took a feeble step to Worley, the friend who tried to warn him. His foolish death glared out to Worley from Boston's hideous eyes. He crumpled to the floor.

The late night respectable men jumped to their feet, staring in shock at Wasted. He gazed back into their ghastly faces. They broke for the swinging doors and stumbled out of the saloon.

Worley jerked about to cringe before Wasted, his pale face gripped in panic. "Don't! Please...don't kill me, Odem."

Wasted looked around the room, seeing the moment as if outside of himself. The blood pooled bright red about Boston, the wool of his green suit soaking it up and turning it dark. Wasted observed with the odd impression of a black mold clawing out from under Boston's body. His green round hat had fallen upturned on the floor, tilted at an angle showing its sweat-stained lining. Wasted thought, *Boston was as empty now as that hat.* Wasted blinked as if waking, turned and stared at Worley. "What?...What name did you call me?"

"Odem. Swifty Bill Odem. But I won't tell! Let me go, Odem," he squealed, "I'm a...nobody. You'll never see me again!"

"Odem..." Wasted whispered. The name ate at his insides, delighted to be set free. Raising his Colt pistols level to his eyes, Wasted stared from one to the other. Worley's terror was reflected in his own eyes. The guns' weight became unbearable, falling from his fingers to clatter on the floor. Worley saw and backed away like a rabbit from a snake. Seeing his chance for escape Worley turned and waddled on those short legs to flee out of the saloon doors.

Odem. The name thundered inside Wasted's head, tearing at his guts and howling like a Stygian chorus. The world spun around him showing...blood...Boston's dead body...the upturned empty hat... Odem...cards about the floor, atop the pool of blood, moving in slow circles...Odem...the Ace of Spades turns round, becoming the dark- haired woman of his dreams, whispering, "...Odem."

Wasted swayed on his feet. Alice stood up, watching him stagger. Fearing he had been shot Alice ran to Wasted, holding to him as he collapsed. The room spun around in a blur, oblivion opened and Wasted was swallowed into its spiral. Everything turned...

Black.

A flash of light appeared and disappeared again and again. Faster. Strobing in and out, forming, becoming a shape that turned into the face of—

A ragged Mexican bandit on a deserted dirt road at night. The man slashed out with a long knife that streaked silver in the moonlight. He thrust it back and forth with no finesse, only ugly power and speed. His eyes gleamed like an animal's in the dark. Hard and cruel. The point of the dagger was coming closer with each swipe.

A flare reflected off his face, followed by the loud eruption of a gun. His eyes bulged in surprise. He was flung backwards to bounce off a boulder and fall dead. Another burst of light and a—

Young slender cowboy stood holding a gun as he laughed in a dark alley. He had the drop on his unseen adversary. Confidently he waved the gun. It was too easy. His opponent moved like lightning, slapped his gun to the side. A shot rang out. The nineteen year old looked up, blinked in surprise. A cold realization seized his features. His eyes turned wide with fear. Blood poured over his lower lip as he tottered backwards and with a bright glare—

An old and dapper businessman in a top hat stood outside a big city drinking establishment. He sneered at his unseen opponent. A two-barreled derringer was whipped out from his pressed coat. A pistol struck out, crashed down on his face. The small gun fell to the ground while the white-mustached senior wobbled unsteadily. He regained his balance and defiantly looked up with dark blood gushing from his nose. A pistol blast tore into his face. His top hat flipped off from the head's recoil. The gun's vivid exhaust erupted in a show of flame—

A barn door exploded into pieces. In stepped a hulking ex-buffalo hunter turned bounty hunter in a coat of shaggy skins along with a double-barreled shotgun trailing smoke. A door opened behind him. Two pistols fired four times out of the darkness, hammering slugs into the giant's wide back. Grunting in rage the man turned and tried to raise his shotgun. He weakly fell to his knees. Boom! He was twisted around by a pistol blast, a hole between his wide dying eyes sprouted a red leak that flooded down his cheeks. Another gunshot to the back of his head kicked him forward before its burst of flame whited out the moment, fading into—

—A darkness that was all-consuming. Shadows moved against a growing light defining shapes that became—

A man and woman held to each other, kissing as black silhouettes. Deep feelings shared in a parlor, they twisted about in their embraces, hungry for the other's touch and the feelings it invoked. There was an urgency to their loving signaling a shortness of time. More luminence drew back the shadows revealing a ravishing beauty of a woman with coal-black hair. She pulled away. The man had sharp handsome Scandinavian features and reluctantly let her go. Their hands reached out to the other while parting. The man made his way to the door. He turned to give his lover a parting glance then walked out of the door.

One gunshot shattered the quiet calm. The lady turned to the door in alarm. Two more shots thundered. The door slowly opened with her man backing slowly through it. He rotated on his feet and stared down. Blood gushed out of the three holes in his chest. He managed to gape up at his darling, eyes wide in panic. He gave a wet, garbled cough and plunged dead to the floor. The woman bent down toward him shaking in panic, trying to reject this horror.

A younger and clean-shaven Wasted stepped through the door, his guns drawn, smoke trailing from the barrels. He was dressed in fine tailored clothes, a man of means. He stared down at the dead body, his face a mask of betrayal and desolation. The beautiful woman stood up, shoulders back, stared at him in defiance and anger. Wasted's features twisted with his fury. He lifted the pistols to point at her face.

Shots blasted from outside. Wasted was hit in the shoulder and his side. As he turned another shot glazed his forehead. He was spun back to stare into the woman's face. Her lovely features changed into a grinning harpy. She threw back her head and laughed wildly at Wasted. Another shot splintered the door frame. Spurred into action, Wasted spun about and returned fire. With a glance of rage at the woman Wasted held to his wounds and continued shooting as he staggered out to face his attackers.

The woman crossed to the door to watch. Out in the darkness guns exploded long flames at each other, the men hidden in the darkness. Gradually the loud shooting and images faded.

Wasted's eyelids fluttered, his eyes opened to stare about a small room. He was lying on a bed. The raven-haired woman of his nightmares rose up from a chair and walked over. She bent down to gaze at him. Wasted strained to see. It wasn't his dream, it was Alice. She held a cloth and reached over to press it against his face. Attentively she dabbed at the sweat beaded about his temples and Wasted realized he felt a strange sensation.

He felt...safe.

Chapter Twenty-Two:

Esther, Alice and Secret Names

Alice observed his confusion and smiled, "Wasted. This is my room. Mister Ardway heard about what happened and had you carried here. So no one knows where you are."

Wasted studied her face. "You... You're Alice."

She looked closely at him, weighing her next words. With a sigh and an embarrassed smile she said, "Alice....is my saloon name. I don't give out my real name to customers." She paused for a moment. "It's...Esther."

Wasted took this information in, wondering why she was telling him this. "I'm a customer."

"Ha! What a customer. Never met a cowboy that didn't drink. You're so...different. So..." Esther dropped her eyes, feeling a blush warming her face. "I don't figure you as a customer. Least, not like the others. I've never told a man my real name since I got here and started work in..."

Wasted was touched. "...In a saloon. Esther. It's a nice name. Fits you. Wish I knew my real—" Wasted tensed up, his face tightened over a thought. "I shot a man." He remembered, "I...killed him."

Esther leaned in, "He pulled a gun. Could have killed me while trying to kill you. You shoved me out of the way. Thanks."

Wasted closed his eyes as he replayed it in his mind.

"So you passed out after that. Ardway got you here. Wasted... You...had fits. Nightmares."

He turned away in frustration. "I kill people in my dreams, Esther. Over and over. Like that man in Molly's. I have guns and... People try to kill me. But I always kill them first. Then, when I wake up...that's when I feel...afraid."

Esther drew back, surprised. "Afraid? You? Afraid of what?"

Wasted stared out of the corner of his eyes at her. "Me. Of who...I really am. Inside."

Esther shrugged this off. "Shush. Everybody that knows you says you're a fine and good man. I...I been asking around."

Wasted looked back, unconvinced. Esther reached over and lifted his head up. She plumped his pillow with her other hand. Gently she lay his head back down. She lightly stroked his hair that hung over his forehead. "Mister Ardway said to rest. He wants you over early to the hotel for breakfast. Sleep. You can't do anything but sleep now. I'll wake you." With both hands Esther's fingers tenderly caressed Wasted's temples. His tension loosened and he relaxed. After a few moments his eyes closed.

"I am tired. And that feels...well, I'm not afraid now." Wasted's breathing slowed. "You're...very sweet...Esther." His voice became softer. "Esther...I like that..." Wasted drifted away to sleep.

Esther stared closely at Wasted's face and moved her head to view it at different angles. She carefully raised a strand of the long black hair and let it drop. Lifting up his beard carefully in her hands, she frowned at finding the small scars on his neck. Something had gripped his throat with what looked like...sharp long teeth. Esther gently lowered the beard back.

As she stood and watched Wasted sleep, a pensive expression worked its way across her face. She walked over to her dresser and opened the top drawer and dug through her things there. Her hands searched, coming up with a brush and a comb. She tossed these aside and then a hair pin and a clip. Her face lit up when she found what she wanted. Esther turned back to stare at Wasted. In her eyes she was weighing a question about how to proceed. Hours later in the early morning Esther watched the pale light take hold and stream through a window into her room. It was growing brighter as she stretched her arms wide while yawning. Gripped in one hand was a pair of scissors.

She stood and continued moving her body to pull at her taut muscles from sitting in the rocking chair for the last few hours. Esther walked to the bed. She tugged at the toe of Wasted's boot and spoke softly. "Wasted. Wake up." He turned over to face her. Breathing in deeply he opened his eyes to signal he was awake.

"You can wash your face," Esther nodded to the corner, "at the basin on my dresser."

Wasted stood up, arched his back and twisted his torso. With a yawn he walked over to the dresser while Esther sat on the bed and watched. A hint of anticipation was reflected in her eyes.

Wasted bent over the basin and cupped water in his hands and splashed it over his face. He rubbed the sleep from his eyes and picked up a towel on the dresser to dry with. When he lowered the towel to look in the mirror he was startled to see an unknown man staring back at him. He drew back then moved his face in close to study his reflection. His beard and long hair were gone, shorn away by Esther. His face had a slight stubble and the neck was bare. The pink scars from the wolf's teeth were there.

A fine handsome face stared back at Wasted as he searched its features, trying to recall this person.

"I hope you're not angry. I thought it might help you to remember. 'Sides, I was curious..." She lowered her head, hiding her blushing.

Wasted stared at every detail like looking at an unknown map, studying the features of this stranger in the mirror. "I'm not angry. I...I guess my beard and long hair was...kinda like your saloon name. It hid me. Now I've got to show who I am...to God and everybody."

Esther spoke up, "That man. Worley. He called you...Swifty Bill Odem. Mean anything?"

Wasted continued to look at his reflection for some hint or memory. "No. Except he was sure I'd kill him as easy as I'd spit over it. 'Cause it was important. Like secret important."

Esther's face clouded up wrestling with this, trying to make it work out okay. "Well, I don't believe you're this Odem. Least...not anymore."

Wasted stared deep into the eyes looking back at him in the mirror. He wondered if he was this Odem. It sure scared the hell out of Worley after he drew and shot Boston twice like it was as natural as breathing. So this Odem was fast with a pistol. A gunman for hire? Too many questions, he'd have to figure it out after he got back to the ranch.

He turned away from the mirror and picked up his hat. Wasted walked over to look out the window. The street was empty in the early morning. The sun shone on his face, he lifted it up with eyes closed enjoying the warmth without a beard and long hair. Wasted turned to regard Esther. She looked up with a smile that warmed him even more than the sunlight. "Esther. You've been so kind. I...I hope I can pay you back...soon. Thank you, Esther." She smiled faintly. He wanted to say more but knew he was expected over at the hotel. Wasted started to leave when he blurted out, "We share a confidence. Secret names..." He rubbed the stubble on his chin, "Whoever I am, I... Well, I hope it's as fine a person as you."

Esther dropped her eyes, charmed at this unexpected compliment. When she looked up again Wasted was gone.

Esther jumped up and rushed to the open door. She watched Wasted walk down the hall and disappear around the corner to the stairs. Esther backed up and closed the door. Passing the mirror she caught her expression and realized she hadn't seen such excitement to her eyes in a long time. Her brow knitted up suddenly, remembering the death of Boston and how frightened that Worley fella was. Who the hell was this Swifty Bill Odem?

Esther was gripped by an uneasiness, an apprehension for Wasted's safety and to be honest, for herself.

Chapter Twenty-Three:

Pettigrew's Coffee

———————————

Preoccupied with his thoughts, Wasted walked down the Spirits Bend main street toward the Ardway Hotel. He noticed it was quiet and glanced up to check his progress. Wasted drew himself up and slowed to a stop. He glanced up and down the street with a growing alarm. Wasted started walking again, picking up his gait, trying not to run to the hotel for drawing attention.

At the Ardway Hotel, Wasted cautiously entered its front door. He scanned about the lobby. There were no locals sitting and talking after breakfast, no hotel guests who had checked out and were waiting with luggage for a stage or train. He looked to the empty front desk. A frown pulled at the corners of his lips. His eyes darted about as he continued to walk toward the "Sticks" dining area.

He entered through the two large oak doors thinking it was strange they should be closed. Glancing around the room he saw Ardway and a tired Bailey slumped in a chair at a table in the back. There were no other customers. He walked to them past dark-stained oak tables covered with white dining cloths, stopping at their table. Bailey yawned and gave him the once-over. With a shock, he jumped up and slapped Wasted on the back. "Good Lord, Mister Ardway. Look! It's Wasted! Peeled like an onion."

Ardway's face dropped in shock as Wasted sat down. He stared sideways at Wasted and then broke out with a grin. "Hell. I almost shot you for a Fendris man."

"Pleased to see you, too," said Wasted.

"How you feeling?"

Wasted shrugged. "I feel...strange and out of sorts, I guess. Still getting used to seeing my new face. And figuring out other things."

Bailey stared, unsure how to take Wasted's shearing. "Well, you don't look nothing like you used to. I hear your voice but...your face! You should stop shaving for a year, I might recognize you."

Wasted shot him a sarcastic look. "Listen, you curly wolf. I'll take your razor to yo—"

Bailey perked up, turned to Ardway. "Yep! It's Wasted."

Wasted gave a troubled sigh, "Yeah..." He looked to Ardway. "That killing last night. There was another man. Worley. Spoke of a...Swifty Bill Odem."

Ardway's shocked face drew back like it was punched. Recovering Ardway spat out,

"Odem is dead! Shot over a whore."

Wasted wasn't expecting that reaction from Ardway. He lowered his voice to the men. "Maybe. I noticed a few off-kilter things coming over here. Nobody was out sweeping or opening up on the street. On a Saturday. Out front the desk is empty. And there's no people in the lobby."

Bailey wearily reached over for the coffee pot and poured himself a cup. "Tarnation, you are too much for me this morning. I was at Nancy's with Lucy all night. I need some of Mrs. Pettigrew's coffee to make some sense here." Smelling the brew he grinned and drank. Bailey's face blanched, brought his hand up too late as coffee spewed out over the floor. Bailey coughed, "That coffee is... full of salt!"

Ardway's eyes darted to the cup. He took it from Bailey, drank and spat it out quick. His face was grave, almost white as he whispered. "Mrs. Pettigrew don't queer her coffee. 'Cept for a reason." His eyes roamed the empty room. "Boys. We're in a bag of nails." The men shifted in their seats, expecting an attack any moment from how solemn Ardway appeared. He spoke low and carefully. "Keep talking. Make like everything's fine. But pull your guns under the table and be ready." He stood up and stepped to a window by the table. Silently raising it open he lifted a boot over the sill and stepped out onto the back stairs. "I'm going to the kitchen to check on Pettigrew." Ardway's face shored itself up for the task. "Pray, boys. That I ain't too late."

Bailey looked around, his eyes wide and anxious. He spoke quietly, more to himself, "Oh. I'm praying..."

Ardway slipped away down the stairs. He was pressing lightly on each step, careful not to make a sound. He jumped a railing to land quietly on the back service porch so he wouldn't be seen out a back window. He pulled his guns, and quietly slid up the wall to the window. Peering in Ardway saw two rough-looking men holding guns on the frightened staff and Pettigrew. Another gunman had his ear pressed to the dining room door, listening.

Inside the dining room Wasted and Bailey waited nervously at their table. Under its top Wasted had his two guns' chambers out and hastily emptied the two spent shells that killed Boston. He added two bullets and quietly clicked the chambers back. Bailey perked up at Wasted's nod. He spoke loudly, "Boy, this coffee's mighty fine." Bailey gasped lower to Wasted, "Hell's bells, this wait...is killing me."

Glancing around Wasted whispered, "Shut your trap about killing. You're the one that's always right, remember?" Bailey's eyes widened in chagrin at the thought.

Outside the hotel five grim-faced men with dark slits for eyes and wearing long gray work coats strode fast, watching doors and alleys for any hint of threat. The men's efficient manner with its practiced defensive strategies propelled them quickly down the street toward the hotel. Each man's head was shaved pale white on the sides in stark contrast to their tanned leather faces and necks. It was a common ritual for up-close intimidation, telling folks, clear the way, bad hosses coming.

The first one to the entrance sported a thick handlebar mustache under sharp eyes that checked out the hotel lobby. Seeing no one he nodded to the others. They entered the hotel with the last member watching the street as he backed in. He looked about twenty-eight years old. His face was unsmiling but his eyes gave off a wild gleam.

He held his pistols straight up and tight against his chest. Backing through the entrance, he kicked the doors shut behind him.

In the lobby each man quickly went about securing the surroundings. One checked the hallway, another the stairs, two on the doors. Satisfied they were safe and clear the men opened up their coats and withdrew their weapons. Three carried twin .44 Smith & Wesson Model 3 revolvers in holsters, military issue. The other two men carried the same but with double barrel, ten gauge Moore shotguns with barrels sawed off to eighteen inches. These were "coach guns" normally used for killing highwaymen on the roads in close battle. This was an assassination squad. Fendris wasn't messing around.

One man had a deep scar from his lip to his ear. The other had a red patch over his left eye with an eyeball painted in white on it. A large pale blue orb, the iris, stared out with a Día de Muertos skull in its center. These two men were the oldest at forty-five years and were also the largest, built like old bulls. Each man inspected his guns in a quick once-over. The clicking off of safeties and hammers cocked ended the ritual of securing the area of engagement and left only the battle. They moved to the dining room doors and stood a foot away. Each man stared beyond the closed doors into the room, waiting for a signal. Eyepatch leaned in to listen to someone talking loudly about how hungry he was and how good the coffee tasted. His one eye tossed a murderous wink to the other men.

Out back on the porch Ardway kicked in the door to the kitchen, his guns spitting flames behind streaking bullets. Two men wheeled toward Ardway only to be slammed backwards as the slugs ripped through their bodies. Their hands reflexively pulled the triggers of the guns. Wild shots careened about the kitchen as each man expired painfully.

In the confusion the cook, two waiters and two busboys instantly conformed their bodies into whatever nook or cranny the kitchen allowed for cover.

The man at the door turned and instinctively clutched Pettigrew to him. He pulled a pistol, jabbing it into her ribs. Ardway had both pistols on the man from eight feet away. The man shouted, "Drop it! Or I'll kill her!" Ardway pointed one pistol up and nodded but kept his other on the gunman's head to warn that he was not giving up just yet.

In the hall outside the dining room the paid killers heard the pistol shots. They kicked open the doors and rushed inside with their guns pointed out and itching to shoot anything that moved. Each looked around in confusion. Their hard faces went slack. What greeted them was an empty dining room filled with tables covered in long white tablecloths. There was no sign of Ardway or his men.

On the floor Wasted and Bailey lay silently, four tables apart, guns pointed ahead at the mercenaries. The white tablecloths hung down two feet above the floor from each table about the room. Wasted and Bailey couldn't be seen by anyone standing at a distance and looking down. Across the room the killers stood with their boots and legs in clear view from below the white cloths. Wasted and Bailey raised guns up to point at their targets. They exchanged an affirmative glance and Wasted fired. Bailey let go, too. The room thundered with the sounds of guns blasting.

The killers' legs were turned into bloody ruins from the volley of slugs. The men collapsed to the floor growling and cursing in pain. But these ex-military had been shot and survived ambushes before, being too damn mean to give in. Wounded and grunting in pain the bastards kept hold of their guns and swung them around to point at Wasted and Bailey.

The sounds of the ferocious battle out in the dining room caused Ardway and the gunman to shift their eyeballs in that direction. The frightened staff crew sweated while cowering behind the supplies and stoves. Pettigrew was squeezed tight to the gunman, the gun barrel poking her ribs. Her desperate eyes locked on Ardway's. She gave him a repeated glance over to the stove.

On the stove in a large skillet several pieces of thick bacon were frying in boiling grease. Next to it in other skillets eggs flapped about in hot lard. Grits simmered in a big pot. The smell of rising biscuits floated from an oven. Ardway saw the skillet of sliced pork bubbling in the brown grease. His eyes flicked two times to the skillet and back at Pettigrew. She closed her eyes and blinked back twice slowly.

The gunman was growing more unhinged with Ardway, screaming, "Dammit, Ardway! Toss them guns!" Ardway kept the one gun held up high and one pointed on the gunman. He slowly stepped away from the stove. The man reacted by clenching Pettigrew tighter and shoving her flat against the stove to keep a better view on Ardway, "I ain't telling you again!"

Ardway nodded to the gunman. "Okay!...Okay. I'm setting one down." He brought the gun down slowly from over his head. He held it out and over a table. Pettigrew stared at the skillet and prepared herself. Carefully her hand touched on a padded cloth by the skillet. Ardway placed the gun down on the table with his hand on it.

Pettigrew understood. She sucked in a deep breath, seized the skillet's hot handle with the hand pad. Bringing her other hand around instantly she grabbed hold of the handle with both hands and heaved the skillet up with all her strength over her shoulder.

Boiling hot grease and frying bacon rained down directly over the gunman's head and face. The gunman shrieked as his face became a raw crimson mask, its flesh blistered and popped open with blood and milky fluid running in streaks under the scalding grease. His hands and body quaked in convulsions, the guns tumbling from his nerveless fingers.

Ardway leapt over to Pettigrew as the man sank yowling to the floor. For a second Ardway stood frozen with his gun pointed at this dreadful face that wasn't a face. The deformed mouth was gasping open and shut like a fish tossed on a deck. Mewling sounds sputtered from it like some newborn abomination. Suddenly the man's head bent up with eyes boiled dull and white with the shock of realizing he was blind. With mangled lips he screamed gibberish, unable to understand or articulate the what and why of his unimaginable pain.

Clasping her hand over her mouth Mrs. Pettigrew gave a muffled squeal then reached over and placed her other hand over Ardway's finger and pulled the trigger. The gun roared, its bullet exploded a black hole between the man's eyes and sprayed the back of his skull and brains over the floor and against the far wall. His body was flung next to the German cook nicknamed "Fritz" who was curled into a tight ball in the corner. Fritz shrieked "Mutter Gottes!" like his guts were coming out. He climbed over a table backwards to run out the back door.

Ardway jerked his head around to Mrs. Pettigrew. They stared with horrified relief for a brief moment before sagging into the other's arms.

Back in the dining room the crippled professional killers fired at Wasted and Bailey from the floor where they had fallen. But the two friends were up, leaping fast onto chairs as the murderers' gunfire blasted around them. The two landed on the top of the tables and kept moving. Wasted fired at the downed executioners through the tables. Bailey joined him, both jumping from table to table to make themselves hard targets. Their bullets violently punctured the tables with wide ragged holes, streaking down at the professional killers whose own bullets tore up through the tabletops, barely missing them.

Carnage played a deadly calliope of disjointed gun blasts combined with bullets hurtling throughout the room. The relentless ex-soldiers were trapped as a showering of hot metal hurled into the area around them. A bullet exploded the skull and scattered the brains of the mustached leader in a bloody mosaic over a rug. The others rolled and desperately tried to avoid the lead missiles peppering their space, their guns firing blindly through the tables.

Wasted sprung from one table to another, his guns blasting down at the killers by following their shots that sheared up through the tabletops. Bullets smashed into the restaurant's roof, shattering it open, raining down paint chips and wood fragments. Dust and blue gun smoke clouded the room while sunlight streamed from windows in chalky shafts of white. Tablecloths were tossed up resembling the milky crests of ocean waves as bullets ripped through them. The cloths sank eerily back onto the tables like the ghosts of dead victims descending, giving last witness to the killers' violence.

Bailey fired wildly and danced over the tables, caught up in the frenzy. Still the bullets streaked up around him. The wounded killers on the floor had fought for decades while pissing at death. To hell with the job and to hell with the money, all that mattered now was surviving by being more vicious and mean. Wasted understood the mercenaries and what came next. There was only one way for this ungodly slaughter to end without Bailey or him dying. Without a thought he dove to the floor between the last two manic killers. Before one bastard with a shotgun could roll over to shoot, Wasted fired first, blasting his heart into Hades. The other one with the red eyepatch turned fast. Reacting by instinct, he jerked himself around to point his shotgun at Wasted. He clicked the hammer back as Wasted tried to get his pistol around. A thunderous blast shook the floor under the tables.

Wasted slowly opened his eyes. The killer's eyepatch was gone, replaced by a big red hole in the man's skull. He toppled over on his cocked shotgun revealing Bailey, bent over low, holding his smoking pistol with a feral expression on his face. Wasted wearily smiled his thanks. Bailey sagged to the floor, blowing out a deep sigh of relief.

They slowly rose to their feet and walked around with guns pointed while they cautiously kicked at the bodies. The killers were deader than Lincoln.

Ardway dashed out of the kitchen with both guns pointed out. Upon seeing Wasted and Bailey he lowered and holstered his pistols. He surveyed the bodies strewn about in the room and its destruction.

"Hell's bells, boys! You didn't waste no lead with this dead meat." Ardway nodded to the kitchen. "That was Fendris's men back there." He looked over the shot-up corpses on the floor. "Never see these here busters before."

Bailey spoke up, "Blazes, they was loaded for bear and tough as iron. They kept shooting at us while they was shot up awful bad. And they never said one damn word or squawked out."

Ardway took off his hat and swatted his leg while staring at one of the men's boots. "Hired killers. Ex-military from those wide-lipped, black boots."

Wasted looked around at the other bodies and nodded in agreement. "Probably needed killing years ago."

Out of the kitchen Mrs. Pettigrew rolled a food cart toward the men. She stopped to show plates of eggs, fried ham and biscuits. She raised a pot and poured cups of coffee while holding a pistol. She handed a cup to Ardway. "Mrs. Pettigrew, this ain't no time—"

"Eat! Look around, Burton Ardway." A severe-faced Pettigrew waved her pistol around the room's shambles and dead men. "This is not over. And Fendris will be hellbent to finish it fast. Now eat. You're in for the fight of your lives. If you live, you'll thank me later. Besides, this food'll just go to waste if you don't eat it. I'm not getting any business today." Pettigrew walked back. At the kitchen door she turned to see Ardway staring after her. "Burton, don't make me tell you twice." Pettigrew disappeared through the door.

Bailey grabbed a plate of food, "Hell, I'm starved!" He began wolfing down the food. Wasted and Ardway shrugged and joined in.

"She's right. As always, dammit," grunted Ardway, "Fendris ain't stopping until I'm dead."

Wasted chewed at a biscuit and ham. "Poking at you is over. Fendris was set off hearing you got a gun man named Odem and..."

"Odem? I told you he's..." A thought hit Ardway, "Dang my melt!" His eyes widened, "Fendris wouldn't start nothing without a man good with a gun. John mentioned this Jurant."

Wasted spoke up, "The one that came out to the ranch?"

Bailey looked up as he chewed a mouthful of food, "I heard of a Jurant out of New Orleans here in town. Killed a lot of men down there."

Ardway's face turned stricken while thinking of Jurant at his home. He leaned in, squinted in thought at his two men. "We need help from the ranch. Wilson and all the men." He regarded Wasted and Bailey and worried over his next thought. "You two. Find our boys here in town. Get them to the livery stable in an hour or sooner. Bring ammunition. Guns. Don't be polite. Just get it."

He turned and charged for the kitchen. Ardway looked over his shoulder and called out as he opened the entry. "I'll see about my friends in town. Stay off the streets. Keep your eyes peeled extra for Fendris's men." Turning, Ardway disappeared out the door.

Wasted finished a long drink of coffee and set down the cup. He started to follow after Ardway when Bailey reached out and pulled at his arm. Wasted turned to Bailey's confused expression. "Aaah... who's this here fella, Odem?"

Wasted sighed deep to himself, wishing he had never heard that name. He flashed on being a drunk again, with no feeling or thoughts of dying, except for that next drink. Wasted motioned for Bailey to follow him. "Let's get the boys. Tell you about Odem on the way."

Chapter Twenty-Four:

We're in a Bad Box, Fellas

A hulking black bear stood on its hind legs, its jaws open and fiercely exposing its large yellow teeth beneath angry eyes. It stared across Fendris's large office on the second floor in his feed store. The stuffed animal glowered across the room which had more than a passing resemblance to Ardway's study but assembled with no cultured woman's appreciation for style or warmth. The walls had been constructed with roughhewn logs. There was a big rock-laid hearth, blackened from ash and smoke. Native American weapons of primitive axes, arrows and knives lined the wall on each side. Two war lances were crossed with some considered respect above the fireplace. Hanging from both spears were gruesome reminders of Spirit Bend's past: Indian and settlers' scalps showing hair of different colors and the dried ragged edges of grey dead skin.

Fendris stood with his back to this while looking out a large single paned window from his second floor. He was dressed in a resplendent dark blue wool suit from New Orleans that was cut with a French flair at the folded cuffs and the pleated pants had brass buttons down a dark stripe on the sides. His long thick hair was brushed back to fall across his back. His two Indian ponytails were braided and tied off at the ends with a slender blue ribbon matched to the suit. Each had an ornate brass button like the ones on the pants. The sunlight from outside gave the clean trim suit a cerulean glow like a piece of the blue sky. Fendris's face was shaved and his mustache and goatee trimmed to perfection against the deep-tanned brown of his skin. This look, and the moment, had the air of a coronation to it as Fendris stared down the far street toward the Ardway Livery Stable. His face was drawn tightly, showing all its lines like wires stretched across and hooked to his pursed lips.

The deadly men Fendris had hired at a great sum of money to kill Ardway had gone into the hotel, but they had not come out. As if to accommodate his mood immense dark clouds had started to gather beyond the town's horizon. A door opened behind him and Fendris turned to it.

Kroeber stepped inside and stood silently. He waited to gauge Fendris's disposition while Fendris instantly guessed as to why Kroeber was not speaking. Fendris let out an angry sigh, looked at the floor in disgust. "My hired men failed to kill Ardway and Odem. And Jurant's not back yet," said Fendris.

"How did you know—"

Fendris cut him off sharply, "Shut." Kroeber closed his mouth. "Things...just keep getting messy." A thought. "Like you, Kroeber." Fendris crossed over to stare up at a large crudely-painted canvas with dull greens, browns and other colors behind his desk. It was of himself standing on a hill overlooking his ranch. There were flatly-rendered depictions of men and horses and cattle. Fendris was in ragged clothes as he first came to Spirits Bed. As "primitive" as the artist was that produced the painting, he captured something in Fendris's eyes. There was a fierce hunger to them. Like the eyes that gazed upon the image now.

Fendris spoke quietly to the rendering of himself in the painting. "It was supposed to be...so simple. Aggravate...Goad...Anger. Then kill Ardway like it was self-defense." He remembered on the moment he might have done that. "I could have ended it that day at the train station. But my hangover made me hesitate. No. That's not right." Fendris sighed at the thought. "It was that silly damn drunk. And he's still spoiling it." Fendris looked over at Kroeber. "He even ruined you. That...filthy tramp. That worthless drunk...turned out to be...Odem. Back from the dead like..." The rancher dryly chuckled to himself, "...like in the Bible."

Kroeber bristled under Fendris's insult. "He's just one man. Got lucky with—"

Fendris's anger exploded loudly, "SHUT!..." He calmed himself with an effort, "...your broken mouth. Hell. He beat you when he was still a sick drunk." Kroeber looked away. Fendris strode quickly over and roughly seized Kroeber by the jaw to force the tall man to look down into his eyes. "Worley said Odem shot Boston so fast that Worley shit himself. Others seen it. Said...it was like...greased lightning. Magic..." Fendris pointed his chin in the direction of the hotel. "Those men I sent to the hotel. Was powerful hard men." He glanced at the ceiling. "They lasted as long as taking a piss."

Fendris raised his hands up in frustration at Kroeber. Suddenly an idea came. He jabbed his index finger into a scab on Kroeber's face, releasing a stream of blood. Kroeber flinched as Fendris stared at the red liquid flowing down his finger. "Well. Least we got the town closed up with Ardway's men. Burton's in a tight spot but shit..." He held the bloody finger up to Kroeber's mouth. "So are we. He won't go down easy. I'll have to finish this..." Fendris lowered his bloody finger to his own lips and gave Kroeber a mocking grin. "...ugly." Fendris licked Kroeber's blood off his finger and smacked his lips. He turned his back and walked over to stare out the window at the gathering clouds.

Kroeber's angry and grotesque face glared at Fendris as his wound drained red in a broken trail over its scars and stitches.

Wasted treaded cautiously through the shadows cast from the sheds and tarp roofs in the back alleys of Spirits Bend. The wind had picked up with the dark clouds crowding the sky. Strange sounds and rustlings came out of corners and from windows. Footsteps creaked over boards, approaching from behind a shack he leaned against. Wasted whipped out a pistol and waited. Esther stepped out past him without seeing Wasted. He holstered his gun and called out. "Esther! What are you doing here and out of your room?"

Esther turned around, surprised and relieved to see Wasted. "Been lookin' for your boys that Fendris ain't got locked up. Mister Ardway said to send 'em to the livery."

Wasted's voice turned angry. "But what if Fendris found out what you was doing? He'd kill you. Get home, now!"

Esther straightened her back. Her eyes squinted hard at Wasted. "Don't tell me what to do. I know the girls that them boys are with and where they are hiding." She softened. "'Sides, Fendris's bunch are looking for them and for you particularly. You forget. I'm just a... just a no-account saloon gal. They all think women like us ain't got the brains God gave a goose and cry over courting flowers." Esther turned from Wasted and looked about the alley in frustration. Wasted stared at her back as both let their anger subside. Esther turned to look over her shoulder at Wasted. They each glanced a little softer at the other.

Wasted sighed and spoke up. "Ain't we a pair..." Esther smiled at this but Wasted wasn't having it. "Now," he continued, "if you don't go back right now, I'm walking you back if I have to throw you over my shoulder."

"Good Lord! That'd get us both killed! And besides, what makes you think you could do it, Mister Wasted?" She stretched the "Mister" out to mock him like the boys did.

Wasted took hold of her arm. Esther pulled away to rush a few steps ahead. She turned to Wasted and was about to say something. She relented and her angry expression folded in to become one of sadness. Carefully Esther lowered her voice. "Wasted. Last night. You said..." Wasted attempted to speak before Esther said, "Who's Ruby?"

Wasted's face fell into itself, so shocked to hear that name spoken by Esther and that he had spoken it in his sleep. He flashed in anger at Esther. "She's dead. Like you if you don't git!" He walked quickly to her, ready to haul her back to her room. Esther jumped and ran a few yards ahead of Wasted. She paused at the corner of a building. Her lip was drawn up, irritably, but she held it shut. Wasted was already walking away, his pistol held up in one hand for any more surprises. He disappeared into the shadows of the back alley.

Esther let out a breath, frustrated and disappointed with herself in the moment. Why did she make Wasted angry? He had enough on his mind without worrying about her. Esther had already combed the town for Ardway's men anyway. She hung on that thought. Alright, she thought, she'd march back to her little room and sit alone and worry about him and Mister Ardway and the boys. But especially about Wasted. Her shoulders sagged as Esther shook her head.

Esther walked in the other direction down the gloomy alley while lost in her thoughts. The backstreet had grown darker and the wind was picking up. Esther lifted her eyes at the large storm clouds circling above and moving in fast. It was going to rain in buckets. Dammit, that's all they needed with this Fendris mess. A cold breeze whipped her hair up and away from her neck, making her uneasy. Esther walked faster. She thought she heard footsteps and turned to it. "Wasted...?"

A shadow loomed over the expanded whites of Esther's shocked eyes. The stitched horror of Kroeber reached down with his massive hands toward her as she screamed.

Kroeber's great paw closed over her mouth. Her muffled shriek was lost among the din of the debris and leaves swirling on the winds of the oncoming storm.

~

A shifting penumbra rolled over the hills and under the clouds moving toward Spirits Bend. Lightning streaked the sky and lit up these great gray masses tumbling against and over each other. The vague play of distant thunder grew closer, becoming a drumbeat counting down to the great rain that was approaching. The louder it sounded the darker the world turned. It was too late to ride ahead of the storm. All you could do was seek shelter and hope for the best.

Wasted peered out an alley into the street toward the livery stable. It had been built on a large mound of land fifteen feet higher than the street. Out back ran a small creek that joined another tributary that led to the great Alasga River. He saw that two Fendris men with rifles had been set up on the street to look for Ardway's crew going to the livery. They sat watching behind stacked wooden crates. The older one, about thirty years old, faced toward the stable and the other, barely sixteen, stared off at the opposite end of the street towards Fendris's store. They were talking to each other while sitting comfortably on some boxes. Things were quiet and each was relaxed despite their job. But why not? You'd be a fool to get mixed up with Ardway given what Fendris had lined up for him. Wasted weighed going around to the creek and coming up the back way. He shook his head at the thought and walked quietly toward the men. The youngster who faced him stood up as he approached and the man turned to see. Wasted was holding up his arms and smiling as he kept coming. "Hey!" he called to the men. "Something going on at the livery?"

Both men were up and staring hard at Wasted. The kid spoke up. "It's closed. You're supposed to be inside. Didn't you hear?"

Wasted kept walking and pointed at the stable. "But my horse is in there. I got to saddle up and skedaddle back home."

The two men had the rifles up but not aimed at Wasted. He slowed amiably up to them. The older man tensed up his face with a sour expression. "Shut up! Now go somewhere far from here and play with yourself until ya go blind. I ain't gon—" With a blur Wasted pulled his gun and slugged the top of the man's skull, knocking off his hat and with it his consciousness. The boy stood with his mouth gaped open. Wasted grabbed the boy's rifle away from his hands and deftly popped him in the chin with the stock. His lights went out as the boy collapsed onto the boardwalk. Wasted picked up the rifles along with two boxes of cartridges set on a box and continued walking over to the stable with no hurry, as casually as if he was sauntering from out of the saloon.

Inside the stable Bailey opened the office door for Wasted with a smug grin. Wasted walked in and looked around. The stable's walls had been stacked up with feed bags and wood boxes of goods, ready for trouble. He noticed a worried Tom, who gestured with his hands held out to say *what the hell kind of mess are we in?* Wasted handed him the rifles and bullets. "Here, Tom. This should make you feel better."

Bailey shook his head at the men. "We sneak around and come in the back. Wasted walks in the front door like he's at a church social and hands out Fendris rifles." The five ranch hands around the room laughed nervously while cautiously squinting out at the street through the openings between their barricades. Jordie gave Wasted a weak smile and a small wave. Wasted nodded at him while trying to show some assurance. Five men. And Bailey. He didn't like the odds.

Ardway walked in from the adjourning stables. He was wearing his old red leather slicker with a ruddy whiskey shine to his cheeks.

He stared at the small group and clapped his arms in defeat to his sides. "Looks like this is all we got, boys. Sent Ben out to the ranch... but that'll be ten hours before anyone comes."

The men looked to Wasted. He studied their troubled faces and said, "We got an hour before they come. Or less."

A loud pounding on the locked back door turned everyone to it. Jordie went to check. A few seconds later Gammill rushed in dressed in a long coat for the coming rain. He took his hat off and wiped the sweat from his face as he looked around. Gammill's face couldn't hide the disappointment. "This all?" He let out a deep breath and thought. "Well, we better hightail it out the back and follow the creek."

The room grew quiet. The men looked to Ardway. Wasted studied him closely. Ardway wore a game face but there was a desperation in his voice. "Where to, John? Fendris probably has men staked out along the creek to pick us off."

Gammill combed his fingers through his graying hair and tried to think. "We're in a bad box, fellas." He shrugged with Gammill's big shoulders sagging in resignation. "Let's pray on it."

Ardway let out a bitter laugh to the ceiling. "Pray? Ha! God's lit out on us here!" He turned to his men, his eyes shiny and red. "You men. Any of you want to leave, I...Go! Get out now."

They stared at each other in confusion. Ardway said to run? Tom's face turned red with anger. He barked to the room but more to Ardway. "No one's leaving, Mister Ardway. We're sticking. Fendris will have hell getting at us here. We've got lots of water. And jerky to eat. They'll have to cross a wide area and we're on the high ground. We just got to last until the ranch boys get here." Ardway's nervous eyes looked away. He was at a loss to speak.

Gammill gauged the room. "Let's bow our heads and—"

"No!" yelled Ardway. "I'm not done having my say." He stared wildly around the room at his men. He searched their faces closely. They waited and watched. Ardway was wrestling with something deep inside that wanted out. His voice was strained and almost hysterical. "I've tried to live my life, my whole life, honest. And upright. But..." He sucked in a deep breath, like someone getting ready to jump off a tall rock into a small pond. "I lied! I lied to my wife. And it drove her off. Drove her off because I...I ran around on her and... loved a whore. A whore that only wanted my damn money."

Ardway fought to hold back the emotions that battered him inside. Outside of the livery the lightning flashed, strobing the light and shadows in the room. "I lied! To my boy. About me. And why his mother left. Now, he knows the truth and...and I don't have a son."

Rain was beginning to fall in discordant sounds that slowly plinked and plunked on the roof before the steady patter began. The men glanced away from looking into Ardway's wild face. He raised a shaking hand and pointed at Wasted. "Look at this man! I...I abused Wasted out of my hurt pride. I judged him! I thought I was justified to kill him if he couldn't...live through the hell I put him through." Wasted looked down at his boots, ashamed for Ardway's break with himself. "Oh. I was high and mighty!" Ardway jabbed a finger at his chest. "Now, God...judges me." Ardway reached his arms out and pleaded before the room. "Me! I sinned. I'm the one that should pay." His eyes were shiny and wet. He looked up and yelled, "Don't you see, boys? God wants Fendris to kill me, not you."

Ardway turned and stepped away, "Now. Get out. Get out while you can." His emotions spent, he weakly went to an empty stall and hung his arm over a rail to hold himself up. Taking a flask out of his slicker with his other hand he turned it up high to his lips and swallowed the whiskey fast at it drained out. Ardway didn't give a damn anymore about what people thought. The rain came down harder, drowning out the quiet. It made the room seem small and disconnected from the world. The men glanced around to each other, unsure how to act or what to do.

Gammill stepped before them. His eyes searched the room from man to man, looking deep inside of each one. He humbly bowed his head. Gammill's deep voice spoke in soft and assured tones. "Now, we pray." The men dropped their heads and began their desperate prayers. Some silent, rocking on their boots. Others whispered like God was standing right there listening. Wasted stared at the ground but his thoughts were not for himself but for Ardway. And to his surprise, of Esther. Gammill opened his eyes to speak. "Dear Lord. Hear us in our hour of need. We humbly ask for your divine counsel and to answer our call—"

An answer came. A shattering explosion that shook the ground under the stable. Inside, the men were tossed to the floor as crates, feed sacks and harness equipment crashed around them. They crawled up from out of the tumbled debris amid a cloud of dust shaken loose in the room. Each squinted about in the floating grit unsure what to make of it like shocked deer after an earthquake. Something crashed through the glass pane of a window facing the street. It bounced across the floor trailing sparks. Like a cat Wasted's arm shot out to seize a lighted stick of dynamite. He spun and slung it back out the shattered window. He and the men leapt to throw themselves upon the floor with hands over their faces and heads.

Outside on the street the dynamite stick went skipping and bouncing down the street in the rain, smoke and sparks trailing its lit fuse. Fendris's men broke in a panic, frantically running and leaping for cover behind wagons and boxes. The fiery eruption of the stick's nitroglycerin created a bright explosion that rocked the street. Plate glass windows in storefronts down the street split in large cracks from the concussion. Frightened horses reared up and jumped on two legs. Others broke their leather tethers and raced away down the street. The explosion heaved earth into the air in a dark cloud until it mixed with the rain. The dirt fell back as mud into the wide crater carved out of the street. For a few moments the street's people cowered inside their hiding places and waited for what was next. It came in the sounds of shattered glass falling from store windows as rifle barrels broke through. Next to this rifles jutted out from doors in dark rooms. Above on the rooftops rifles swung over their ledges. All were pointed toward the livery.

Wasted stared out from a window and saw the lightning gleam off the gun barrels lined down the street and taking aim at the stable. He shouted, "Rifles! Get down!" He and his friends threw themselves behind any cover available. A barrage of gunfire ripped through the building. Walls splintered. Boxes were ripped into shreds. Feed sacks tore open in bursting clouds of grain. Each man balled up tight, grimacing in panic and terror, waiting for death.

Bailey threw his arms up reflexively as a slug tore into his back, rolling his eyes up white into his head.

A bullet cut through Gammill's thigh, blood shot out in a long stream. He cried out in agony, "Holy Jesus!"

Shattered glass, wooden shards and scraps of leather flew about with the bullets careening around the room. Wasted and Ardway were hunched down behind a big oak desk while slugs smashed into it, sending splintered wood shards flying around them.

The gunfire tapered off to a few shots and then stopped. Dust floated about in a thick curtain through the shattered office and its debris. Moans and sighs of pain were heard from the men moving among the rubble. Wasted and Ardway exchanged glances and cautiously rose to crouch low, ready for more gunfire. They stared around the room to check on the men. Ardway saw Gammill tying a bandana around the bloody wound on his leg. He quickly stepped over to him. Gammill looked up at Ardway and gasped, "It's not bad." He grunted as he tried to move. "Hades blazes, but it hurts like jabbed with a pitchfork!"

Wasted carefully sidled up to a destroyed window to get a view outside. Fendris's voice called through the falling rain from down the street. "Ardway dead?"

Ardway snapped his head up from tending to Gammill. He shouted out a window to the street, "Fendris! Come in here and I'll settle our hash, you yellow bushwhacker!" Wasted and the others listened from their cramped positions of cover.

"Damn it to Hades, Burton. You're alive." Fendris shouted back. He sighed. "Alright. See to your wounded. Come to my store in an hour. Noon. Do that and I'll let the rest of your men live."

Ardway looked at the bloodied men around the room. He felt his stomach sink. No one could survive another of those rifle fusillades.

"If you don't come, well..." He paused. "It's your choice, Burton." Lightning strobed outside and leaked inside the stable, pasting the men in a hellish white pallor as Fendris's meaning sunk in.

Jordie called out from a stall in the other room. "Wasted! Mister Ardway. Hurry. It's...Bailey."

Wasted and Ardway shared a glance at each other's surprised faces. They quickly crossed to the stall. Their faces switched to shock, then concern at seeing— Bailey resting askew atop a mound of straw in the stall. A wet shiny red covered the yellow straw beneath him. Bailey's skin was fast losing its color, turning a bluish white. His bright clear eyes had become trembling black gashes. Thin pale lips spoke with a raspy and forced whisper. "Mister...Ardway?...Wasted?"

Wasted leaned in close to his friend. He grabbed Bailey's hand and squeezed. It was ice cold. Wasted had an odd sensation of déjà vu. This wasn't a new feeling..."I'm here, you curly wolf."

Bailey managed a tight smile. "Good. Don't wanna...die alone." Wasted and Ardway exchanged a miserable glance. "Wasted. Take my...shaving razor. In my...boot sleeve." Wasted reached down to Bailey's boot. He pulled out the long razor filed off in a sharp point at the end. He lifted it before Bailey's face. Bailey reached up slowly with great effort and touched it. "I don't have...much. I want you to have it. To remember..." Bailey's voice had grown smaller, farther away. Wasted bent closer to hear. "It...it was...my daddy's." Bailey wheezed softly as his life departed his body.

At that moment Wasted sniffed hoarsely before he turned away. Ardway gazed sadly at Bailey a moment more. He closed his eyes then rose to stand. Ardway opened his eyes to stare around the room at his battered men, seeing all their pain and suffering for being loyal to him. His eyes landed on the wounded Gammill and the hurt was too great. He made a decision. Ardway pulled his pistols and started dumping the spent shells. He thumbed in new bullets from his gun belt. "I ain't waiting an hour," he said, speaking aloud to himself. Wasted heard. He stood up to watch Ardway finish, snapping the guns' chambers shut. Ardway strode quickly toward the front door.

Wasted grabbed him by the arm, holding him to the spot. Wasted's eyes were wet with pain and anger as he spoke. "No." Ardway, blindsided by this, frowned at Wasted. Gammill and the men looked to each other with confusion. Ardway wrenched his arm from Wasted's grip. He started to walk away. Wasted seized his arm again and jerked Ardway closer, face to face. "I'm planting Fendris. You're staying."

The other men stepped back. This wasn't in the cards.

Ardway pulled his gun, fast. Wasted was faster. He grabbed his hand. They struggled for a moment. Wasted's fist streaked at Ardway's chin, punching him so hard it made Ardway's eyes cross. He dropped the pistol and staggered on unsteady legs. The gun hit the ground and went off, making the people jump back. Ardway fell on his back. The gun twirled across the floor to slide before Jordie's feet. He grabbed it up.

Ardway shook his head. It cleared to find Wasted standing over him. Ardway wrapped his legs around Wasted's feet, locking his spurs together. He twisted and caused Wasted to smash hard into the floor. Ardway was on top, swinging his fists in a rage, pummeling Wasted about the head. Wasted turned his head and caught Ardway's right arm by the wrist. He pinned it to his own chest. Then kicked up to land on his heels, raising his legs and Ardway upward. Without the use of his pinned arm, Ardway was forced by gravity to topple. Unable to brace himself Ardway tumbled forward, off Wasted and onto his head. Wasted moved like an old hand at this. He was on his feet and charging Ardway before he could get up. Grabbing a shovel, Wasted slammed it hard over Ardway's head. The older man groaned and fell to his knees, then slumped over face-first to the ground and unconscious.

Wasted stumbled back against a stall and tossed the shovel away. His chest inhaled heavily, gasping for air. He glanced about the room. The shocked faces of Gammill and the men stared at him, perplexed and angry. Wasted shrugged it off. "I had to. Don't wake him until after I'm gone." Jordie and Tom stepped over to care for Ardway.

Gammill watched as Wasted went to Bailey's dead body. He removed his friend's gun belt and pistols. Retrieving Bailey's razor, he gazed at it a few seconds, then turned and cut a hole in the sleeve of his boot and inserted the weapon. Wasted rose as Gammill realized there was no stopping him. "Fendris," said Gammill. "His men. They'll kill you."

Wasted extended his hand out. "Give me your belt and guns."

"No. There's too many—"

Through clenched lips Wasted sneered, "Your leg is shot. You ain't got a say." Gammill stared deep into Wasted's cold angry eyes. Something was different with Wasted from before, when he entered the livery. Hell, different from entering Molly's, where he played cards amiably and then killed a man faster than any witness had ever seen. Gammill had spent most of his life dealing with hard customers. He was staring at one of the hardest now. Gammill unbuckled his gun belt.

Ten minutes later the stable was a dark outline in the violent squall. Down the streets and alleys the storm lashed wind and rain over Spirits Bend. Water poured in cascades off its roofs to form rippling pools that spread about the open lots and roads. The front door of the stable slammed open. Thunder rumbled overhead, drums to herald a battle call. A tall man strode into the tempest in Ardway's red slicker. With the collar strapped up around his neck Wasted stared down the muddy street, his face hidden in deep shadow under the wide brim of Ardway's hat.

Wasted stopped at the large dynamite crater in the street. Wasted turned his head to the stable for a brief moment, his thoughts on Bailey, Ardway and his friends. Then he stared down into the gaping crater where the trapped rain was rising fast, muddy black waters churning in the violent storm. He wondered who would show up at the end of the street in front of the Fendris feed store — him? Odem? Or someone in-between? And would he be man enough to do what was needed? The red slicker flapped wildly around his tall figure in the wind. Lightning cracked open the sky. He started walking to Fendris. The scarlet reflection of Wasted shimmered then disappeared from the crater's seething black water like something escaped from Hell.

Wasted marched in the mud down the center of the street as the cloudburst bore down on it like a river. He slogged on through the silt and clay pulling at his boots, turning his head to better see the street left and right. Silhouettes of men with rifles pointed down at him from the rooftops on either side. Rifle barrels extended from the gloomy openings of doors and broken windows of the storefronts. The lightning strobed over it with an apocalyptic eeriness. The downpour pounded harder at him and grew louder with each step. Wasted had seen enough.

He turned to his right toward the raised planks of the boardwalk. Up he stepped, kicking and stomping the mud from his boots while continuing to walk onward fast and steady. Ahead, a door cracked opened. A man stood in its shadow with a Winchester rifle pointed at Wasted. Wasted had his hand on his gun inside the slicker.

The man commanded, "Halt! Or I'll sho—" Wasted drew his pistol and fired. One shot. Through the heart. The body was blown back into the darkness of the store. The rifle was left to rattle on the walkway. Wasted bent to pick it up without stopping. The storm raged on about the street.

Further up the boardwalk another door creaked open with a rifle barrel. Wasted fired his Winchester. Crack! A man fell through the door. Wasted caught him, took his rifle and shoved the body back into the room. He shut the door, continuing on with two rifles pointed low, hidden along the sides of his legs. Wasted kept moving, picking up his pace against the heavy rain beating down in sheets. The squall was doing a good job of covering for the gunshots with the thunder and wind. Up ahead a couple of buildings, two men leaned over from the roof and aimed their rifles at Wasted. The stouter of the two shouted to be heard over the storm, "Was that shooting? What happened?"

Wasted walked on, ignoring them. The second man was short and scrawny and not having it. "Hold up!" Wasted continued walking into the driving rain.

The big man yelled, "Stop right there, you bastar—" Wasted spun around, fired with both rifles up at the men. The thick man was hit dead center in the chest. He fell backwards and out of sight on the roof. The little man caught a slug in his throat before getting off an unchecked shot from his rifle. The bullet ripped into the wall above Wasted's head. Shattered wood fell in pieces over Ardway's hat. The little man gripped his neck to stumble and fall off the roof. His body crashed into part of the walkway and flipped to drop with a splash into the flooded road. Blood flowed out like a red ribbon streaming around his sunken face, with the mouth and eyes staring wide open in shock, and disappeared down the street. Wasted watched the blood trailing the body and fading into the muddy waters. It made him think of a soul slipping away into nothingness.

Three cowboys with rifles heard the shots and charged out of the building ahead. They gaped at the grotesque face bleeding out in the street unsure just what had happened. Hidden by the blinding rain they didn't notice Wasted leaning against the wall. One of the cowboys turned and noticed an outline of a man with Winchester rifles. Wasted flipped the guns forward and back holding the levers, loading their chambers with bullets. The man brought his rifle up at Wasted. Too late. Wasted fired both guns to slam the man backwards with his feet up in the air. He landed in a roll with his ass up as Wasted dropped one of the rifles.

The other two men reacted in confusion and fumbled trying to bring their rifles to bear on Wasted. He worked the Winchester's lever like a pump, firing it until empty. The slugs hammered into the men as fast as the rain falling. They spun about so abruptly both their hats flew off to sail away in the wind. One stepped off the sidewalk and fell face first into a jumbled heap in the mud. The other man sagged to his knees in a daze, his head tilted down at the neck, forced to witness his life gushing crimson out of his chest. He coughed up a phlegmy red vomit and slumped over dead.

Wasted tossed the rifle away, turned and went on his way. Ahead loomed Fendris's store. Its shape appeared black and indistinct in the storm's sweeping torrent. A pale light burned dimly from the large second floor window. Wasted knew that was the room where he would kill Fendris and die for it.

Wasted stepped out of the rain inside a doorway nook, gazing about in the haze. He pulled his gun and opened the chamber. With his thumb and index finger he plucked out the spent cartridge and tossed it onto the sidewalk. As he started to put in the new slug he stopped and stared at it. A voice came to him warning never lose a moment to refill your irons. The bullet you replaced could stop that next man from killing you. Wasted wondered where did grim thoughts like that come from? Gammill knew. Ardway knew. Fendris, too. The wind made a shrieking howl through Spirits Bend to say something terrible was waiting for Wasted. No, he thought, it wasn't waiting, it was pursuing him. Were these old memories from Odem, or Wasted creating these new thoughts? He couldn't tell. Abruptly a face appeared out of the shadows behind the large window. Wasted's gun appeared at once, the hammer cocked and trigger ready to kill.

A gun was pointed back at him. He leaned in to peer closer. The stranger did the same. Wasted was staring at his reflection. The expression was cold. The eyes black in the bleak light. He and his double relaxed and both spoke, "Howdy. Swifty Bill...Odem..."

They both finished the sentence. Without speaking aloud, their lips mouthed: "Your call...to drop—"

Lightning streaked the window in silver. Thunder shook the glass until it cleared. Wasted's ghostly reflection, or Odem's, shimmered and faded as he turned and continued on toward Fendris's store.

Chapter Twenty-Five:

Fendris's Turn to Drop the Ball

The Fendris Feed Store was framed against an ashen sky that seemed to have broken open awakening its angry deity to drown a city of apostates because of the intrusion of civilization in this nature god's untamed world. One that the Lakota and others had kept a faithful covenant with allowing their Great Spirit to sleep for thousands of years. Whatever the reason the storm was as biblical as that night the dark clouds rolled in and stole the light of Spirits Bend with a drape as black as sin. One man had entered that world and walked a journey of purpose between life and death like a cricket that called to life and a widow that gave it death for daring so. Today the deluge closed and opened its curtains like life and death, hiding the street then flashing a stark glimpse under an arc of lightning. Out of this walked that man of purpose in a red slicker and hat. Five men in gray raincoats stepped out of the store with pistols drawn to meet him.

A man named Knob with dark long hair flying wildly under the brim of his hat stepped forward before the others. He shouted, "Ardway! Stop right there or be cut down!"

Wasted paid no attention and kept coming toward the men. If they thought that he was Ardway then they must have orders from Fendris to kill him. Wasted hadn't counted on this. He planned he could get into the store as Ardway and fight it out from there. Wasted remembered bitching to himself about how hard his first two weeks as junior foreman were. He kept staring at the ground, leaned into the rain and marched on with his sleeves stuffed in the slicker's pockets.

Knob turned to the men and smiled. "Together..." The men raised their pistols to aim directly at Wasted. Knob counted off, "Three. Two—" A ball of lightning streaked down before the men and abruptly raced away down the street. The sleeves of the slicker flew out of its pockets to flap wildly above Wasted like the red wings of death. Knob and the men hesitated for a fraction of a second, wondering if this was real before the white brilliance of the lightning. Hidden inside the the buttoned slicker Wasted had both pistols drawn. The guns fired, punching slugs through the coat. Knob and his men were struck, flinging them backward, their bodies whipped around like rags in the wind. They fell zigzagged and wrapped about each other in a bloody heap, watching each other's life drain away.

Knob staggered back against the store's wall. He coughed up his red juice with one hand holding in his guts. He weakly tried to raise the gun in his other hand to point at Wasted who closed fast upon him, shoving Knob's gun to the side, loosening a wild shot across the street. Wasted took away the pistol as Knob gasped, "I'm shot! Oh, God. Help me..." Wasted turned Knob toward the store's door and steadied his body from behind. Bent low Wasted quickly opened the chambers and reloaded his guns. Done, he shoved Knob's gun into his belt. Then he grabbed Knob, turned the door handle and opened the door slightly. Knob wheezed in fear, "No. Don't...Waiting inside—" Wasted shoved Knob through the door while low behind him. Inside Wasted dived fast for the goods aisle on the right. The explosive burst of a double-barreled shotgun caught Knob's body and hurled it out the door and into the street, leaving a long trail of pinkish-gray and red intestines.

The feed store was a maze of heavy shadows cast by the single source of light— the storm's bleak gray through the front glass window. No lamps were lit but the multitude of blasts from Fendris guns popped bright flashes in the dark. Wasted had landed on the floor between two tall wooden shelves. Several rows of shelving and wares blocked the light and kept the store almost completely black. He rolled on his back between the shelves as bullets whizzed through the air and about, trying to make him. Two attackers fired from the opposite ends of where he laid. Wasted extended both arms and fired two shots, killing each man.

There were hints of movement in the darkness as men moved with the flare of guns going off. Bullets shredded the goods on the shelves above Wasted. A thought blazed to his mind. He braced his boot heels against the heavy shelf above his knees and strained to push it with his legs. More bullets ripped the space above him, tearing the goods open, spraying feed and splintering boxes. The shelf tipped forward and then rocked back from Wasted's efforts. He pushed harder, glad now that he had been put through all that back-breaking work carrying buckets of water at the ranch. His face red, he puffed his cheeks and pushed with his back. The shelf tipped further forward and rocked back hard. He put everything he had into it on the next shove forward. Bullets tore up the wood boards braced against his boots, spraying sawdust and shards over him. The shelf hung for a second on its pitched edge. Before it could tip back toward him, he kicked it as hard as he could. It toppled forward.

It fell with a loud crack onto the next shelf knocking it over at an angle, creating a domino effect of heavy shelves colliding against the others. This continued as men broke in panic, unsure what the hell was happening. Some were caught in the calamity, pinned by the shelves or swamped under the deluge of falling goods. Wasted rose up in the chaos. The air was fogged by bullet-tossed powdered wares, blue gun smoke and the years of dust from the fallen shelves. Wasted pulled his bandana over his nose and jumped to the peak of a toppled shelf and fired his pistols, picking off the figures running below and those unfortunate enough to have been pinned under the debris. The explosive roars of the guns added to the confusion, echoing about the walls of the large cavernous store. Wasted watched it all from high above in the dark, leaping from one fallen shelf to the other. As soon as someone figured out that he was in one place he jumped to another. Fendris's men fell and died on the floor below and never saw him coming or his gun firing.

Wasted sighted his pistols on four men in shadow. The guns clicked empty. The men heard and turned to see Wasted and aimed. Wasted slung off Ardway's slicker, revealing several gun-belts and pistols strapped about his body and limbs, all taken from Ardway's men back at the livery. He fast-drew Bailey's guns from the holster about his chest and cut down three of the men. The fourth man threw up his hands in surrender. A shaft of lightning outside flashed through the store window, casting the room in a pale dreamlike flash. It was the pear-shaped Worley, the fat-assed man who recognized Odem in Molly's. His eyes stared in terror at Wasted while his arms shook like tree limbs outside in the storm. Wasted lowered Bailey's guns. There was another flash of lightning as Wasted caught his breath, "You... told...Fendris. About Odem."

Worley choked on his tongue for betraying him. His frightened eyes spread open wider like they were going to pop out. Wasted growled, "Run to Fendris." Wasted fired one shot. It tore Worley's earlobe off, splattering blood over half his face. Worley screamed and raced for the stairs at the back of the room.

Wasted trailed Worley through the store from above on the shelves. More men turned to hastily fire at Wasted, but missed their target and then ran like frightened rabbits. Wasted shot them in the backs and they died stumbling over themselves. Wasted had only one thought — these yellowbelly scum got themselves killed like how Bailey got dry-gulched.

Bailey's guns clicked empty. Wasted discarded them, pulled new ones that were strapped about his body. He crossed over men trapped below under the wrecked shelves and goods. They fumbled with their guns while trying to fire on him. They aimed but Wasted was faster and pumped lead into each one, Fendris rats caught in a trap.

Wasted jumped from one toppled shelf to the other. He closed on Worley at the stairs. Men hiding nearby had heard him coming by the gunfire and screams. Each was unnerved at Wasted's ease under fire and his deadly accuracy was beyond anything they had known. He killed without mercy. Cold. Remorseless. They fired their guns at Wasted but he escaped their shaky aim. Each man was terrified by how casual Wasted appeared as he killed. To Wasted it was like a game he used play over and over. They fired. He fired back. They died with one shot. One shot was all he needed. A thought struck him during this chaos, "Just like old times..."

The gunfire faded away. Wasted stopped and stood on the toppled shelves above the moaning and the cries for help. Worley cowered before him from behind a thick oak railing to the stairs. Wasted aimed and shot, shattering the railing into long sharp wooden pieces. Worley shrieked like a child and raced up the steps. Nearby a man screamed out repeatedly in pain. Wasted stepped to another shelf and without looking pointed his gun and shot him dead. Others immediately muted their groans, fearing Wasted's attention, whimpering to themselves among the silent dead. The room was quiet except for panicked breathing. Wasted glanced around at the death and ruin. Worley had caused this. For money. Or maybe for revenge concerning his friend. The reasons didn't matter now. It was kill or be killed. Only Fendris's death would end it.

Wasted leapt down to the floor. He carefully stepped around the fallen shelves and stared out at the stairs. Ten men had gathered there and up along its steps to hold its ground. He looked up at the top from where Worley held a bloody handkerchief to his ear, gazing down on Wasted with wide frightened eyes.

Wasted fired shots up the stairs, slaying two men by Worley who fell and rolled down the steps. This drew everyone's attention as Wasted ran the twenty feet to the bottom of the stairs. He moved up the staircase, shooting two more men. One fell into Wasted's arms. He slung the body as a shield over his shoulder and fired both pistols up the steps, killing men. The dead bodies fell and slid and tumbled down the steps as Wasted walked over them.

The last three men on the stairs panicked at watching Wasted march up the steps and kill anyone in his path. The men turned and ran up the steps, knocking Worley over on the floor. He stared in horror as Wasted stopped at the top of the stairs. Wasted shot the fleeing men in their backs. They each screamed and crawled away to die. Squirming backwards like a worm, Worley stared up at Wasted. Wasted dropped the dead body from his shoulder over the railing. He leaned down to stare directly in Worley's bloody face. "My call... to drop the ball. Ain't that what you said?"

Worley's face cracked like a broken mirror. He twisted around and padded away on all fours before getting up speed and running to Fendris's office. Wasted stepped off the stairs into its darkness. Ahead, Worley looked back to Wasted and stumbled the last few yards to the door of the office. A shot from below the stairs fired up at Wasted. He turned and shot back, a scream his only answer, dying along with its maker.

Worley pounded on Fendris's door. "Fendris!" Worley shouted hysterically, "Odem! He's here. Let me in!" The door opened in a burst of light, bathing Worley in illumination. He slipped inside, the door closed, turning the hall dark. Wasted fired shots through the door. Light broke out in small yellow shafts from six holes. Wasted quickly jumped to it, pressing his ear to the holes. The familiar tell-tale clicks of guns being cocked sent him spinning to slam up against the wall. From inside the room a volley of shotgun blasts and pistol gunfire shredded the door into large ragged holes.

Silence. Except the sound of the rain on the roof. It was the first time since entering the building that Wasted had become aware of the rain outside. Light stabbed out from the holes in the shattered door, brightening up the hallway. Then came the sounds again of guns being quickly reloaded. A voice called out from far back in the office. It was Fendris. "Mister Odem. Do I have your attention? I hope you're not dead."

Wasted stepped away from the wall. His eyes darted about in frustration. He looked to his guns and became angry, yelling, "Soon, Fendris. After I kill you."

"Mister Odem, why would you want to do that? Just what are you doing here? And by that I mean, in Spirits Bend?"

Wasted's face drew up in surprise but didn't answer.

Fendris waited, then continued, "A miserable broken drunk... with no memory...comes here, of all the places in this big wide world." Fendris paused. "Don't you want to know why?"

A curious doubt took hold in Wasted's eyes.

Fendris spoke, "It would please me very much to tell you. Because...only I can, Mister Odem. And I'd also like to suggest a proposition." He paused again. "Then you can decide if you still wish to kill me."

Wasted tried to shake it off. He gripped his guns tightly to his chest. "You're lying, Fendris."

"Am I? You may not recall much about your past but no one forgets a woman like...Ruby."

Wasted lowered his guns, stunned. How did Fendris know that name? Unless...

Fendris asked, "What do you say, Mister Odem?"

Inside the office ten burly men held shotguns and pistols aimed at the splintered door. Wasted's voice called from the hall. "No shooting. I'm coming in." Wasted cautiously tapped the toe of his boot against what was left of the door. It creaked open. He slowly stepped inside, his guns held up high but gripped in his hands and ready. In the room's light the blood and gore splattered about his face, clothes and body painted him as a terrifying figure.

Worley lay spread out dead on the floor, his face twisted up with those terrified eyes still looking ready to pop out, only now in a rictus of horror and blood.

Men quickly surrounded Wasted with their guns pointed at him and fingers ready on the triggers. They knew what he had done today to reach this point, and they also feared him by reputation. Worley's dead face spoke for them all. Benito cautiously stepped forward holding a pistol out and with his free hand stripped the guns and gun belts from Wasted's body. Even with him disarmed the men anxiously backed away from Wasted.

Worley was dragged out by his heels from the office. Benito took two steps backwards, carrying Wasted's holsters and guns slung about his neck and his arms. He still held his pistol on Wasted as he nodded to Pete. Pete turned around to the big desk and spoke, "He's ready, Mister Fendris."

The armed men surrounding the desk moved away. Fendris sat relaxed in a padded leather chair behind the large desk, his angry-eyed painting behind him on the wall. It was quite a contrast to the calm smile on Fendris's lips that greeted Wasted.

"Before we get started, what do I call you?"

"Wasted."

"Fine! Before 'Wasted' sounded quite pitiful. Now, it's more like a calling card."

Wasted glared coldly at Fendris. "What's your card say? Talk men to death?"

Fendris bit his lip. He started to snicker, then broke out laughing. "Maybe, Wasted. After you hear what I'm going to say...it might just kill you."

He continued to chuckle, looked to Pete and Benito. They were not smiling. Neither was Wasted. Fendris waved off his men. "All of you. Out!"

"Hell no, Boss!" barked Pete.

"Go clean up downstairs with the others. We've reached a gentleman's terms." Fendris grinned at Wasted. "Wasted won't kill me. And I won't kill him. Least not 'til he hears about what I know about him and everyone else's sad misfortunes."

The open hatred that Pete and Benito glared toward Wasted could not have been more clear; it said, *shoot this rabid dog now and be done with it.* Fendris knew that look well. His face hardened in a way which signaled the two better leave it alone before he got nasty about it. Benito sighed and waved at the other men to leave. But Pete would not let it go and spoke up defiantly. "Benito will stay, dammit!...Just outside the door." With a sneer to Wasted he barked, "I don't trust that son of a bitch."

The men left. Wasted and Fendris were alone. A streak of lightning outside shot a terrific blaze of silver that glared across the large window with its surface of shifting raindrops, draping the room in spiderwebs of eerie shadows and gray light. The office was plunged into a purgatory. Life and death swayed around these men, waiting, their fates unwritten but sure.

Fendris rose out of his chair to step toward the end of the long desk where there was a decanter of whiskey and a pitcher of water with two glasses. He poured whiskey into a tall glass for himself. He filled the other with water and handed it to Wasted.

"Killing's thirsty work. Don't you remember that...after all the people you've killed?" He tossed the whiskey over his lips in one long drink.

Wasted kept his eyes on Fendris. He raised the glass and quickly drained the water. With a gasp Wasted held the glass out for more. Fendris poured Wasted another then more whiskey for himself.

Wasted said, "You remember any of the people you've killed?" He held the glass up high and drained it in one long gulp. He wiped his lips with the back of his hand as he set the glass on the table and stared directly at Fendris.

Fendris, sipping his whiskey, gave a nonchalant shrug. "Some. A few more than others. I pay for a killing now. So I don't have to remember." He finished drinking the liquor. "That's where you came in."

Fendris hopped up and sat down upon the corner of his desk. He began swinging his legs like an anxious young cowboy.

"See. Me and Burt made this territory what it is, now. This town. We either own or bankrolled everything in it. Well, excepting the whorehouse and Molly's but we let that happen with our approval. We was always trying to outdo each other. More this. More that. For bragging rights, I guess." He leaned over to Wasted, "Shit, and for what?" Fendris waited for Wasted to answer. Wasted shrugged he didn't know. Fendris looked disappointed.

"A legacy!" He poured another glass of whiskey and took a sip. "I had a wife. Gunilda. Part Crow. Mostly Swedish. Good woman. Died in childbirth. Gave me Clayton...Clay."

Fendris slid off the desk to walk over and looked out the window into the storm. The rain still washed down in torrents. The sky was a dark turbulent ocean with clouds that churned like crests of white waves among the lightning.

"Burt married a very fine woman," Fendris continued, "Patricia, from back east. Had a boy, too. Burt, Junior. Seven years after Clay. They were...happy."

He turned around to face Wasted, staring directly into his eyes. "I was not." For a moment he glanced up as he remembered. "My son...My son grew up to become a no account coffee boiler. Not 'cause I spoiled him, hell, I hardly saw him. But...people around here did. To try and sidle up to my good side." He poured more whiskey into his glass and sipped at it.

"Burt and Patricia raised a good son. His mother made sure of that. Avoided my mistakes, keeping him out on the ranch. She schooled him at home. Away from town and...temptations."

Hearing this Wasted's eyes shifted about the room in thought. He glanced back to Fendris and spoke, "Legacy."

Fendris got excited, "Yep. You're catching on. Seeing Burt's legacy and happiness...just about killed me."

Fendris looked up at the crude painting of himself, wishing it could speak and he didn't have to remember the pain that came out in his voice. "I ran off to New Orleans where I could cry in my beer and no one knew me. I played cards. Badly. I didn't care. Drank like there was a hole in my foot. And with all this I chased fancy whores with my money." Suddenly he straightened up and brightened. Fendris winked at Wasted. "Then...I found the scratch for my itch."

Wasted stared back at Fendris. Parts of his memory shifted inside him. Something was unlocked. He walked over to the window and stared out beyond the room and the moment. "Ruby..."

Fendris came over to stand beside him and join his gaze out into the furious rainstorm outside. "The most beautiful woman in New Orleans. And that's saying something. Half Choctaw Indian, half French mademoiselle...All devil." A relaxed wistful expression took hold while Fendris remembered that time. "Ruby learned early that she could charm the bark off a tree with a smile. Break the bank with a kiss. Get anything. Anything. With her body—"

Wasted interrupted, blurting out his thoughts. "You broke up Ardway's marriage...with Ruby."

Fendris raised his glass to Wasted. "She shamed ol' Burt like a Jezebel. Much more than I paid her to."

The anger and revulsion became a blaze in Wasted's eyes. He grabbed Fendris by the lapel of his coat and jerked him close, holding him inches from his face. "Enough of this. Tell me about Odem."

Wasted slipped his hand about Fendris's throat. His fingers tightened about the neck. Fendris smiled, delighted at watching Wasted's anger as the pieces of his fragmented memory began to fall into place. "Tell you, Wasted? Why...I'll show you."

Wasted relented. He removed his hand from Fendris's neck. Fendris backed up with his eyes on Wasted as he walked over to a door in the far corner. He took a shiny brass key from inside his coat pocket that was attached to a gold chain. Fendris inserted it into a lock and opened the door. Inside a pitch black room waited.

With an odd excitement, Fendris motioned with his index finger for Wasted to walk across the room to the dark opening. "Come on. Don't be afraid..."

Chapter Twenty-Six:

Odem

Wasted stepped into the room. It was so dark that it seemed strange and unnatural. Like being deep within a cave where no light existed. The only light was from the lamps in Fendris's office and even that died within a few feet of the open door. The rumbling sounds of the storm with its rain pelting on the roof added to the feeling of disorientation. What could Fendris keep in here that could have any connection to Wasted's past? Fendris shut the door and the effect was that of being swallowed by a great creature. The click sound of the key locking the door was both comforting for the reality it represented in Fendris's hidden realm but also a bit terrifying for Wasted, realizing he was now its prisoner.

A match was struck, flaring into a yellow flame. With it Fendris ignited the kerosene-soaked wick of a lantern and dropped the glass chimney over it. The lantern hung from the wall on a hook. Fendris adjusted its flame to increase the sphere of its glow and lifted the lantern free. He walked ahead with Wasted following. Fendris crossed the room and reached up with his free hand. He pulled back a heavy black curtain on an overhead rod, dragging it to the side. A gray light shone from a large window like the one in Fendris's office, only this view was from the back of the store, looking out on the secluded trees and hills as they were lashed under the downpour. There was no road or open space under the window and the thick brush came right up to the building. No one was likely to see up through the window from below.

With the help of the window's ghostly light Wasted's eyes were starting to recognize shapes out of the darkness. A small desk was set next to a two-person table with two chairs. All else in the room was covered in gloom like a thick black cloth. Wasted walked to the window then turned to stare about the dark room. Fendris set the lantern on the table. "Is there anything that you remember?" asked Fendris.

Wasted stared into the shadows at the other end of the room and thought of the small fragments of a memory he could never trust as being true or just dreams. "Just flashes. Dreams." He remembered and his face turned grim. "Nightmares. I kill people. A woman stands there. Watching. Ruby? I'm not sure. Something... went wrong."

Fendris stepped to the edge of the darkness that Wasted was staring absently into so that he could observe him as he spoke. With each word Fendris's excitement increased in his eyes.

"I'm angry...and afraid." Wasted shuddered. "I...killed someone. Someone important. Important to..." Wasted trailed off, unable to remember.

Fendris stood half in darkness and half in the light. "That you did." Wasted stared into Fendris's eyes. They matched his own intense gaze. "But before that I have to tell you something about Ruby. I'll skip the particulars except that after she burned Burton's marriage to hell, she got...damn greedy. Tried to blackmail me over my part." He chuckled to himself. "That whore wanted me to marry her!" Fendris shook his head at the thought. "Hell, Burton didn't just fall off the turnip wagon. He'd know the score about my part in this if I did that."

Wasted put it together and drew himself back a few inches at the discovery, his eyes wide. "You...You hired me. To kill her."

Fendris cocked his head in agreement to Wasted. "Someone handled the details. I didn't know it was you."

Wasted slumped wearily into one of the chairs, adrift inside himself. "I killed Ruby."

Fendris gave Wasted a rueful smile and sighed. "If only you had..." Wasted snapped his head around to Fendris, his eyes confused. Fendris continued, "Ruby bent men like soft taffy. And...you were a man." Fendris enjoyed how this added to the look of Wasted's uncertainty. "You went to kill her. She wanted to live...She lived. And you. You fell in love."

Wasted's mind reeled, his face opened wide in shock. "Me?"

"Ass over heels. You two ran off. Hid real good."

"But...you found us."

Fendris remembered, smiled sadly. "No." Wasted's face couldn't hide his bewilderment. Fendris saw and took some pleasure in replying, "You found out that Ruby was only using you. She cared for another. With the promise of big money." He leaned forward, looked closer into Wasted's eyes. "You suspected, and waited. And finally, you caught them together."

Thunder rattled the room as a streak of lightning turned everything white. The dreamscape inside Wasted played its story again. As before in Wasted's dreams a couple made love but in the light and not silhouetted in shadow. A man and Ruby. They reveled in their passionate kisses. The man left the room. Outside three shots were fired. The man staggered back into the room where he collapsed. Wasted followed him into the room from outside and watched him die. As Wasted turned to Ruby three more gunshots through the open door caught Wasted. One bullet opened a bloody crease to his forehead. Ruby laughed hysterically as Wasted stumbled out the door. This time Fendris appeared in the doorway. He saw the dead man and the laughing Ruby. He turned and took chase after Wasted as guns fired in the night.

Fendris spoke as Wasted relived his nightmare. "I wouldn't marry Ruby. So she took my son who would inherit my ranch and wealth. I trailed Clay when he disappeared. But like you, I didn't know Ruby was behind it. I got there as you killed Clay. I shot you then without knowing who you were."

An arc of lightning brightened the outside hills as thunder shook the room. Wasted rose up from the chair and moved to the window. His reflection stared back at him. Wasted pulled his hair back off his forehead to study the pink scar that was given to him that night by Fendris.

Fendris appeared behind Wasted in the reflection. Wasted took his hand away and let his hair hide the scar again. He glanced over his shoulder and spoke to Fendris. "Legacy. Your legacy..."

"Clay wasn't much. But he was all I had. My legacy. Wasted, something deep inside your sotted brain pulled you here to Spirits Bend...over your legacy. And now to me." For the first time Fendris sounded weary and tired.

Fendris reached up into the dark beyond the window. He pulled a cord attached to a velvet black curtain hanging from a rod. The curtain opened the width of the room, revealing a large brass bed, covered in a rumpled sheet and blankets bathed in pale light. A moan drifted up from under the pile. The bedcovers rolled and tumbled away.

A coil of black emerged and fell in glossy cascades of hair. It parted and out of that a female face with a perfect bronze complexion awakened with large and blinking green eyes. Ruby at twenty-six years. Even in this disheveled moment, her combination of Native American and French beauty was intoxicating. Maybe even more so for it. With her long neck and supple bare shoulders she was all that Fendris had claimed and more.

"You had one damn job, Odem. Kill Ruby." He heaved with a deep sigh, "But...neither could I."

Ruby's eyes adjusted to the light. They expanded in shock at seeing another person other than Fendris. Ruby squinted to focus her eyes. Her mouth dropped when she realized it was Odem. Fendris watched them both with amusement, entertained by her confusion and Wasted's astonishment.

"He's real, Ruby. It's Bill. Bill Odem."

Ruby continued to stare at Wasted, unsure and not believing. She buried her face in her hands. "No! It's a trick!" Ruby looked up at Fendris with hate. "You're the devil, Ash."

"Don't tempt me to prove it, woman." Fendris reached to a vase by the table and pulled out a leather riding crop. He walked over to Ruby and struck her viciously across her back. Ruby screamed. Fendris raised the crop to hit her again.

Wasted shouted, "Stop!"

Ruby dug herself beneath the blankets for protection. Fendris was suddenly aware how this looked to Wasted. He lowered the crop and gave a weak smile. "Our arrangement...must seem strange. You see, Ruby hasn't seen anyone since...Clay's death. Excepting, me..."

Fendris motioned Wasted over to Ruby while he softly patted on her back. She cautiously emerged from under the blankets to stare at Fendris with a wary eye. He looked over to Wasted. "Here. Show her. Show Ruby that you're real."

"Since Clay's death? How many years is that?" Wasted asked.

"Ummm, over three years. Probably when you turned into a drunk with no memory. But here, Odem. Help Ruby understand she isn't seeing a ghost."

Wasted moved closer to Ruby. He gently laid his hand on her shoulder and sat beside her. "Ruby..."

Ruby guardedly searched Wasted's face, glancing about and remembering the man named Odem. "He...Ash shot you. You can't be—"

"No. I'm here. I...I thought you were dead." Wasted made a troubled smile at Ruby. "I'm...pleased to find out that you're not."

Ruby rose on the bed to study Wasted closer. She reached up to pull the hair away and touched his scar. Suddenly tears welled up in those beautiful green eyes. They spilled down Ruby's exquisite cheekbones. Her beauty was overwhelming in that moment of vulnerability. With a grateful warmth she pulled Wasted to her in a desperate embrace. "Oh, Bill...Bill. If you love me..." she looked over Wasted's shoulder and gave Fendris a cold baleful stare. "...Kill Ash. Now."

Wasted drew away from Ruby. He glanced from her hateful face to Fendris's amused expression, unsure which was more disturbing. Fendris laughed wickedly, "Same ol' Ruby."

Wasted stood up from the bed and turned to Fendris. "Why...are you doing this?"

Ruby dropped a bare foot upon the floor. Then a heavy chain rattled loudly and fell next to it. Wasted turned surprised eyes to the chain and gaped at it in confusion.

The chain led to Ruby's ankle and a padded shackle locked to it. His eyes followed the chain to where it was secured to a link embedded in the wall. Ruby stepped away from the bed and its blankets. She moved toward Wasted as the blankets fell away revealing...

A simple, silk white slip covered her form and tightly clung to the round swell of Ruby's pregnant body.

Wasted stared with eyes wide, unguarded and incredulous.

Fendris grinned, enjoying Wasted shocked expression. "Took a couple of years to clean her up from the drinking and drugs. But once she did... Well, Wasted. You know all about the changes a body goes through when you cut the liquor off..."

Fendris reached out and put his hand upon Ruby's swollen womb that held his child. "See, Burt might patch it up with his son. I can't allow that." He stared at the round shape in his hand and Ruby. "If Burt dies...ol' Junior will sell me that ranch he hates so much. I want that land, along with my holdings. For my son here." Fendris swelled up with pride, "My legacy."

Wasted's anger grew, becoming a sneer he directed at Fendris, "You murdering—"

"Ha! Odem. You may call yourself by a new name but you've killed more men than I ever wanted to or even thought about. For less reasons and in less time. Don't forget, I've got a lot of years on you."

Wasted's angry expression faltered. He stepped back at a loss to answer.

Fendris continued, "And don't think Ardway's an angel. We fought and killed alongside each other in the beginning when there was nothing here but bear, bad men and Indians. I can tell you stories..."

Wasted turned away from Fendris at these allegations. Because inside he knew that they were true.

"Fendris. Why? Why let me live to tell me...this?"

The frontier cowboy tapped his riding crop to his lips, carefully thinking over his words before speaking. "Ranching life...burns the candle at both ends. Hell, I've burnt the middle. The way things are, a sickness or falling off a horse could lay me up. I figure I've got five years or less. Seen it happen. And if I'm stoved up, well..." Fendris made a fist with his thumb up, then turned it down. "I'll eat a bullet 'fore I have to spend my end in a bed." He pointed the tightly woven leather crop at Wasted. "But you. You're still spry. And the only thing you're good at is...killing."

Wasted shook his head uneasily. He sat down, his body slumping tiredly in the chair. "What...do you want, Fendris?"

"My child will need a strong man to protect him. After I'm dead." Fendris stared keenly at Wasted, sizing him up from top to bottom. "Odem. Or Wasted. This is the best offer you will ever get in your life."

Wasted leaned heavily with one arm on the table, seemingly stunned at hearing this overture. His other hand slowly reached under the table and down to his boot. Fendris walked over to the table, bending down to gaze into Wasted's face.

"All you have to do...to get all the money...the land...all the power, and hell, even Ruby, is..." He moved in closer, staring directly into Wasted's eyes. "...kill Ardway."

Wasted whipped out Bailey's long razor with its filed point from his boot. He slashed upwards at Fendris's throat.

Fendris jerked back like a rattlesnake for a strike, avoiding the razor. Using the riding crop he expertly blocked Wasted's next two thrusts of the blade. With a speed honed from decades of pressing an attack, Fendris lashed the crop across Wasted's face, slicing the cheek open. Blood splattered across the table. Fendris slammed the crop down on Wasted's hand. The razor was flung across the floor next to the bed. Fendris regarded Wasted with disgust.

"Son. You disappoint me."

Wasted leapt up from the table at Fendris. Fendris whisked a two-shot derringer from his coat's pocket and stuck it in Wasted's face. Wasted froze in place with his fists out as Fendris made with that wild-eyed look that seemed more animal than man.

"That's right! You bet you better hold up 'cause I'll blow both your eyeballs out the back of your skull."

Wasted dropped his arms down. Fendris pulled a handkerchief from a pocket and tossed it to him. Wasted folded and placed it against his cheek, closing off the blood.

"Odem, you were a worthless drunk. A waste of space. Burt, he worked you like a slave. Near killed you. Without a thought to it." Fendris shook his head sadly, "Don't you see? I'm offering you everything! And more—" Fendris abruptly grunted in shock. His eyes flared wide with pain. His back stiffened as he turned his head to lock eyes with Ruby and her grinning hate.

Wasted saw that Bailey's razor was stuck to its hilt in Fendris's back and Ruby was holding its handle. Blood was growing in a large purple spot on his expensive blue coat. She released the blade and giggled at the shock and agony in Fendris's eyes. It grew into howling laughter just like all those years ago when Wasted was bleeding out from Fendris's bullets. She had stabbed Fendris like a black widow chewing a cricket's head off, because of a nightmare growing inside both her body and mind.

Because of the pain, because of the hate Ruby expressed for him, Fendris couldn't hide how furious he was. Like with with Jake Altenhofen at Rouget's Mill, someone was going to pay. "You...crazy...BITCH!"

Fendris whipped the derringer around and shot Ruby, instantly forming a black hole where her beautiful green right eye had been. Her blood splattered over his enraged face and in his eyes. Ruby collapsed dead in a red jumble at his feet. Fendris wiped the blood away from his eyes with the sleeve of that French cut, royal blue suit. He stared down at Ruby. Looking up in horror Fendris realized what he had done. "No...No!"

Wasted jumped on Fendris, raining punches about his head. They struggled for a moment. The derringer fired its second and final shot. Wasted slipped away from Fendris, slumping to the floor while holding a bloody wound in the left side of his ribs.

Fendris staggered backwards, knocking the lamp off the desk. It smashed to the floor, spilling its kerosene to spread flames about the room. The black velvet window curtain went up in a crackling orange blaze.

Fendris tottered in pain to the locked door with the blade still in his back. He pulled the brass key on its chain from his coat. After a couple of tries he found the hole and inserted the key, unlocking the door and pulling it open. Standing before the entrance Fendris reached over his shoulder and jerked the blade out of his back, making a tortured shriek. His hand dropped the bloody razor as he spun around to gaze at the room. Fendris's desolate eyes blinked white through Ruby's blood. He gaped at his heritage, lost forever in the growing inferno.

Wasted held to the chair and rose from the floor. One hand gripped about the wound in his side. Moving on unsteady legs he zigzagged across the room toward Fendris.

Fendris saw a figure approaching out of the flames. Shaken from his bleak torment he focused and realized Wasted was trying to escape. Fendris turned, the pain stabbing everywhere about his back and shoulders. He slowly walked with great effort through the door. Looking back, he saw Wasted tripping along, almost at the opening. Fendris slammed the door just as Wasted pitched forward.

Wasted managed to shove his arm in the door as it smashed across it. Wasted cried out, his hand clutched in a death grip to Fendris's coat lapel. Fendris was fumbling with the key, trying to insert it into the lock.

With a savage effort Wasted jerked Fendris to him. Fendris's head slammed against the door's edge. Stunned, Fendris leaned against the door as Wasted lurched past him. Wasted turned and slung a hard punch into the back of Fendris's skull, knocking him back into the secret room to stumble and fall upon the floor. In anguish Fendris forced himself up on his knees to stare out. The room was clouding with smoke and flames.

Wasted clung to the door. He noticed that the key was in the lock, the chain trailing to Fendris's coat. Fendris saw and crawled fast for the door, his blood-splashed face and white eyes a terrified mask of desperation. He reached out to Wasted, "Odem, no!"

Wasted slammed the door shut and turned the key, locking it. The chain was caught in the jamb. The sounds of Fendris beating his fists on the door came from the other side. His muffled cries sounded through the door. "Not this! Not my...My legacy!"

Chapter Twenty-Seven:

Jurant

Wasted pulled the key and jerked the chain, breaking it. He tossed it to the floor. There was Bailey's razor. It had been kicked into the room. Wasted gasped and howled at the pain to pick the razor up, sliding it in his boot sleeve. Smoke was trailing up from the slender bottom and top openings of the door, seeping in from the other side. Fendris's pounding on the door slowed, became erratic and finally went silent.

Wasted grunted from the throbbing in his side as he veered back and forth toward the wrecked door in the office, leaving a snaking drip trail of blood behind him on the floor. A gunshot rang out from the hall outside the office. Wasted's eyes snapped toward the door. Kroeber held his pistol out as he walked in the room and saw Wasted, his eyes filled with that familiar hatred. His twisted monstrous face sneered as he pointed the gun at Wasted's face. Glancing wildly about the room for some kind of weapon, Wasted saw the Native American weapons on the wall but — Kroeber fired. Wasted's body flinched. The bullet zipped past his head and shattered a hole in the wall. Kroeber stumbled over dead to the floor, blood pooling around him. Confused, Wasted looked down at Kroeber as he painfully skirted around the body.

Esther's frightened face appeared through the ragged open spaces of the door. She rushed in and saw Kroeber lying face down in a puddle of his own blood. Looking up she saw Wasted and quickly ran to him. They held tightly to each other. "Esther, what are you—"

She was trembling. "Kroeber. Fendris...made him...bring me here. So...you'd kill Ardway."

Wasted saw how frightened Esther was. "You shot Kroe—" He followed the gaze of her terrified eyes toward the door and the hallway. Jurant stepped inside, one gun trained on an alarmed Benito. He stopped. His other gun was pointed at Esther and Wasted. A gun belt hung over his shoulder.

Jurant glanced at the smoke slowly flooding the room's ceiling from the far door. "Kroeber was a dead man long afore I sealed the deal. You knew that. Like I knew you'd kill Fendris, Odem."

Esther blurted out, "Odem's dead."

Jurant jerked his head toward the floor and the stairs. "Tell all those bodies out there." He turned to Benito. "Get the rest of the town to gather outside the building. To be witnesses. You understand? Don't disappoint me, Benito."

Benito gave a series of quick nods.

Jurant yelled, "Go! Now!" Benito ran out of the room.

Esther tried to suppress her shaking and worry for Wasted, "Mister Ardway says his ranch men will be here soon, and—"

Jurant cut her off, "I looked for Ardway last night. At his ranch. Or I'd have been here sooner."

Wasted's eyed widened in alarm as he looked to Jurant. "Wilson?"

Jurant answered with a murderous gleam to his eyes and nodded, yes.

Wasted stared back over his shoulder. The smoke was seeping in faster, blanketing the ceiling. His gaze went to Esther's worried face and then back to Jurant. "Let her go."

Esther cried out, "No!"

Wasted's guns and belt landed on the floor at his feet, tossed by Jurant. Wasted and Esther stared at the holstered guns. Jurant spoke to Wasted, "Outside. I want people to know who killed you."

Esther glanced quickly to Jurant, "But...why? Fendris is dead. He can't pay you now."

Wasted picked up his gun belt and looked to Jurant, sizing him up. Jurant understood what Wasted was doing. "Oh, Fendris is paying. With his ranch. That's the reason for putting his killer in the ground. No one'll fuss...with the man who killed Bill Odem."

Esther perked up, "Mister Ardway and Sheriff Gammill will!" Wasted and Jurant glanced knowingly to each other with icy eyes. Esther saw this. Suddenly her eyes sprung wide in shock. "You.... You're going...to kill them."

Jurant's voice turned stern. "Hobble that lip, woman! Or I'll make it everlasting."

Wasted's eyes darted to the holstered guns in his hands. Jurant smiled and cocked his guns, pointed at Wasted. "That's what I want to see." He started backing away and through the shattered door. "Hurry down, Odem. We wouldn't want this fire to burn up your lady friend." He disappeared through the doorway.

Wasted checked his guns, tossed the spent shells, poked in the new bullets. He began strapping his gun belt on. Esther watched him, speaking in an agitated clip.

"Wasted, I...I saw Jurant. Shoot...Kroeber." She shuddered. "He's too fast. And you're hurt. Bad hurt. You can't—"

Wasted took a step, grunted in pain from the wound in his side and leaned away from it. He looked to Esther. "Help me walk, Esther." She hesitated but saw the determination in Wasted's face. Realizing that it was useless to argue, she stepped to Wasted's bloody side and put her arm around him. They both shared a desperate glance that spoke of their fears.

"Wasted. If..." Esther trailed off. She shook it off and piped up, "I swear. This is the hardest thing I ever did...for a man."

Wasted leaned on Esther. She felt his warm blood soak into her dress. Esther shivered as her face went pale. Wasted felt her body tremble and declared for the third time that day, "Ain't we a pair..." And in that moment Esther knew. Knew that Wasted needed her more than a crutch in a bad moment. There was a kindredness, a connection, to it. She got under the hook of his arm and shored him up with all her strength. They both walked awkwardly together out of Fendris's office. The black smoked had filled up its ceiling and there was no staying any longer, even if they wanted to.

Outside, the storm clouds had cleared as if that nature god knew the real show was about to begin. The clouds has receded to the west and smoke was collecting just above the street. Heat lightning was breaking across the sky on the horizon. The roof of Fendris's store was blackening under the twisting sheets of flame inside. Black smoke rose out of the windows in rolling swirls to obscure the sun.

Pools of water covered the street end to end like shiny mirrors. The fire was leaking out of the corners and windows of the building. Its yellow and orange colors danced in the bright reflections of the water. A blue haze of thickening smoke hung over the street as white and red ash floated in the air.

Jurant stood leaning against an oak tree thirty yards down the street from the entrance. The lights and shadows of the fire played eerily over his relaxed expression.

Wasted limped out of the building while leaning heavily on Esther. The cut on his face was swelling and turning purple with dried blood caked around it. His left side was dripping wet in his red gore and Esther's dress was soaked in it. On the sidewalk across the street a bruised and bandaged Ardway stood along with Wasted's friends. They stared at their bleeding hurt range foreman and shared grim faces. Gammill was out of sight at the doctor's office with his shot leg. Esther helped Wasted struggle to stand on the boardwalk. "Please, Wasted. You can barely stand. Don't go through with this."

"Jurant will kill me whether I draw against him or not. Now go. I can't do this if...you're still here." He gave a glance to Ardway across the street. Esther saw and looked to Ardway. He motioned with his hand for her to come.

Esther walked to where wood planks had been laid across the swampy road. She turned back to Wasted. He nodded with his head for her to continue. She slowly walked across the planks. Esther stopped at seeing the unconcerned Jurant. He smiled at her. Esther ran the rest of the way to Ardway. He pulled her to his side where Claudine and Pettigrew stood. They both embraced her and held her tight. Ardway raised up his rifle and gave Wasted a stern nod of confidence.

Jurant's voice called out, "Odem!"

Satisfied that Esther was protected, Wasted turned to gaze down the walk where Jurant waited. The New Orleans gunman stared at the blood covering half of Wasted's body and the wound forcing him to tilt like an old man. He saw the shiny beads of sweat rolling down Wasted's face, the ugly gash down his cheek. Jurant shifted his weight and stretched his back in anticipation. He called out to Wasted. "I wanted your best, Odem. Not this."

Above them Fendris's store roof fell into itself. Orange flames and black smoke leaped up into the sky amid the roar and clatter. Their reflections shimmered hellishly in the pools about the street. Hot ash drifted down to swirl about the men. Wasted wiped at his eyes with the sleeve of his coat that wasn't covered in blood. He spoke to himself, "My best..." Wasted peered up at the surging fire consuming the Fendris building, then over to his friends. Esther and the others looked on, their faces tight with anxiety and worry. He stared further down the street lined with the town's citizens. The train station manager. Kenton, the piano player from Molly's. Benito and Pete. Their eyes and lips were grim with an anticipation that Spirits Bend was on the cusp of a terrible change. And all they could do was watch helplessly and wait for it.

Wasted turned his concentration back to Jurant. He yelled to him with a voice loud and defiant. "My best, Jurant!" A confident and knowing smile crept over his lips. "I'm pleased to oblige you."

Jurant saw and thought, was Wasted mocking him? Something had happened to him. Odem wasn't afraid, he was confident. Too damn confident for a half dead man. And for the first time ever, deep inside of Jurant, a nerve twitched. A slight irritation took hold in Jurant's features. His brow knotted up as he watched and knew that this was all Odem he was facing, not Wasted or something in between. He shrugged it off with a slight jerk to his shoulders.

Wasted's eyes narrowed into needles of cold light, never taking their gaze off Jurant. Miraculously his body straightened, the pain pushed aside with sheer concentration. His back curved slightly while the shoulders expanded. The arms extended with the hands open, the fingers loose and nimble.

Wasted's face and expression changed. His features drained of anything human. The features had become rigid; muscles, bone and skin fused into a ghastly appearance poised with every fiber in his being to the task. Wolfish eyes bored into Jurant as if nothing else existed. Wasted spoke something that sounded Indian, "Šung'manitu Tanka."

Everyone on the street saw this transformation. Ardway unconsciously put his hand out in protection of Esther and the others. Gammill was watching the crowd from the doctor's office. He saw their startled looks. Gammill turned to study Wasted with one thought...a hard case. On the sidewalk Ardway gripped his rifle closer to him. Esther took a step back, blinking in disbelief. She whispered, "...Odem."

In that moment confusion seized Jurant but with an anger at feeling it. His hands blurred to his guns in an instinct for survival.

Wasted's guns materialized before him like sorcery. With a demonic glee Odem had escaped the purgatory known as Wasted bringing a wolf's pride and a black widow's purpose. Two shots blasted split-seconds before Jurant's pistols got off their shots.

Both men stared at each other in the echo of the guns' roar. Both waited, watching the other.

Jurant's furious eyes became fixed in place as their light faded. His tight-lipped grimace had cracked open, exposing teeth crimson with blood. It trickled red over his lips as his jaw fell open to his chest, a grotesque exaggeration of Jurant's shock at dying. A dark crimson stripe leaked down from his mouth to the two bullet holes punched through the center of his chest. Jurant's pupils rolled up in their sockets leaving a soulless white stare. His guns fell from lifeless fingers. Jurant dropped to his knees and collapsed into an ignominious pile. A pile of what Cajuns referred to as *merde*.

A defeated groan of wood twisting and giving way warned that the Fendris store was crashing into the street. Odem stood defiant and stared with a vicious cold smile at Jurant's body lying among this hell. Then Odem's body sagged, like when Wasted first walked out of the building. His legs buckled and Wasted fell to his knees. Looking about, his eyes searched for someone.

"Wasted!" screamed Esther.

Wasted turned and saw Esther with Ardway. He smiled in relief.

Flaming debris and fiery ash spilled into the street with a tremendous boom that shook the surrounding grounds. The storefronts trembled and creaked at the force of the destruction. Those with large plate-glass windows cracked in unison down the boardwalk from the massive vibration. A giant plume of blue and black smoke rolled out to fill the thoroughfare. Wasted disappeared under the inky fumes and blazing cinders.

Ardway and Esther ran over the wood planks to where Wasted had fallen. They were caught in the firestorm rain of soot and ruin blanketing the street. The sun disappeared above. Spirits Bend was once again thrown into a pitch black veil like at the beginning...

Epilogue:

The Hymn and Gammill's Bible Quote

Darkness.

A female sang with a pleasant lilt to her voice, like the Molly's showgirl. It echoed as though coming from the end of a tunnel.

"Take my hand my darlin'
In this savage land
Hold me in its garden
My soul to God's true plan..."

White light seeped into the dark. It flared and expanded with a blinding arc to become like a train's headlight. Colors and images blurred from out of this. They became solid and clear.

Wasted was in a bed, his body, face and limbs wrapped in bandages. He blinked awake to Esther humming a hymn. Wasted glanced around to see Indian arrowheads and a pair of rusty spurs on the wall. He slowly became aware that he was in Junior's room at the Ardway Ranch.

Esther sat in a chair by his bed while sewing on a man's shirt. A stack of the ranch hands' ragged clothes were in a basket beside her. Esther turned and saw that Wasted had his eyes open and was staring at her. Her face widened in excitement. She shouted out the door to the hallway, "He's awake! Everybody! Wasted is awake!"

Esther rushed to kneel at the bed and before Wasted. She gazed down into his face and couldn't hide her happiness. A commotion was happening downstairs. Someone was running up the steps to the hall.

Ardway appeared at the doorway, his lips spread wide with delight. He was bandaged about his face with some cuts. But his hair was cut and the beard shaved off. He had a trim mustache like when he first appeared to meet the train. He strode up quickly behind Esther. Both their faces beamed with grateful relief.

"Wasted! You're..." Ardway laughed from how good seeing Wasted awake made him feel. "Good! I'm tired of doing your chores." The wetness of Ardway's eyes betrayed his joking. "You had us worried. It's been three days and—"

Wasted looked at Esther. "I heard you singing."

Esther was pleased. "It's a hymn. We used to sing it in our church back in Arkansas."

Wasted held to Esther's eyes, remembering his own past. "We sang it back in Missouri. Where I grew up. I thought I was there..."

Ardway spoke up, "Damn. Then...you remember...Everything?"

Wasted thought about it for a moment, gently nodded that he did. Ardway raised his eyebrows. "Well?"

Esther and Ardway looked on Wasted with excitement and anticipation. The sunlight was streaming through a window and a breeze lightly tossed the linen curtains. Wasted turned his attention to it and felt a lightness inside pulling at his heart.

In that moment Wasted let go and drifted out of the room. He sailed through the sky to look down upon the ranch. It looked idyllic in the fresh clear air and in the day's bright light. His friends worked about the ranch at its chores. The tall green grass swayed in the slight breeze and the cattle grazed on the land peaceful and contented. But there was more. On that hill in the clearing Wasted saw Miss Claudine tending the graves of Wilson and Bailey and the other good boys, next to her roses and Indian Paintbrush blooms.

"Wasted!" called Esther.

Wasted was back in the room. His grateful eyes had tears but for the joy of his new life.

Ardway spoke, "You left us there for a second. You sure...you're feeling okay?"

Without being told, he knew that Ardway had quit drinking. That Esther worked at the ranch now. And that Odem died with Jurant.

Wasted opened his mouth to speak and stopped. He searched but could not find the words. Wasted nodded yes, drawing his lips apart in a wide open grin...like a young and happy farm boy from Missouri.

Luke 15:32

"But we had to celebrate and be glad,
because this brother of yours was dead
and is alive again;
he was lost and is found."

Thank you for reading

WASTED

by Sam F. Park

*please leave a review
on the website of
your favorite bookseller*

SAM F. PARK

Sam F. Park is a screenwriter, film producer, and comic book creator. He was the West Coast Editor of the award-winning **Monsterverse Comics**.

He writes novels now.

Look for more.

MORE GREAT READS FROM HENRY GRAY!

THE LAST STAGE by Bruce Scivally

In his final days, lawman Wyatt Earp dreams of one last showdown—gold, gunmen and love with his devoted wife, Sadie.

VEIL OF SEDUCTION by Emily Dinova

In 1922, journalist Lorelei Alba infiltrates a gothic asylum for "troublesome" women—and falls into the orbit of a dark, mysterious doctor.

THE UNDERSTUDY by Charlie Peters

A kidnapping plot during a high-stakes merger quickly unravels, exposing every flaw in a "perfect crime."

THE DEVIL IN THE DIAMOND by Gregory Cioffi

First on a WWII battlefield and later on a baseball diamond, two soldiers, once enemies, find themselves bound by history, family, and the game they love.

THE MAN FROM BELIZE by Steven Kobrin

Dr. Kent Sterling's perfect life in paradise shatters when his past as a government hitman catches up—and the Viper comes calling.

SINS OF THE RAVEN by Steven Kobrin

Dr. Kent Stirling returns to face adversaries from his past, forcing him to confront buried secrets and fight for his life before the sins he thought forgotten consume him completely.

A PRAYER FOR THE DAMNED by Joe Cornet

Bounty hunter Cole faces a deranged preacher and seeks a lost Confederate treasure in a town on the brink of violence.

SHELBY'S VACATION by Nancy Beverly

Shelby runs from heartbreak into the arms of Carol, a woman carrying her own relationship scars. Together, they discover love worth risking.

TOO MUCH IN THE SON by Charlie Peters

Mistaken identity plunges Leo Malone into a twisted web of lies, gangsters, and family deception.

I CONFESS: DIARY OF AN AUSTRALIAN POPE by Melvyn Morrow

An Australian pope battles corruption, blackmail, and betrayal as he tries to reform the Vatican from within.

SEARCH FOR FUN WITH PAPA ROCK!

PAPA ROCK'S HORROR MOVIES WORD SEARCH
by Rock Scivally & Jeffrey Breslauer

150 puzzles based on horror films from *Frankenstein* to *Godzilla* equals 150 reasons to keep the lights on all night!

PAPA ROCK'S SON OF HORROR MOVIES WORD SEARCH by Rock Scivally & Jeffrey Breslauer

Looking for more Word Search chills? In this edition, monsters from the 1960s and 70s haunt every page!

PAPA ROCK'S REVENGE OF HORROR MOVIES WORD SEARCH by Rock Scivally & Jeffrey Breslauer

Looking for more monter Word Searches? Here you'll find the classic movie monsters from the 1980s and 90s!

PAPA ROCK'S ROMANCE MOVIES WORD SEARCH
by Rock Scivally & Jeffrey Breslauer

From *Casablanca* to *Titanic*, here's 150 Word Searches based on romance movies, so pick up a pen and turn on the love light!

PAPA ROCK'S WESTERN MOVIES WORD SEARCH
by Rock Scivally & Jeffrey Breslauer

Hop into these 150 Word Searches and ride with John Wayne, Randolph Scott, Clint Eastwood, and cowboy favorites!

PAPA ROCK'S ANIMATED MUSICALS WORD SEARCH by Rock Scivally & Jeffrey Breslauer

You'll be humming along as you do 150 Word Searches on favorite animated musicals from *Snow White* to *Strawberry Shortcake!*

PAPA ROCK'S WAR MOVIES WORD SEARCH by Rock Scivally & Jeffrey Breslauer

Climb into your foxhole and challenge yourself with Word Searches based on classic war films from *Sergeant York* to *Saving Private Ryan*.

PAPA ROCK'S SCI-FI MOVIES WORD SEARCH by Rock Scivally & Jeffrey Breslauer

Relive science fiction's greatest hits with these Word Search puzzles covering classics from *Metropolis* to *Star Wars!*

PAPA ROCK'S DETECTIVE MOVIES WORD SEARCH by Rock Scivally & Jeffrey Beslauer

Solve 150 puzzles inspired by classic detective films, from Sherlock Holmes and Sam Spade to noir favorites.

PAPA ROCK'S MOVIE COMEDY TEAMS WORD SEARCH by Rock Scivally & Jeffrey Breslauer

From the Marx Brothers to Abbott & Costello to Martin & Lewis to Cheech & Chong, celebrate the greatest comedy teams with this laugh-out-loud puzzle collection!